
★

THE LITTLE HOUSE WAS WARM, THE SMELL OF BLOOD IN THE AIR.

Sheila knelt beside Francine and reached for her wrist to seek a pulse. As soon as her fingertips touched flesh, however, she recoiled. Already the body was stiff.

Her own ... e of unexpected ... leasant people di... e swallowed a lu... ly back to where N... phone.

"Ambulance will be here in a minute." She took one look at Sheila's face and leaned heavily against the sink. "Dead?"

Sheila nodded. "I think we better call the police."

Nell's eyes widened. "Po-lice? Again?"

★

MURDER

in the Charleston Manner

PATRICIA
HOUCK
SPRINKLE

W✺RLDWIDE.

TORONTO • NEW YORK • LONDON
AMSTERDAM • PARIS • SYDNEY • HAMBURG
STOCKHOLM • ATHENS • TOKYO • MILAN
MADRID • WARSAW • BUDAPEST • AUCKLAND

To Hank, Betsy, and Anna Beth,
and their wonderful house

MURDER IN THE CHARLESTON MANNER

A Worldwide Mystery/May 1993

First published by St. Martin's Press, Incorporated.

ISBN 0-373-26119-5

Printed in U.S.A.

In Charleston, South Carolina, everything moves slowly. Languid mules, pulling ancient carriages around The Battery. Carpenters, restoring buildings first refurbished long before the Civil War. Sailboats, lazing across the bay. Bees, buzzing away spring afternoons. Nothing hurries. Not even murder.

ONE

THE BEGINNING

IT WAS LATE AFTERNOON, and still Francine had not come. Dolly tried once again to pin her soft hair into a bun on top of her head, but arthritis made stiff sausages of her fingers and sent waves of pain up her forearms.

"Oh, bother!" She was more annoyed with her body than with her absent nurse. After all, she had given Francine the afternoon off. But why was the woman so late? Dolly fumbled for the gold watch that swung from a chain around her neck. Ten past six. In another five minutes it would be time to go down, and she had especially wanted to put on a fresh wrapper. This week was so hot for March. Still, it was not half as important to change clothes as it was to get downstairs first. Dolly liked to be in the living room, sherry in hand, before Cousin Annie and the Judge arrived. It preserved, she felt, a modicum of dignity, a shred of the illusion that she was still in control of her life and her family.

It was Wednesday, when the whole family came for dinner. They came other times, too, of course, flowed in and out so often that a stranger might wonder who actually lived in the old Wimberly house and who lived elsewhere. But on Wednesdays they washed their faces and changed their clothes before they came.

Every Wednesday Nell brought out the damask tablecloth and napkins, soft as butter from many washings and faded to the color of a spring sky. She planned a company dinner that took her all afternoon to prepare. Marion came home early from the shop to pick roses for the cut-glass bowl on the table. One of the twins arrived soon after six to lay the gold-rimmed plates and heavy silver their thrice-great-grandmother had successfully concealed from the Yankees. Buddy left the restaurant by half past, to pick up the other twin on his way. And just before Cousin Annie steered Judge Black by one elbow up the sidewalk from the house next door, Francine wheeled Dolly into the elevator and—for the only time all week—downstairs for dinner.

But where was everyone tonight? With difficulty Dolly propelled herself to the doorway of her bedroom and listened intently. She heard Marion ask a question, Nell rumble a honey-soft reply. No lively chatter from Rake or gentle hum from Becca.

Mildly troubled, she returned to her mirror. She hoped no one was ill. Then, illogically, she hoped someone was. What else would Marion forgive? "Don't borrow trouble, dear," she told her reflection with an insouciance born of years of putting up with her elder sister's tart temper. "Your immediate problem is what to do with that mop of hair."

Her hair was one of Dolly's glories. Still honey-brown with only a few threads of gray, it flowed past her shoulders in waves to curl impudently at the ends. But it was too soft for her unwilling fingers to control. She reached for another pin and tried again. When she dropped the pin behind her and heard it hit the wide old floorboards, she could have wept with frustration.

Instead, she knotted her hands in her lap and took three deep breaths. Jamison had been blunt last week about the condition of her heart, and she certainly wasn't going to get upset over hair streaming down her back. "It isn't worth dying for," she reminded herself, brushing it as well as she could.

She wheeled herself awkwardly out into the hall and across to her sitting room with its bay window overlooking the street. En route to the window she changed direction toward the loveseat, fumbled beside a cushion, and almost crowed in triumph. Rake, who scattered possessions like a queen distributing bounty, had left an interesting new hair clip there yesterday. What would it look like on a woman past seventy?

A few minutes later she picked up her hand mirror to survey the results: a cascading ponytail with a few soft curls around her face. "Not bad," she murmured. "Maybe even nice, for a change." She arranged one of the curls to her satisfaction and reached for a puff to cover her face in a layer of soft white powder. Dolly was not a vain woman, but she did, in her own words, "like to look nice."

When her reflection met her approval she rearranged the ruffles on her ample bosom and resolutely wheeled herself over the threshold and into the small elevator beside the stairs. Just because she'd never operated the elevator before was no reason she couldn't.

But once inside, she found she had miscalculated. The elevator, installed where hall closets had been on each floor, was too tiny for her to maneuver her chair. No amount of twisting could force her stiff arms to reach the button over her left shoulder. Not for the first time, Dolly wished her grandfather had built larger closets.

By the time she had backed into the hall and turned around, she was trembling with weakness, damp from perspiration, and close to tears. With relief she heard Marion mounting the stairs.

As soon as Marion reached the landing and could see her sister's wheels, she spoke. "Not a soul is here yet, and I can't think where they could all be." Her voice was sharp with irritation, not worry. Marion never worried, but considered tardiness a capital sin. Her antique store opened promptly at nine, and lagging afternoon browsers were surprised to find themselves brusquely steered onto the sidewalk by five.

Marion's head appeared over the top step and her eyes widened. "What on earth have you done to your hair?"

Dolly smoothed it with a sunny smile. "Do you like it?"

Except for the shape of their chins and a certain way they carried their heads, no one would have known they were sisters. Where Dolly was round, Marion was angular. Where Dolly was soft, Marion was firm. Dolly's eyes could have been made from chips of sky, Marion's from bits of bright coal. And unlike Dolly's fine, brown hair, Marion's was thick, the color of old pewter, and worn—as she herself would have said—sensibly short. Her mouth twisted as she surveyed her younger sister's newly arranged curls. "Not on a woman your age. But it's too late to do anything about it now. I just heard Annie coming up the sidewalk." Deftly—for Marion was still strong—she pushed Dolly into the elevator and jabbed the button.

"Where's Francine?" she demanded.

"I gave her the afternoon off. Nell was in the kitchen, and I couldn't stand to have anyone puttering around me. It's too hot."

"She's not supposed to leave you alone." Dolly could almost see Marion's lips tightening. "And I can't imagine where she could have gone this late."

Dolly hesitated. She hated to upset Marion further, but she'd know soon enough. "I think she and Buddy went out to Boone Hall."

"Humph." Dolly couldn't tell if Marion's snort was for Buddy's taking Francine somewhere, or for his taking an afternoon off. Thank goodness they reached the first floor before Marion could say more.

They found Cousin Annie and the Judge hovering just inside the screen door, looking uncertainly first into the living room then into the dining room across the hall, where Nell moved around the table like a portly dark shadow. Annie often looked like a bird. Tonight, peering from side to side in a pale-blue double-knit suit and a pink blouse that strained over her plump chest, she only needed a perch to make the resemblance complete.

"Come on in," Nell was saying, not breaking her rhythm distributing silverware. Under most circumstances she would have greeted the old couple at the door.

What creatures of habit we are, Dolly marveled silently, when four people late for dinner can throw us all off our stride.

The Judge's almost toothless mouth widened into a grin as she rolled into the hall. "Now that's what I call a coiffure, Dolly! Why don't you do that to your hair, woman?"

Annie peered from beneath her scraggy, too-often-permed bangs. Before she could make an acid comment, Dolly motioned Marion to push her into the living room. "Who's ready for sherry?" she asked gaily. "I certainly am."

As usual, Annie made a quick, negative motion. Also as usual, the Judge ignored her. He shuffled to the couch and planted himself at one end, hands clasped on his ebony cane and chin tilted defiantly. "Pour it quick, before my old woman objects. She's always going on and on about saving my heart. At eighty-nine, who the hell does she think I'm saving it for?"

He cackled at his own wit. In two gulps he downed the small sherry Marion had handed him and held out his shaking hand. "More than that, Marion. That scarcely wet my whistle."

She refilled his glass, saying with the familiarity of one who'd lived next door most of her life, "That's all you get."

For a few minutes they sat in silence, ears strained to hear approaching cars or the telephone. "Where is everybody?" Annie finally asked, making a point of not touching the drink she held.

"I don't know where the girls are. Buddy and Francine went out to Boone Hall, and I guess they got caught in traffic." Dolly brushed away a tendril of hair and enjoyed her own sherry. Marion only permitted her one a week, and she always savored it to the last drop.

The Judge leaned so far forward he almost fell off the couch. "That traffic gets worse and worse," he said in a quavering tone. "They just fly up this street. Take Heyward Bennett, now—comes speeding in here like a bat out of hell. I gave him a piece of my mind last week, and I would've given him a piece of my cane, too, if he'd been close enough. Rhoda needs to control that boy."

"Heyward's all right," Dolly said indulgently. "Sowing no more wild oats than you did at twenty-six, I'd wager."

"A sight less," he boasted, "but I didn't run over old men while I was sowing."

"Are you going to Women of the Church tomorrow afternoon?" Annie asked Marion. "They're showing the video from the preacher's trip to China."

"I promised to take a cake." Marion nodded. "Nell will bake it in the morning. I'll pick you up about three."

Relieved that she didn't have to ask, Annie sat back in her chair and almost relaxed. "How are you getting along with Francine?" she asked Dolly.

Dolly shook her head. "Nearly drives me crazy, puttering around. I'm too healthy to need a full-time nurse."

"She ain't full-time nursing." Judge Black chuckled. "Meeting Heyward under the magnolias in the dark. Probably takes him in the house, too, when you ain't looking."

"There's no such word as 'ain't,'" Annie burst out. "And why a man with your education and experience—"

"Woman, when a man has my education and experience, he can say any damn word he pleases. And what's got you so riled up ain't my language. It's the thought of what them young 'uns might be up to. Once an old maid, always an old maid," he said to Dolly in a very audible aside, "even if she has been married nigh on fifteen years."

"I could kill him," Annie muttered. "Sometimes I could just kill him."

It was time, Dolly felt, to change the subject. "I've been thinking of asking Francine to write a little history of our family. What do you think?"

Marion raised a skeptical eyebrow. "What on earth for?"

Dolly shrugged. "The girls, I guess. When we're all gone, there's so much nobody else would know."

Annie made a face of disgust. "Don't speak of such things, Dolly. It's bad luck."

"What you worrying for, gal? I got a good fifteen years on you, and I ain't worrying about dying." The Judge held out his glass. "Marion, give me one more sherry."

Marion filled it half full, then turned back to her sister. "Why, Dolly? You've never been interested in history before. Aunt Bella and I tried for years—"

Dolly interrupted with an impatient wave of her hand. "I'm still not interested in the United Daughters of the Confederacy, Marion, nor the South Carolina Historical Society. I just want a little record of our family, for the girls. Nobody's ever done one before."

Marion sipped her sherry and shook her head. "For a very good reason. There's nothing to say. It's a very ordinary family, Dolly."

The Judge leaned back and worked his thin cheeks in and out importantly. "Oh, I wouldn't say that, Marion. Your mama—"

Marion turned sharply, but Dolly interrupted again. Like most placid women, she could be remarkably stubborn. "No matter how ordinary it is, Marion, it's *our* family. I'd like the girls to have some notion of where they came from."

The two sisters confronted one another across the room—
Marion lean and tanned, crisp in white linen, Dolly flowing in
ribbons and ruffles out of the chair that tried to contain her.
Marion spoke with a trace of asperity. "You'd do better to help
them decide where they're going."

Dolly sighed softly. The girls seemed to irritate Marion more
these days. Becca by getting so serious about marine biology
when Marion had set her heart on leaving her the shop. And
Rake...

She picked up her sherry and sipped it to keep from saying
"Rake's all right, Em—not much different than I was at her
age, head full of parties and boys. She'll settle down." Saying
that wouldn't do any good. Marion hadn't approved of Dolly
in those days, either. Better to stick to her guns. "I still want her
to do it."

"But Francine's a nurse, Dolly, not a historian. What would
she know about writing history? If it's just facts you want, I
can..."

Dolly shook her head. "No, you don't have time and she
does. All I want is a few pages, saying who married whom and
what they did for a living. Francine can do it in the afternoons
while I'm resting. But she'll need your help to find any old letters or things that are in the attic. I'd do it, but..." She spread
her hands to encompass not only the chair, but her reasons for
being in it.

Marion hesitated, then relented. "I'll see what I can find."

Judge Black leaned even farther forward, until Annie
grabbed his coat and pulled him back. "You want hist'ry,
gal,"—he punctuated each word with his empty glass—"you
tell Francine to come to me. I've forgotten more hist'ry about
your family than you ever knew. And I wouldn't mind spending a few afternoons with that bit of fluff. You tell her—"

"Speaking of Francine"—Annie quivered on her perch—"I
do hope nothing has happened to them."

As if on cue, a car door slammed in the street beyond the
open front window. Feet trooped along the porch, and the
screen door banged. Four voices spoke in unison:

"...sorry we're late."

" . . . glad you didn't go with us, Aunt Em."

" . . . nothing we could do."

Rake's voice rose dramatically over them all. "We could have all been killed!"

TWO

TWO WEEKS LATER, in an expensive condominium overlooking Atlanta's ever-soaring skyline, two women sat reading. One, a petite elderly woman curled into the corner of a rose velvet sofa, was scanning a letter written on lavender paper. The other, a long slim woman of nearly forty, was sunk into an ivory chair with her long legs stretched over its matching ottoman, her dark head buried in the *Atlanta Journal & Constitution*.

The old woman looked up. "Sheila, how long has it been since you were in Charleston?" Her voice was husky, and seemed much too deep for her tiny frame.

The younger woman peered around the paper. "Charleston? I've never been to Charleston, Aunt Mary."

Her aunt's brown eyes widened in disbelief. "Never? How could that be, dear? I spent so much of my girlhood there."

"I spent my girlhood in Japan," Sheila reminded her, "until I came to live with you for high school."

She dropped the newspaper to her lap and lazily stretched her arms high above her head, letting a midafternoon yawn engulf her. Only belatedly did she give her mouth a few ritual pats. She felt as lazy as Alfred, the big white Persian sunning himself on a blue rug under the window.

"Do you need a nap?" her aunt suggested.

She shook her head. "No, I'm just basking in doing nothing."

"You've had a strenuous winter." Aunt Mary spoke absently, her attention back on her letter. "I'm glad you got a spring break."

Sheila let her head drop to the high back of the chair and considered. Was it actually "strenuous" to lose your husband in a mountain-climbing accident while you were home reading haiku, to oversee efficient embassy servants in packing up your belongings, to walk straight into your first job three months later, or to solve a mystery by sitting in an elegant coffee room chatting with various students? It didn't sound as strenuous as the work done daily by Mildred, Aunt Mary's maid, or by mothers of preschool children. But strenuous or not, Sheila felt as if she had been beaten with a thick stick. What she wanted—what she had left Chicago's spring slush and flown to Atlanta determined to get—was two weeks of shopping, plays, and sitting deep in Aunt Mary's wonderful chairs to read the newspaper.

Of course, she risked something by coming to see Aunt Mary. Sheila could still hear her father nearly twenty-five years ago, as he put her on the plane in Tokyo. "Living with Mary won't be physically tiring, Sheila. Getting Mary to stir herself is like pouring molasses in January. But watch out for yourself. Trouble follows that woman like fleas on a dog." Sure enough, being around Aunt Mary had gotten her involved in more trouble than she planned to remember on this April afternoon.

Just now, however, Aunt Mary looked harmless enough, reading through enormous glasses like a wise little owl. Sheila settled deeper into her chair with the *Constitution* and for nearly five minutes silence reigned. A thin woman in a starched rose uniform brought iced tea and cookies. "You want anything else before dinner, Miss Beaufort?"

The older woman looked up at her absently. "No, thank you, Mildred."

"Then I'm planning to serve about six. You're due at the theater at eight." She carefully set one of the glasses at Sheila's elbow.

As Mildred left the room Aunt Mary reached for the other glass and asked, a shade too casually, "How's Mike?"

Sheila sipped her own tea. Bless Mildred, she'd remembered not to sweeten it. "He's fine, so long as I stay off his turf. He sent you his love." The big Chicago detective had growled like a bear when Sheila and Aunt Mary had solved a case for him in February, but now he dropped by at least once a week to boast of cases he was solving by himself.

"And David?"

Sheila let herself fully enjoy the homemade chocolate chip cookie before she answered. "He's fine, too. He's suggested that I come over to Scotland in August to meet his sister Fiona."

Aunt Mary peered over her glasses. "Are you trying to tell me something, Sheila?"

"No, Aunt Mary, I'm trying *not* to tell you something, because there's nothing to tell. As I told you several months ago, being single suits me for now. David is a very special friend—I've never really had a man friend before—and Mike is fun, when he's not being obnoxious. But"—she picked up the paper again and turned to the business section—"I can live these next two weeks without mentioning either of them again."

"That's fine." Aunt Mary seemed, for some inexplicable reason, relieved. "Then Mike need never know that you've been."

Sheila answered automatically, her attention on a corporate merger. "Of course he knows. He drove me to the plane."

"But he needn't know that you've been anywhere else. If he calls, I can just keep putting him off until you get back."

Sheila again put down her paper, puzzled. "Back? From where? I just got here last night."

Her aunt gave her a look of mild reproach. "From Charleston, dear. As we were discussing." She tapped the lavender letter gently against her silk lap. "Of course, there may be absolutely nothing wrong—Dolly does get into flaps over very little. But this seems different, somehow."

Sheila dropped the paper onto the floor beside her chair and regarded her aunt with tolerant amusement. "I have no intention of going to Charleston or anywhere else, Aunt Mary. But are you going to tell me what this is all about, or am I to piece it together from odd remarks?"

One penciled eyebrow rose in gentle rebuke. "Sheila! I never make odd remarks. And of course I am going to tell you the whole story—as much as I know of it from her letter."

She sank into thought again until Sheila prompted, "Whose letter?"

"What? Oh, Dolly Langdon's. We were at Ashley Hall together."

That at least explained the reference to Charleston. Even Sheila had heard of Charleston's most prestigious school for girls.

"Dolly and Marion were both there," Aunt Mary continued, "but Marion was five years older than we were. That seems like so very much when you are children." She paused, lost in reminiscence.

Sheila brought her back to the present. "About the Langdons."

Aunt Mary shook her head. "It isn't the Langdons, dear, it's the Wimberlys. Marion and Dolly Wimberly they were, and Marion still is. One of Charleston's old, moderately distinguished families. They lived directly across the street from my own Aunt Mary, and I went to live with her just after Mama died so I could go to Ashley Hall. Dolly and I were in the same class, so of course we spent a good deal of time together after school, as well. We've remained friends ever since. Marion is tall and serious, good at anything she does—schoolwork, tennis, running a shop, just anything. Dolly is shorter and a bit flighty, but exceptionally pretty. She never cared a rap for grades. Her mind was always on the next party. Poor Dolly."

Sheila was giving the conversation only half her mind. The other half was wondering whether it would be cool enough for her wool spring suit that evening. "*Poor* Dolly? She sounds like lucky Dolly to me."

"She was, then. When she left college to marry Alva Langdon, we all envied her. I've never seen a bride glow like Dolly. They had one daughter, Margaret, and lived in Columbia."

She paused. When Sheila didn't prompt her again, she demanded, "Sheila, are you attending to what I am telling you?"

"Of course, Aunt Mary." Sheila decided to wear her new dress instead. "It's just that I thought we were discussing Charleston, and now you're in Columbia."

"I am explaining," Aunt Mary said with dignity. "Pay attention, please. About ten years ago Alva dropped dead one day at work. Margaret was married to Buddy Endicott by then, with twin girls, and lived in Charleston not far from Marion. Marion invited Dolly to come back and live with her in the old homeplace."

"Southern ladies of leisure." Sheila didn't mean to sound derogatory, but she wondered how they stood it—day after day with nothing to do but visit friends, go to church meetings, and flit through a house cleaned by a maid who also cooked. Of course, it wasn't much different from her days as an embassy wife, but even before Tyler's accident she had known she had to find something else to do before she ran screaming through the streets of Tokyo. Aunt Mary was the only woman she knew who found indolence thoroughly satisfying.

Aunt Mary corrected her. "Oh, no, dear. They both worked. Practically everybody in Charleston had to work after the War."

Sheila knew which war Aunt Mary discussed in capitals. "Let me remind you, Aunt Mary, that the Civil War ended nearly fifty years before the Wimberlys were born."

"In Charleston, Sheila," Aunt Mary informed her in an icy voice, "they call it the War of Northern Aggression. You will need to keep that in mind. It left deep and lasting scars." She sighed deeply. "It was not until after World War II that Charleston got back on its feet. They used to say they were too poor to paint and too proud to whitewash. When you've been vandalized and victimized . . ."

Sheila knew better than to let a South Carolinian get started on the Battle of Charleston. "What did the Wimberlys do?"

Aunt Mary subsided and fanned herself delicately with the letter. "Marion inherited an antique store from her Aunt Bella, and Dolly helped her out. Marion still runs it herself, although she must be . . ." Aunt Mary recalled just in time that to discuss Marion's age would be to discuss her own. " . . . well able to hire help," she finished smoothly. "Marion is a good businesswoman. She's done very well."

Sheila stretched her long body in the comfortable chair and lazily sipped her tea. "What about Dolly?" She didn't really care, but listening to Aunt Mary tell stories from her past was as good a way as any to spend a vacation afternoon, so long as no exertion was called for on Sheila's own part.

Aunt Mary grew grave. "Dolly helped Marion in the shop for several years, then some years ago—it must be six or seven—Margaret became very ill. Cancer, I think, but Dolly never said.

Dolly cared for her that last year until she died. Three weeks later Dolly herself had a massive heart attack, and her heart's been very bad ever since. In addition, she'd got severe arthritis. For two years she's not been able to walk. Marion fixed up the front bedroom on the second floor as a sitting room and gave her the bedroom across the hall. Dolly spends her days there in a wheelchair. She keeps busy taking phone calls for some organization, as a volunteer, and they installed a small elevator between floors so she can come down occasionally, but most of the time she's alone. Poor Dolly." Aunt Mary tapped pearly nails on the letter that lay in her lap.

Sheila was still puzzled. "And you want to go cheer her up?"

Aunt Mary shook her head. "Oh, no, dear. Dolly is the most cheerful soul you can imagine. But she's worried. Here." She handed the letter across the coffee table. "Read it yourself."

The letter was written in a hand that must once have been round and childish, but now wavered almost as erratically as the syntax.

Dearest Mary,

　　Please don't think me a fool. Em does. Probably right. But it's too many accidents. The twins' car got smashed, then Judge Black went, all of a sudden. The t.v. had a fire and Em got a flat. Could happen to anybody, but Roy Luther's never mixed up my bottles before. I had a terrible time. Fine now. Don't worry. Em says I'm silly, but I keep wondering. When will it all end? Wish you were here, old dear! Always able to see clearer than I. Please write— or *come!* I'm not going anywhere. Nell's here too.

Love, Dolly

Sheila read the letter through, then her eyes met her aunt's. "You said Dolly is a bit flighty?"

Aunt Mary nodded. "Even imaginative. But she sounds worried, don't you think?"

"Could her illness have made her extra nervous?"

Aunt Mary sighed deeply. "I just don't know, Sheila." She untucked her feet from beneath her on the couch and slid them into tiny shoes. Gracefully she pulled herself to her full five feet. "I think I'll give her a call." She trotted out of the room.

In less than ten minutes she was back. "You need to go, dear, and soon. There's been another accident, a more serious one. While Dolly's granddaughter took her to the doctor this afternoon, Marion came back to the house for something she had forgotten. When Dolly and Becca returned, they found Marion lying at the foot of the stairs. She had fallen from the landing."

"Is she badly hurt?"

"Just a sprained wrist. But Dolly is convinced there's something Marion is not telling her. I want you to spend a few days there and see what you think. Ferret out the truth, if you can."

"Why me?" Sheila protested, her vacation rapidly receding. "They were your friends."

"That's why. I can't go poke and pry about my friends' business like that. It would be highly rude."

"While for me, an absolute stranger..."

Aunt Mary waved away the rest of her sentence. "You can be the soul of tact, dear, when you make an effort. You can run over for a couple of days to find out what's going on, and still be back in time for the ballet next week."

"But you," Sheila pointed out, "could stay as long as needed. And don't worry about me—I'll stay here with Mildred and do very well."

Diamonds sparkled as Aunt Mary laid one slim hand on her heart. "Nonsense, Sheila. You can't really expect me to travel to Charleston in my condition."

"What condition?" Sheila asked brutally. Aunt Mary's excellent health was legendary in the family.

The old woman did not deign to explain. "Besides, I have an important meeting with Charlie on Friday. And you just said you've always wanted to see Charleston."

"I said I've never *seen* Charleston. That's not the same as saying I've always *wanted* to see it. And I'm sure Charlie would be glad to postpone." Sheila knew enough about Aunt Mary's financial advisor to say it with confidence. What Charles Davidson suffered helping Aunt Mary manage her fortune, Sheila never dared imagine.

"Nonsense, dear. Everyone should see Charleston. And this meeting with Charlie is absolutely critical. He's been putting money in the wrong places again." Aunt Mary's tone indicated a con man out to swindle poor little old ladies, not one of Atlanta's most conservative financiers. She started back across the room. "Now, dear, if you'll excuse me, I think I need a short nap before dinner." She paused at the door. "You might start packing. I told Dolly to expect you tomorrow afternoon."

THREE

SHEILA LEFT Atlanta late the next morning, fuming. Why didn't she have the spine to say no to Aunt Mary? Neither a quick shopping trip to purchase clothes suitable for warmer weather nor the loan of her aunt's sleek gray Cadillac (without Jason, its usual driver) made up for the injustice of losing her Atlanta vacation.

The Cadillac, however, was a joy to drive after her own much lighter car. Keeping one eye out for zealous officers of the law, she let the speedometer climb as the car sped along Interstate 20. Just beyond Augusta she decided on impulse to leave the interstate, expecting to find long country roads with few patrol cars to monitor her speed. Instead, she found herself behind country drivers out checking their fields.

"Move it!" she muttered to one particularly exasperating old man hunched down in an ancient Ford, an equally ancient cap perched on the back of his head. After meandering along for miles, he came to a dead stop to make an elaborate right turn into a rutted driveway.

She ate barbeque from a roadside stand in a town whose name she would not remember, and continued to ramble toward the southeast. Finally, just when she'd begun to think she'd find a way back to the interstate and forget the scenic route, she spotted a solitary crane standing in a cypress swamp. Almost at once the road was arched with a green corridor of huge live oaks draped in Spanish moss, and when she breathed deeply, she could smell the sea.

She passed estates as old as the nation itself—Middleton Place, Magnolia Plantation, Drayton Hall—and hoped she'd have time to come back for a relaxed trip through the colonial era.

If the outskirts of Charleston still remembered the Revolutionary War, its suburban sprawl had lost the battle to the Kentucky Colonel and the hamburger Scot. As she crossed the Ashley River Bridge into Old Charleston, Sheila shuddered to think that future historians might conclude that she and her contemporaries preferred concrete to grass, fast food to leisurely dining.

When she finally reached the old city, she was surprised at its scale. Charleston was almost a doll's town, with exquisite narrow houses and pocket-handkerchief lawns. The streets were also narrow, and almost immediately she made a wrong turn and found herself in a maze of streets that inexplicably sprouted "Do Not Enter—One Way" signs halfway down. Proceeding on the incorrect assumption that she could go around a block and get back where she'd started, she was soon hopelessly lost.

She pulled to the curb in front of some modern Georgian town houses and pored over a wholly inadequate City of Charleston insert in her South Carolina map. All she could tell from it was that she was probably on the south side of Calhoun Street.

A slender man with skin the color of mahogany and a grizzled beard put down the scraper with which he had been attacking peeling paint on a shutter. "May I help you, ma'am?" He bent nearly double to peer in her window and beamed her a friendly smile. "Havin' a little trouble?"

She gave a heartfelt sigh. "Am I ever." She handed him the slip of paper on which Aunt Mary had drawn a precise (but, Sheila was now certain, inaccurate) map.

While he made sense of Aunt Mary's directions, Sheila breathed deeply of the fresh sea air. "You're not far," he assured her. "Go right on down Legree Street to Tradd, turn left on Orange to Broad and take another left. On Ashley, by Colonial Lake, take a right and that will lead you up to here." A bony finger indicated a spot on Aunt Mary's map.

Sheila started to put the car in gear. "That sounds easy enough. How do I find Legree Street?"

"You're on it." The sign he pointed to said "Legare." As she drove away, Sheila reflected that Charlestonian might be almost as hard to learn as Japanese.

The man's directions, however, were excellent. Colonial Lake was easily identifiable, ringed with palmettos and black benches. In less than five minutes she reached the Wimberly house.

There was a fire hydrant right in front, so she pulled into a vacant spot in front of the next house. She cut her motor and sat for several minutes, feeling sticky (she'd driven most of the way with the windows down) and useless, wishing she had the courage to find a hotel and drive straight back to Atlanta tomorrow. What on earth was she doing in Charleston trying to find out why two elderly women she'd never met were having accidents? She carefully went over in her mind what she would like to say to Aunt Mary—and never would.

After a time she became aware that she was under well-bred scrutiny. A woman diligently weeding a border across the sidewalk never looked at Sheila directly, but shot occasional sidelong glances from beneath a large straw hat. Embarrassed into action, Sheila dragged a quick comb through her hair, noting it was already frizzing in the humidity.

The woman rose and came toward the gate to meet her as she got out. Sheila knew that her own cotton skirt and sweater were in good taste, but this woman made her feel rumpled and gauche. She was dressed in white slacks and a soft white blouse with a neckline decorated with cutwork—not what Sheila would have chosen for yardwork, but her clothes were spotless except for the stained gloves that she flung to the ground. With a graceful gesture she removed her hat and held it beside her.

She was one of the most beautiful women Sheila had ever seen. She must have been close to fifty, but her thick white skin was flawless, her blue eyes wide and ringed with long lashes. Her blue-black hair looked freshly styled in a salon where cost was never considered, and her long nails were polished to match her lips. Her face showed absolutely no emotion whatsoever as she asked, "May I help you?"

"I'm looking for the Wimberly house." Sheila waved one hand in its direction. "Will it be all right to park here?"

The woman gave a bored shrug. "It's public property."

"Thanks." Sheila didn't think the exchange merited a smile.

She'd turned to go when the woman asked, "Are you related to Marion?"

"My aunt is a friend of Dolly's. I'm Sheila Travis."

"How do you do? I'm Rhoda Bennett." She extended her hand as if they were at an embassy function and said her name as if it meant something and Sheila should know what.

All she could think of to reply was "I'm glad to meet you. Your home is lovely." It was an inane remark. The house was magnificent—a large box of pale-gray stucco with black shutters and white trim, it covered almost half a lot that was twice as large as any other on the street. In common with many Charleston houses, it was built near one property line with a two-storied porch facing not the street, but the lawn that stretched from street to alley on the other side. A tall fence of iron railings surrounded the lot, anchored by stucco columns topped with fat white pineapples. Brass pineapples gleamed on the wrought-iron gates, and in the center of the lawn a small green boy held aloft what Sheila at first took to be another pineapple, spouting water. Only a second glance assured her it was actually a green fish perpetually filling a pond full of fat orange brother and sister fish.

The dignity of the house was softened by masses of flowers that reveled in its manicured yard. Purple pansies lifted their faces from white concrete planters. Lavender and violet irises marched in front of ivy beds and boxwoods, while pink and white azaleas circled huge magnolias and oaks. Sweet peas in pink, lavender, and a delicate, unexpected yellow bowed next to a walk of old bricks laid in a herringbone pattern. Pink and white roses climbed a trellis just beyond a gleaming white concrete birdbath. Even hydrangeas massed against a distant alley wall had been bred to a perfectly purply pink to blend with the rest.

"Thank you." Rhoda permitted herself a small smile of pride, then inclined her head as if waiting for another remark.

Sheila had not felt so at loss for polite conversation since her first embassy party. What could one say to a well-groomed, beautiful zombie with a lawn out of *Southern Living*? She was relieved when a blue sports car lunged to the curb across the street and disgorged a young man obviously intent on joining them.

He was dressed in cut-off jeans, a faded sports shirt, and a captain's cap, but even before he reached them, Sheila knew he was Rhoda's son. He had the same perfect nose, delicate black brows, raven hair, and navy eyes. He also had a deep tan and a cocky smile that was a welcome contrast to his mother's frosty respectability. "You wanted to see me?"

Sheila thought for a moment he meant her, but Rhoda said coolly, "Yes, I do." She was not, however, easily distracted from propriety. "Sheila, this is my son, Heyward. Heyward, this is Sheila Travis. She's come to visit Dolly and Marion for a few days." Her voice was as flat as a computerized recording.

Heyward's eyes crinkled at the corners when he smiled. They crinkled now as he stuck out a lean, well-shaped hand roughened by the weather. "Welcome to Charleston, Sheila. If you'll come by Bennett's Sailing School, I can give you a good price on lessons."

"I've sailed since I was a child," she said, smiling, "but not for nearly a year. Could I just rent a boat for an hour or two?"

Heyward's eyes crinkled again. "For a beautiful woman, anything is possible. Look me up."

It was clearly a dismissal, and it was time in any case for her to go on her way. As she loped down the sidewalk she heard Heyward ask again, "You wanted to see me?"

Rhoda's reply was muffled, as if she had returned to her weeding. "Not out here. I'll be in in a minute."

"Well, don't be too long. I've got a student at five."

By now Sheila was standing in front of the Wimberly house. It was just as Aunt Mary had described it: narrow, three-storied, and painted a crisp white with the ubiquitous black shutters. "They look black, dear," Aunt Mary had informed her, "but actually they are what is known as Charleston green. It's black with just a soupçon of green."

In her present mood, Sheila would have defied anyone to find the soupçon of green. She couldn't help admiring, though, their crispness against the white clapboards. This house was smaller than Rhoda's, but she preferred these graceful milled cornices and bannisters, the horsehead hitching post beside the gate, the waist-high wrought-iron fence, and deep-red roses climbing a trellis beside a deep bay window on the front. The lawn was not as elegant as its neighbor, either, but contained respectable borders of pansies and sweet peas and several bushes heavy with fat roses. Above the heavy Charleston green front door, a screened upstairs porch looked inviting.

"Piazza." Sheila murmured it in surprise. She'd never used that word that she could remember. It must have risen from some ancient racial memory. Was that the right word, or was it "veranda"? Either word conjured big rockers and iced drinks, which she hoped would soon be forthcoming.

At the gate she hesitated once more, looking up and down the street in the faint hope that something would happen to send her back to Atlanta. She was surprised that other houses on the street seemed in various stages of repair—and disrepair. Across the street a scaffold propped up an elderly chimney. Down the street a new roof rose above peeling boards and unkempt bushes. Apparently there were still some people in this part of Charleston too poor to paint.

The warm, light breeze fluttered her skirt, bringing a tang of the sea. Soon, she vowed, she'd find all that salt water she was smelling. It reminded her of Japan.

Well, she might as well get on with it—whatever "it" might be. With a deep breath—for she really did hate coming to stay with perfect strangers without a prior introduction—she opened the gate and mounted six steps to the brass knocker.

"Hey, there. Can I help you?" A man's cheerful voice called from behind. Sheila turned.

He was handsome for a stocky man, solid rather than fat, with friendly brown eyes and lighter brown hair only slightly thinning on top. He looked about forty-five and was expensively, though casually, dressed in tan slacks and a creamy shirt open at the neck to show a mass of curly dark hair. He wore a gold chain around his neck and a thick gold bracelet on one wrist, which Sheila usually disliked intensely. On him, she admitted to herself, it looked good. He mounted the steps and stood slightly taller than her own five nine.

She put out her hand. "I'm Sheila Travis. I've come to spend a few days with Dolly Langdon."

If the man was surprised he was too well-bred to show it. "Welcome, Sheila. I'm Buddy Endicott, Dolly's son-in-law. I saw you talking with the Ice Maiden"—he jerked his head toward the Bennett property—"and thought maybe you were doing a survey. A classy survey," he amended.

His smile was so warm she smiled back. "I was—a survey of where I could legally park."

He unlocked the door for her with his own key. "Rhoda would have charged you if she could, but lucky for us all she doesn't own the street—yet." He pushed the door open with a flourish and stood back for her to precede him. "Come on in."

She stopped, surprised. The door led not into the house, as she had expected, but merely onto the end of a downstairs porch. The actual front door of the house stood halfway down, open behind a screen.

Buddy chuckled. "I thought that door would fool you. This is what Charlestonians call a 'single house,' one room wide and several rooms deep. I've always wondered why Great-grandpa Wimberly invested in such a solid front door when you can just as easily come up those steps down in the middle of the piazza."

"It *is* a piazza!" Sheila exclaimed, delighted. Then, to keep from explaining, she added, "It's a bit like a train, isn't it?"

Buddy flashed her a look of approval. "Yes, a European train, with a corridor along one side. A writer said long ago that 'Charleston houses stand sidewaies backward into their yards and onely endwaies with their gables toward the street.'"

Did he really have a good eighteenth-century accent, or was that just Charlestonian again? Before Sheila could ask, he'd taken her elbow and steered her gently along the porch and down the center steps. "And let me show you something else." He pointed to the rear. Just beyond the house, set slightly back and also facing the yard, was a tiny white house with its own shutters. It was two stories tall and could scarcely have more than one room on each floor. "The caboose," he said.

"It's charming! What is it really?"

"It used to be the kitchen, put out back to keep kitchen fires from destroying the rest of the house. I don't know when, exactly, but at one time there was a law in Charleston that the kitchen had to be far enough away from the main house for green grass to grow between them."

"Sounds sensible," Sheila agreed. "What's the house now?"

"For a long time it was where Marion stored extra furniture. For the past two months Francine, Dolly's new nurse, has lived there." He led her briskly back up the porch toward the screened door.

"Do the houses face sideways so there's more lawn?" Sheila wondered aloud.

He shook his head. "No, it's to keep cool and get the breezes. We've built like this since 1733, before air conditioning or even fans. The piazzas all face south or west, to shade the houses from the sun and let in the breeze."

He held open the screened door for her and called in, "Nell? You've got company."

Sure enough, the downstairs was dim and cool even without air conditioning. It was also empty—that was easy to see. From a large hall arches opened into the living room on the left and the dining room on the right. Beyond the dining room, an open swinging door led into the kitchen. From the hall, a staircase ascended to a landing then curved back on itself to the upper floors. Next to the stairs was a small elevator door.

Sheila had a quick impression of space, airiness, and beautiful old things well kept. The pale-blue walls rose at least twelve feet to ceilings painted the same creamy white as the woodwork. Oriental rugs covered polished pine floorboards like sapphires and rubies. A tall Chinese vase of eucalyptus added its musty smell to those of furniture polish and homemade rolls. In the dining room, silver candelabra gleamed on a mahogany sideboard and were reflected in a mirror edged in gilt. In the living room, brocade chairs and drapes set off the glow of mahogany tables.

Buddy didn't give her time for more than a glance. "Do you have a suitcase in your trunk?" When she nodded, he held out one hand. "The gray Caddy, right? Let me get it for you. Nell must be upstairs. Go right on up. Dolly's sitting room is directly over the living room." He took her keys and went out with a quick light step.

Sheila heard footsteps, heavy and hurried, and a stout woman in a gray uniform hurried down wiping brown hands on an enormous white apron. "You must be Sheila. I'm Nell, the housekeeper. Sorry I wasn't down here to greet you, but Miss Marion wanted me to help her get some things out of the attic this afternoon." She stuck out one hand, as forthright as her name. "Dolly told me this morning you were comin', and we're both glad. If you're anything like your aunt, you'll do her a world of good." She eyed Sheila dubiously. "You don't look much like her, do you?"

Mentally comparing her inches with Aunt Mary's diminutive frame and her thick dark hair with Aunt Mary's silver curls, Sheila had to agree. Nell, however, was looking for similarity and finally found it. "You got her twinkle in your eye. That's good."

"When did you meet Aunt Mary?" Sheila asked her.

Nell's chuckle was deep and rich as honey. "Law, child, we met when she first come here as a little girl. About seven she'd have been, I reckon."

Nell certainly didn't look that old. Her smooth hair was only lightly touched with gray, and her round face was unlined. She asked with the easy confidence of one who is at home in her work, "Can I get you something to drink before you go up? Iced tea, a Coke, some lemonade?"

Sheila knew from experience that "iced tea" meant sweet tea. "Lemonade would be lovely."

Nell had started toward the kitchen when a voice inquired from the landing, "Nell, do we have a guest?"

The woman coming down the stairs had short gray hair, stylishly cut, and a bandage on one arm. Her face was tanned to the color of caramel and lined with wrinkles, her voice as deep and raspy as Aunt Mary's own. Was it the South Carolina water, Sheila wondered, or years of secret smoking that caused these Tallulah Bankhead voices? And how did the women manage to look so cool and fresh in this heat and humidity? In yellow linen, Marion Wimberly looked as if she had just dressed, not gone through an attic.

She came down the stairs as Nell spoke. "This is Sheila Travis, Miss Marion, Mary Beaufort's niece. She's come to visit us for a few days."

Only by a flicker of her eyelids did Marion show that this was news to her. Almost at once her face arranged itself into a formal smile and she held out her hand. "Welcome, Sheila. I hope you'll enjoy your stay with us. Charleston is lovely at this time of year."

Her handclasp was firm, her dark eyes alert and intelligent. Sheila realized that much of her dread had been the thought of spending time in a house full of old women, but neither of these fit her stereotype. Perhaps Charleston wouldn't be so bad after all.

Marion looked about her. "Did I hear Buddy, too? He called and said he wanted to talk with me about something."

"He's gone to get my suitcase," Sheila explained.

"And I was just going to get her some lemonade."

Nell started back to the kitchen, but Marion put out a restraining arm. "I think it would be a good idea for us to ask Rhoda and Heyward over this evening after dinner—Rhoda knows Mary. Could you make us something special for dessert?"

"I already made it," Nell assured her. "Strawberry shortcake. Dolly told me—"

What Dolly had told her, they would never know. Just then Buddy Endicott called cheerfully at the door, "I've got her suitcase, but before I carry it up, did I hear Nell mention lemonade?"

He set down the case and headed toward the kitchen. "Boy, is it stuffy in here! What's the matter with the fan?"

He flipped a switch, and three things happened simultaneously. Something whizzed through the air, something crashed to the floor, and Nell began to moan.

FOUR

THEY RUSHED TO THE kitchen and stared in disbelief. One blade of the fan had detached itself and spun through the air, carrying a large jar of rice in its trajectory.

"Lawdy, Miss Marion," Nell said, groaning, "if you hadn't stopped me, I'd of been right in that thing's path. It would have been my head instead of rice lying all over that floor." She leaned against a cabinet, hands covering her face. Buddy put his hand at Sheila's waist, a gesture more protective than sensual.

A very small young woman with freckles and sleek platinum hair ran down the stairs. "What happened? Is anybody hurt?"

Marion crossed the dining room. "Everything's all right, Francine. A fan blade slung off, but no one was hurt. Tell Dolly it must have just worked loose."

But Francine wasn't going upstairs just yet. She crossed the dining room and Buddy's hand fell from Sheila's waist like a dead weight. Francine gave him a smile, showing a mouth full of small, pointed teeth that protruded slightly. "You okay, Buddy?"

"I'm fine, honey," he replied.

Francine put out a hand to Sheila. "Hi, I'm Francine Jenkins, Mrs. Langdon's nurse." As if to prove it, she looked about the room and reached for Nell's wrist. "Are you all right, Nell?"

"I'm fine," Nell said heavily, "but it gave me quite a shock."

"And you, Miss Wimberly?"

"I'm fine," Marion said with a trace of asperity, "but I think Nell could do with a drink of water."

Francine moved to a cabinet and stood on tiptoe to take a glass from an upper cabinet. Everything about the nurse was angular—sharp elbows, pointed nose and chin, eyebrows with high arches penciled above eyes that slanted slightly. But her soft yellow sweater and black slacks clung to curves Sheila would once have coveted and her smooth white hair swept her shoulders provocatively as she passed Buddy. Beneath a soft bang her eyes glowed green and complacent in her thin freckled face.

Buddy followed her across the kitchen and bent to pick up some glass. Francine brushed against him lightly as she handed Nell the glass of water.

Nell's hand trembled so badly that Marion helped her hold it. "You've had a shock, Nell. Perhaps you should go on home. I'm sure Francine can . . ."

Her suggestion was the tonic the housekeeper needed. "Go home? With comp'ny for dinner?" She was clearly scandalized. "I'll be *fine*, as soon as I catch my breath. Everybody clear out and let me work. But get *that* stuff"—she kicked at the rice with one sturdy foot—"off my floor."

Marion hesitated, then gave a short nod. "Very well, perhaps work is what you need. Buddy, if you would clean up this mess?" He nodded. "And I'll be in my office upstairs, if you will come up afterward. Francine, if you'll show our guest up to Mrs. Langdon's room . . ."

"I was going to help Buddy clean up . . ." She trailed the sentence and waited.

The older woman gave the young one a long, icy look, then yielded. "Very well. Sheila, let me pour you that glass of lemonade, and I'll take you up myself."

As they climbed the stairs, she turned to say dryly, "This isn't a typical Charleston welcome, but it's one you're not likely to forget."

On the second floor she ushered Sheila into the front room. "Dolly, here's your guest. Sheila, this is my sister—and Mary's friend—Dolly. Tell Dolly what the ruckus was downstairs." With that she left the room and went upstairs.

Sheila's first impression of the room was of lavender—pale-lavender walls, deeper lavender drapes, lavender flowers on the ivory chintz slipcovers, even touches of lavender in the flat tweed carpet that covered the floor, making it easier for a wheelchair than shiny floors. In a garment of lavender and rose organdy that ruffled around her throat and down her magnificent bosom, Dolly sat in the front bay window, a tall glass of iced tea at her elbow.

As Sheila crossed to her, Dolly turned her wheelchair with a warm smile of welcome. "How nice of you to come, Sheila. You've got glorious weather for your visit." She patted a large wicker armchair with plump cushions. "Come sit in the window, where there's a breeze—and do tell me what that ruckus was downstairs."

Her imitation of Marion was so droll that Sheila laughed as she sank into her chair. "A fan blade blew off in the kitchen and demolished a year's supply of rice."

"Do!" Dolly exclaimed, her eyes wide. Sheila smiled. She hadn't heard that expression in years. Dolly was already chattering on. "The fan doesn't matter, but you'll soon find we like our rice in Charleston. Oh well, we'll let Nell worry about that. Tell me about Mary."

As they talked, Sheila considered her hostess. Aunt Mary had been right. Even past seventy, Dolly Langdon was an exceptionally pretty woman—and a charming one, as well. She was plump, her soft white skin so powdered she seemed dusted with flour. Her blue eyes twinkled and her honey-brown hair escaped a large soft bun on top of her head in curling tendrils that she brushed away from time to time as if they were flies.

"I was so glad you could come," she said, as if Sheila had been invited for purely social reasons. She looked about her room. "I don't get out much, so the world has to come to me." Lest Sheila feel sorry for her, however, she added, "But I am surrounded by memories—years and years of them."

She certainly was. On every surface in the room small framed snapshots and formal studio portraits brought Dolly's memorable past into her limited present. "Is that you?" Sheila asked, indicating a tinted photograph over the mantelpiece. A petite bride stood beside her handsome groom, her golden curls almost as high as his. They surveyed the world with identical blue solemn gazes.

"No, that's Mama and Daddy. They sent that to Aunt Bella when they got married. Daddy was at Yale, you see, and in disgrace..." Her eyes twinkled and invited Sheila to ask the obvious question.

"Disgrace?"

"Because he chose a Yankee college. Granddaddy never forgave him—especially after he met a Yankee woman and married her up there. Granddaddy had a stroke and was paralyzed for the rest of his life." She reached for another photo, of a fierce old man in an old-fashioned wheelchair, holding an infant. "That's him with me, just before he died. They'd come home by then," she added unnecessarily.

Dolly lifted another picture from the table. "This was my Alva. He'd have made two of Daddy!" While Sheila examined that picture, Dolly wheeled herself to the bookcase. "I have something here you might like to see." She chose a small sepia snapshot framed in pewter. It showed three girls, one tall and scraggy, two short and pudgy, all wearing school uniforms and standing beside what Sheila recognized as the Wimberlys' horsehead hitching post. The two small girls had blond ringlets, the largest looked like her darker hair had been shaped around a pudding bowl. All three scowled.

Sheila examined it, then, as Dolly chuckled, looked more closely. There could be no doubt. One of those two plump little girls, the one with her tongue peeping from the corner of her mouth and one foot twisted behind her in a most unladylike manner, was someone she knew very well.

"I may want to get a print of this," she told Dolly, "for blackmail purposes."

Dolly returned the photo to her shelf. "I'll show you others later. How is Mary's health these days?" Only after she had completed a Southern welcome did she broach the real reason for Sheila's visit.

"Mary told me you've done a bit of, well, detecting in the past."

Sheila nodded. "Some. But I'm not at all sure I have anything to offer here. Aunt Mary made me . . ."

Dolly threw back her head and laughed in delight. "You sound *exactly* like Mary herself, railing against *her* Aunt Mary for making her wear an undershirt! You don't look much like her, but you're very alike after all."

"Not at all," Sheila assured her. "For one thing, I don't foist relatives off on friends in the vain hope that they can help them."

"Oh, but you'll help just by being here," Dolly replied. "You've done me a world of good already. I don't feel so anxious any more."

"But so far the accidents have been pretty harmless, haven't they?"

Dolly twisted the satin ends of her sash in her lap. "You'll probably think me a proper fussbudget." She paused, unsure how to go on.

The room was silent except for the hum of a bee in the roses outside the open front window. Then, abruptly, above them they heard Marion say icily, "I will not be bullied, Buddy. Mr. Adams has been at me all week to sell that parcel, and now you. I tell you, I've made up my mind."

"It's not right!" Buddy declared hotly.

"Close that door, please," Marion replied. They heard it shut.

Dolly shook her head. "I wish—" She broke off, as if lost in thought.

"Tell me about the accidents," Sheila prompted her, "and what worries you most."

Dolly sighed and reached for a fan, which she moved lazily. "It all sounds like nothing when I try to talk about it, and Marion thinks I'm downright silly." As she brushed away a tendril of hair from her neck, Sheila saw that her hand was trembling. "If you don't mind, I don't think we'll tell anyone why you are really here, especially Marion. Let's just say you wanted to see Charleston."

"Won't she think I'm imposing on you?" Sheila wondered.

Dolly's chuckle filled the room. "Laws-a-mercy, Sheila, how could Mary's niece impose on us? Marion's always glad when someone comes to visit." Her voice lowered almost to a whisper. "She worries, you know—thinks she ought to give up the shop and stay home with me. But the shop is her life. That and Charleston history. She's miserable if she can't go down and dust her precious bits and pieces every day."

As if to prove her point, the door upstairs opened and they heard Marion descending the stairs. She paused in the doorway, her face showing no sign of the tempest they'd overheard. "I'm going back to close up the shop. Do you need anything?" Dolly shook her head. "I'll be back for dinner, then."

Almost immediately Buddy stuck his head in the door, his face cheerful. "Hello, Mama-in-law. Just wanted to report that the kitchen is back to normal, and Nell's about to make her famous broccoli soup. Get your taste buds ready. She's even promised me the recipe, as a reward for good sweeping." He clumped down, whistling.

"He cooks?" Sheila asked, curious. Buddy looked like a man who would prefer being cooked for.

"Oh, my, yes, dear." Dolly's laughter rippled across the room in waves. "He owns a restaurant, Harbor Lights. One of those places that are all fish nets and driftwood, where the lights are so dim you can't see the menu, much less your food. But the food is excellent. It and a restaurant actually called Buddy's are two of the best seafood places in town. In the family we refer to our Buddy's and their Buddy's." She took a sip of tea and wiped the sweating glass with a napkin. "But our Buddy has something they don't have—Nell. He calls her his secret weapon, and gets all his best recipes from her."

"Oh." That explained, Sheila still wanted to hear about the reason she had come. "You were about to tell me about the accidents."

Dolly nodded. "And that Marion thinks I'm a fool for worrying about them."

If Aunt Mary had been there she could have said "Don't mind Marion, dear," her husky voice confidential as two old friends can be when discussing a third. Sheila chose to be matter-of-fact instead. "Why don't you just tell me what's happened?"

Her tone seemed to give Dolly confidence.

"Very well. It began nearly two weeks ago. The girls—that's my granddaughters, Buddy's daughters . . ."

Sheila nodded. "Aunt Mary filled me in on your family, so I think I'll recognize the names, at least. Let's see, they are Rachel and Rebecca. Is that right?"

Dolly nodded. "Yes, but we call them Rake and Becca. They are sophomores at the College of Charleston. Rake's a drama major and a wonderful little actress. Becca is studying marine biology. But to get back to my story, they took an out-of-town friend to see Boone Hall Plantation, and while they were inside, a tree limb fell on their car. Nobody was in the car, and they thought it a great adventure. But..." Dolly shook her head to complete the sentence.

"It must have been inconvenient," Sheila murmured, "to get back to town."

Dolly shook her head again. "No, it so happened that Buddy and Francine were also there for the afternoon. I'd given her the day off"—Dolly let out a small sigh—"and Buddy has been squiring her lately." She shook her head in disapproval, then her lips curved in a wry smile. "I'm very proprietary about my son-in-law, Sheila. He's been more like a son to me."

"He seems to feel the same."

Dolly nodded. "Which is why I won't say a word even if he"—her voice quavered only slightly—"marries the girl. Though I'll admit to you that I hope he doesn't. Now, where were we?" She smoothed the ruffles on her lap.

"Buddy and Francine were at the plantation."

"Yes. They brought the girls back, and Buddy sent a man for the car. As I said, it was only an adventure at the time."

"But then?"

Dolly shook her head, as if in disbelief. "From that time on, it's been one thing right after another. The very next afternoon Judge Black—our neighbor to the south—died of a heart attack while his wife—who's our cousin Annie—and Marion were at a Women of the Church meeting. When they got back, Marion dropped Annie off and went back to the shop—she always likes to close up. Annie went in and found him lying on the floor, dead." She pursed her lips and shook her head again. "I can't get used to his being gone. It's like losing the last tie with my parents, somehow. He was fifteen, living in that same house, when I was born. His father, the first judge, was Daddy's law partner, and the judge handled all our affairs until he went to the State Supreme Court—that was just before Aunt Bella died. And then he married Annie, our cousin, some years ago, which put him right in the family. I couldn't say why, though. Emma, his first wife was such a lady—a Rutledge, you know.''

Talking with Aunt Mary had accustomed Sheila to historical sidetracks, but listening to Dolly was like unraveling a skein of yarn. Sheila decided to forge ahead rather than go back through those last sentences. ''That wasn't really an accident, though, was it? I mean, he must have been . . .'' She paused, trained by Aunt Mary to know she was treading dangerous ground discussing the age of a man whom her hostess had just said was fifteen when she was born.

Dolly had no such modesty. ''Nearly ninety. And I guess it wasn't an accident, but it was strange. He'd been over here the night before for dinner, chipper as could be. Even talked about how he wasn't afraid of dying.'' She shook her head and sighed. ''Then Marion picked up a roofing nail in her back tire.''

''A roofing nail?'' Where had Sheila seen a new roof lately?

Dolly told her. ''Probably from Annie's. The Judge had already ordered a new roof before he died, so she went on and had them do it. Once you've gotten those men to say they'll come, it doesn't do to postpone, no matter how it looks right after a funeral.''

''And they left a nail in the street?''

''They must have, mustn't they? Because when Marion came out of church on Sunday, the tire was flat and there was a roofing nail stuck in it. So annoying, and Buddy already at the restaurant.''

''What did she do?''

''Well, luckily Francine's brother Lamar was visiting her that day, so Marion called her and he went over and changed it for her. He's the one who fixed Buddy's television, too. He's very handy to have around the place, if he weren't so surly. But it was hard for Marion to ask for his help.'' Dolly looked as if she were about to say more, then didn't.

''Tell me about the television,'' Sheila suggested.

"There's not much to tell. It was something to do with a worn wire, I believe. They were sitting there watching it when they began to smell smoke. But it had been fine that afternoon, so Annie said." Seeing that Sheila wasn't making the connection, Dolly tried to explain. "When she was in watching her story. She didn't have a color television yet—the Judge wouldn't allow it—so she went to Buddy's."

"Every day?" Sheila found it hard to believe that anyone could be that attached to a television program.

Dolly nodded. "She did then. It's just around the corner and up the block." She waved one hand in a generally southeasterly direction.

"I see. What happened next?"

"Oh, Annie bought herself a color set the week after the Judge died," Dolly said. She leaned forward confidentially. "Marion thought that was awful, unseemly somehow. But we've none of us got enough years left to worry about that kind of thing. I say if she wants a color television and can afford one, get it!"

She seemed to expect some sort of agreement, and Sheila murmured one, but inwardly she was fuming. Had Aunt Mary sent her all the way to Charleston to investigate the death of a ninety-year-old heart patient, a nail in a tire, and a worn television wire? She would spend the night, she decided, and bid her charming hostesses farewell first thing in the morning. But there were two accidents still to account for before she went for a well-deserved rest with a good book. "What about your medicine?"

Dolly pursed her round mouth into a rosebud. "That was so aggravating. I get my medicines from Luther's Pharmacy—always have. Roy Luther and I went to Sunday School together as children, and I trust him. My hands aren't strong, so he gives me easy-to-open caps." She reached into a pocket beside her wheelchair and brought out a plastic vial. As she spoke, she flipped the top open and shut as if to show herself how easily it could be done, but this time she did not lose her thread of conversation.

"A few days after the flat-tire incident, I woke in the night with a pain." Her blue eyes clouded like a summer sky at the memory. "I reached for my pain medicine—a new bottle—and it had one of those childproof caps on it. You know the kind I mean?"

"The kind every child can open but adults find difficult."

"Exactly. I couldn't get it off, and Marion didn't hear me call. I tried and tried to open it, but I never could."

The next question was one Sheila hated to ask, but must. "How serious could that have been? Is there anyone who might want to do you harm?"

Dolly shook her head. "My nitroglycerin, now—that could be serious, like it was for the Judge. But these are just pills for pain. I had a worrisome night, but after I slept a good bit the next day, I was fine."

"Have you talked with the pharmacy?"

"Yes, after I asked Francine why she had gotten the wrong cap. She always picks up my pills. She said she'd asked Buddy to pick it up that day on his way here for dinner. He said he'd told Annie to get it, and she said it was already bagged when she went for it. Then I called the pharmacy. Roy said I had called him and asked for the childproof cap because children would be visiting. Now, Sheila, what was I to say? He's known me forever."

Sheila carefully controlled her voice. "What kind of medication are you on?"

The elderly woman flapped her hands with a flutter of ruffles. "Now don't *you* start that, Sheila. Marion already suggested I ordered that medicine under sedation. But I don't make phone calls under sedation. I sleep. I did not make that phone call."

"Who else might have?" Sheila asked. "And why?"

Dolly gave her a look of approval. "Exactly what I've been asking myself day and night. Nobody in this house sounds like me."

Sheila smiled appreciatively. Dolly's voice was half talk and half laughter, and in spite of the seriousness of her physical condition it rippled like a friendly stream. Probably, Sheila thought, nobody in the whole world sounded like Dolly Langdon. But in that case, why had Mr. Luther made what could have been a most serious mistake?

"I suppose it could have been an accident," she mused.

"Yes, dear. They *all* could have been accidents—even that fan blade slinging off this afternoon. But they are *so* annoying—and time-consuming, too. Francine spent half a day cleaning up at Buddy's after the fire, and she had a time with me the morning after I couldn't open the medicine. Then Marion missed half a day of work trying to get hold of my doctor. The flat tire meant Sunday dinner was nearly two hours late, which gave Nell a fit, and deprived Marion of the little free time she allows herself. Just tell me, Sheila, why we're having such a rash of accidents all at the same time?"

Sheila shook her head. "I have no idea—yet. Tell me about Marion's fall."

Dolly's brow puckered. "There's not much I can tell, but I don't think Marion's told me all there is to know. Becca drove me to the doctor yesterday afternoon as she always does on Tuesdays, and as we got home Francine was coming back from an errand. We all came in together, and"—Dolly's voice trembled slightly—"found Marion lying at the foot of the stairs." Dolly reached for her tea and took a sip before she continued. "She was just stunned, thank goodness, and Francine soon brought her around and checked for broken bones. Marion insisted she was fine, and except for a sprained wrist, she seems to be. But there's something about that fall she doesn't want me to know."

"And you'd prefer for me to try to find out without asking her directly?"

Dolly nodded, and her eyes were grave. "If you can find out what's going on, Sheila, I'll be most grateful. But you must be very careful. I may just be a silly old woman, but I think there's more to it than pranks. No one has gotten seriously hurt so far, but Mary would never forgive me if you were the first."

FIVE

"How dramatic I sound! And it's probably about nothing at all." Dolly concealed a yawn behind one hand. "I usually lie down for a while before dinner, Sheila. Has anyone shown you your room?"

Sheila gave her a wry grin. "We were otherwise distracted. But if you'll tell me where it is . . ."

Dolly shook her head. "I'll show you, but you'll need to push. I'm tuckered out by this time of day." She directed Sheila out into the hall and then, to Sheila's surprise, to the wide door leading onto the upstairs porch.

"In Chicago this would never work," Dolly said with a twinkle over her shoulder, "but this is Charleston. When we were girls there were three bedrooms and one huge bath on this floor, but when I got incapacitated and needed to be upstairs most of the time, Marion moved up to what had been her office at the front of the third floor and had part of the attic fixed up for a new office. My bedroom is over the dining room"—she nodded to the first set of windows—"and two small baths were put into what used to be the one big old bath. Now the only way to get to the guest room is along the piazza here. I hope you won't mind being isolated—at least it's private."

Sheila returned Dolly to her own quarters, then retraced her steps with relief. An hour of quiet was what she needed to unwind from the trip and decide how to explain to Aunt Mary that there was nothing here worth worrying about.

Nothing could have looked less sinister than the Wimberly guest room. Creamy walls were broken only by the door and one tall window on the porch side and two windows in the north wall that gave a feeling of spaciousness beyond the room's modest dimensions. A soft beige Oriental rug bordered in soft pinks and greens covered most of the polished pine floorboards. All the flowers from the yard seemed to have moved indoors to brighten the chintz drapes and matching cover on a large wing chair, and were echoed by two prints from the Calendar of Flowers hung over the dresser. Grassy green chintz formed the ruffle around the four tall mahogany posts of the bed and the dust ruffle beneath its thick white spread.

Sheila took off her shoes and wiggled her toes on the silky old carpet, then padded over to open one window on the north side to let the breeze encircle the room while she unpacked. She was putting her suitcase away in the bottom of the small closet when Nell spoke at the screened door. She held out a telephone.

"Sheila? Your aunt wants to talk to you. I brought you the living room phone. We almost never use it, so you can keep it up here." She dropped to her hands and knees and plugged it in beneath the bed before Sheila could offer to help.

Aunt Mary scarcely waited for Sheila to say hello. "You didn't call to say you'd arrived."

"I've only been here an hour or so, Aunt Mary." Sheila waved good-bye to Nell, slipped off her shoes, and lay back against the pillows on the bed. "It didn't occur to me you'd expect me to call before the rates went down."

Aunt Mary ignored the barb. "What have you found out, dear?"

"In an hour?"

"Well, what *have* you been doing?"

Her tone conveyed that Sheila had been malingering at the very least. "I went for a sail and toured Middleton Plantation, and . . ."

"Sheila!"

"Very well, Aunt Mary, I've spent most of the time visiting with Dolly. She's a dear. Frankly, the accidents all sound pretty tame, but I can understand how they'd get on her nerves. Especially since we had a little demonstration right after I arrived."

"Demonstration?"

Sheila explained. For a wonder, Aunt Mary listened without interrupting before she said, "You watch out for Francine."

"Don't you think a final vote is a bit premature?"

"She's certainly not suitable for Buddy, dear."

"He seems to think so," Sheila pointed out. "Isn't that what counts?"

"You won't know for sure until you get better acquainted with him. I had forgotten he was eligible . . ."

Sheila permitted herself an audible snort, which Aunt Mary ignored, ", , , but you may find you have a good deal in common. He was stationed in Japan at one time, I believe."

What Aunt Mary thought soldiers and embassy wives might have in common Sheila didn't plan to imagine. It was a moot point in any case, now. "I won't have much time to get to know him, Aunt Mary. I'm thinking about coming back to Atlanta tomorrow." (Now why hadn't she said "I am *coming* back"?)

"Nonsense." Southern Bell managed to convey a raised eyebrow and tilted chin. "You went there with a task to do, and you haven't even begun. In fact, from what you tell me, things have gotten worse."

"That wasn't my fault!"

"Nevertheless, I hope you won't leave before you accomplish what you set out to do. And Sheila?" Aunt Mary sounded worried. Could she possibly be concerned, for once, about her niece's safety? "Be very careful. Charlestonians have such nice manners."

The temper she'd been controlling all day flared. "Aunt Mary, I have eaten dinner with two presidents. Surely my manners will be equal to dinner in Charleston."

Aunt Mary paused. "I certainly hope so, dear. Just take your cues from the others."

"Given the way accidents happen around here, you might show a little concern for my safety instead of my manners."

"Oh, fiddlesticks, Sheila. You're perfectly capable of taking care of yourself. Call me tomorrow."

Sheila hung up and slid off the bed. Maybe she *should* start detecting—before she threw a vase against a wall.

SHE STROLLED DOWN to the kitchen. Nell, fully engaged with dinner, scarcely noticed as she peered up where the fan hung crippled and still. "Do you know where Buddy put that fan blade?" she asked. "I'd like to take a look at it."

Nell opened a cupboard and took down a key. "Miss Marion's workroom, most likely." She jerked her head toward the screened door that led from the kitchen directly onto the porch. "It's the next door down."

The workroom must be directly beneath Sheila's, but instead of comfortable furnishings it was filled with a hodge-podge of tools and what looked like valuable furniture pieces—a drawer from a chest, the skeleton of a chair, a lovely small round table, and, in one corner, a pile of old bannisters that must have been replaced on the porch. Because all the windows were closed, the air was thick with heat and dust. A space was cleared in the center around a lovely old sideboard in the final stages of stripping. Shelves along one wall held stripper, wire brushes, sandpaper, and other implements for refinishing fine furniture. Apparently Marion's high standards meant she refinished some of her pieces herself.

The fan blade was propped near the door, leaning tipsily to one side. Even a quick examination showed it had not torn loose. Sheila rubbed one finger around the three screw holes and found them all smooth. Had someone deliberately loosened the screws so that when the fan was turned on, the blade would sling off from the vibration? Or could all three screws have worked loose at the same time?

"Does Miss Wimberly know you are here?" The voice, like a light splash of cold water, made Sheila turn quickly to the door. Francine stood with one hand cupped to the screen door, peering in.

"Nell does." Sheila set the blade down and joined Francine on the porch.

"Miss Wimberly does not allow anyone to enter her workroom without permission." Her eyes scanned Sheila's hair, face, and clothes as she spoke, searching for flaws.

"My hair frizzes, I have a mole on my left earlobe, and I wear size ten shoes." Sheila was tempted almost unbearably to say it, but just in time she remembered Aunt Mary's caution. Surely her manners were up to this exchange. "Have you worked here long?"

"About two months." Francine followed the brief statement with a question of her own. "Why have you come?" Her brows rose above her green eyes like ellipses.

"To visit Dolly." Sheila gazed around the yard. "Charleston is so lovely at this time of year."

"Did she *ask* you to come?"

Sheila was beginning to enjoy this. "Oh, yes. When Dolly found I was visiting my aunt for a short vacation, she invited me."

"I see." Francine's eye dropped, as if accidentally, to Sheila's bare left hand. "Are you divorced?"

"Widowed."

"Very long ago?"

"Last November."

"I'm sorry." Francine didn't sound sorry. She sounded as if she was thinking things over. She made a move as if to go, then turned back to ask carelessly, "Did you know Buddy and I are engaged?"

Sheila shook her head. "I hadn't heard." If Francine expected congratulations, she was doomed to disappointment.

Perhaps Francine had expected nothing at all. "We aren't announcing it, until he gets my ring. And until I . . . work some things out. But we're getting married soon. I thought you might like to know." She turned. "Well, I have to get back to work. I'm doing some research for Mrs. Langdon. Family history and stuff." She, at least, was impressed with her assignment.

"And I'd better get changed for dinner," Sheila said cordially. She didn't know what else to say. Would Francine be eating with the family?

Apparently so, for she called as she glided down the porch, "See you later."

Sheila returned to her own room and lay down on the bed to think things over. But the lazy hum of the bees and the soft sea breeze were so soothing that she was soon fast asleep.

SIX

SHE SLEPT SO WELL that she was almost late to dinner. Quickly she slipped into a new dress of beige silk and tied a colorful scarf at the neck. She went downstairs to find the house filled with people drinking sherry from antique glasses. Dolly sat in the arch leading to the living room, listening to a plump old woman with a round head and large, beaked nose. Her body bulged out of a brown double-knit suit that hadn't been fashionable ten years before when it was new, and the red blouse she wore with it made her look distinctly like a robin.

From the dining room, Francine came into the hall to join Buddy and Marion at the foot of the stairs just as he was saying in a low voice "But Rhoda won't, Marion." To which Marion didn't reply.

Nell was lighting candles and calling to someone behind her in the kitchen. " . . . sure was. If Miss Marion hadn't called me just then, you'd be cooking your own supper from now on."

Sheila's slight pause on the landing had the effect of making everyone stop talking and look up. Embarrassed, she started down the final steps feeling like Miss America on the gangway.

Dolly wheeled over to meet her. "I think you have met everyone, Sheila, except Annie and the girls." She lifted her hand and her companion came across the hall. "This is our cousin, Annie Black. She lives next door." In the plain house with the new roof, Sheila concluded. Annie was as plain as her house.

She peered with snapping black eyes through frizzy gray bangs. "How do you do?" She was standing so close to the bottom step that Sheila, bending to shake her hand, felt at least three feet too tall.

"Fine, thanks." She took another step down and Annie finally shifted slightly to let her pass.

"And these," Dolly continued, beckoning with one hand, "are our twins." Two young women came obediently from the kitchen, wearing smiles of welcome. Confronted with identical rose-blossom complexions, perfect noses, and big brown eyes, Sheila felt ancient.

Introductions complete, one of the twins smiled gently. "Until you know us better, Rake's the one with the crimped hair." Her own fell straight to her shoulders from an Alice-in-Wonderland band.

She could have also said, "Rake's the one with the makeup and the dramatic clothes." Becca's soft blue dress almost blended into the walls, while Rake had chosen a magenta cotton sweater, pleated cotton skirt in a pink, blue, yellow, green, and magenta plaid, and a vivid green scarf flung casually over one shoulder. Rake's eyelids were also magenta, Becca's a soft gray. But beneath the paint and clothes, the girls were hard to distinguish.

Sheila smiled. "I'm going to need to remember that."

As the twins turned back to help Nell bring dishes in, Buddy came to bring Sheila a sherry. "There's an easier way to tell them apart. Rake talks, Becca listens."

The table was set with china so fine that Sheila knew it must have a history, and hoped she could ask about it in a day or two. For now, she contented herself with admiring the orange birds and turquoise flowers on a huge soup tureen and with counting the candles that glowed on the table, on the huge mahogany buffet and in sconces around the wall. There were fourteen in all.

"Aunt Em won't permit lights for dinner," Becca murmured, sliding into the chair beside Sheila. "But she likes a lot of candles."

Candlelight was kind to the old woman. That face was too strong to have ever been pretty—its jaw too square and the brown eyes too piercing—but as she sat regally at the table's head, candlelight lent her network of tiny wrinkles a patina of beauty that even the lovely twins might envy.

As if they had never quarreled, Buddy sat automatically at Marion's right. He was a perfect host. If he minded being the only man in the room, he gave no sign as he carved the ham to a delicate thinness. Francine had started to the seat beside him, but Rake slid into it with a too-sweet smile. Buddy gave Francine a smile of apology and she took the seat across from him with an expression Sheila couldn't see around Becca.

Dolly occupied the other end of the table—it was impossible to think of any place that Dolly sat as the "foot." Sheila had been given the place of honor at Dolly's right, Annie was on her left.

"Seen much of Charleston?" Annie asked her as soon as grace was over.

"Not much, yet." Sheila helped herself to green beans from the dish Nell was holding. They had been simmered for hours with bits of pork, and she wished once again that Southerners could be taught the delicate art of stir-frying.

"It's too hot to do much sightseeing," Annie grumbled. "Too hot already, and just April. I don't know what we'll do..."

"We'll give you some guidebooks tomorrow." Marion spoke as if Annie were no more important than a raucous crow outside the window.

Rake wrinkled her nose and made a face her great-aunt couldn't see, then demanded, "Somebody tell us about the latest accident." She sounded aggrieved to have missed it.

Neither Buddy nor Marion spoke, but out in the kitchen Sheila heard Nell give a heartfelt "Uh-huh!"

"Perhaps you could ask Sheila," Francine suggested with a sideways look across the table. "She was looking at the fan blade afterward."

Sheila opened her mouth, wondering how to reply to this direct attack, but Marion spoke first. "Nell doesn't need to be reminded of that. Neither does your grandmother."

Rake threw Dolly a quick apologetic look. "Sorry, Gram. This ham is great, Aunt Em." She speared a piece on her fork with zest.

Dolly answered her. "You'll have to thank Rhoda Bennett, dear. She sent Heyward over with it this morning. Her brother sent it from Virginia. He never does remember she hates ham."

"Speaking of such things"—Rake looked archly around the table—"you'll never guess who I've asked to our sorority dance." Her eyes gleamed with mischief.

"Why should you ask anyone?" Annie demanded. "In my day, young men asked us."

Rake caught Sheila's eye but Sheila took a sip of water to avoid smiling back. Rake turned back to bait Annie. "I thought this would be a lot more fun. The guys at school are so young, and those at the Citadel so *boring.*" She drew out the last word in disdain.

Dolly was immediately hooked. "Whom did you ask instead?"

Rake wasn't telling at once. "Anyone else interested?"

"I'd rather watch you pop." Buddy grinned.

She wrinkled her nose at him, then leaned forward and said as if imparting a confidence, "Heyward Bennett himself!"

Sheila felt the girl beside her grow very still. Across the table, Francine's eyes narrowed. A frown creased Marion's forehead. In the kitchen, Nell muttered, "My, my!" Even Dolly looked perturbed.

"He's too old," Buddy said flatly.

Rake's hair was a soft bush as she tossed her head. "He's twenty-six, I'm nineteen. His daddy was over forty years older than his mother. The Bennetts prefer much younger women." She said it as if throwing down a gauntlet, and got two immediate responses. Francine inhaled a quick breath and Becca knocked over her water. With a brief word of apology to Marion she rose and went to the kitchen to mop her skirt.

Before Buddy and Rake could continue to argue, Marion quickly asked, "How did you girls do in the tennis finals?"

Becca called from the kitchen with soft pride, "We won."

Rake was more forthcoming. "Becca was great! The other team didn't return a single one of her serves! I didn't do that well, but at the end we were tied forty-all and I slammed a backhand just inside the line. They thought it was going out, so they didn't even try to return it. Boy, were they surprised!" She turned to Sheila. "Aunt Em taught us to play, Sheila, so she always wants to know how we did."

Marion caught Sheila's unguarded moment of surprise. "I don't play anymore, of course."

"But she did until just a few years ago," Rake said with pride. "Aunt Em had a *marvelous* backhand."

"Aunt Em now has a marvelous biscuit," the old woman said tartly, "which is waiting for the butter." But she favored the girl with a frosty smile as she accepted the butter dish.

After the main course, Becca rose to help Nell clear the table. Marion suggested they adjourn to the living room for coffee. "Rhoda and perhaps Heyward will be joining us for dessert. But you behave yourself, Rachel, and you, too, Buddy."

"I always do," the irrepressible twin assured her.

"Don't worry about me," Buddy said cheerfully. "I'll be as nice to Rhoda as she is to me."

When the Bennetts arrived, Sheila saw what he meant. Rhoda arrived dressed in blue the exact color of her eyes. She murmured a greeting to Rake and Sheila with a frosty smile, spoke briefly to Annie and Dolly, then sauntered over and dropped gracefully beside Marion on the couch as if Buddy and Francine were miles away. Only when she was seated with her perfect ankles neatly crossed did she say in a cool voice, "Good evening, Buddy. I thought you might be down at the restaurant."

"Oh, it runs itself," Buddy replied, leaning just a fraction closer to Francine. Rhoda still ignored the young woman.

Heyward, on the other hand, seemed intensely aware of her. He paused in the doorway as if trying to decide which of two vacant chairs to take, but his eyes kept returning to Francine and each time he gave her a long, thoughtful look.

"Wish the sailing school ran itself," he lamented. "I've got three boats that need scraping, and when I'll get to them, heaven only knows."

"Poor Heyward." Francine's smile of sympathy was as warm as her voice.

"I could help," Becca volunteered shyly from the dining room.

"Couldn't ask you to do that, kitten," he replied over his shoulder. "It's nasty work."

He finally crossed the room and took the seat by Sheila. "How're you doing tonight?" he asked. His smile was charming, but it was obvious he'd forgotten her name, and it was hard to be flattered by his attention when the only other seat was beside his mother. He leaned across her to give Rake a con-spiratorial wink. "How's the future Miss Broadway? Ready for tryouts tomorrow?"

"Ready as I'll ever be. If I don't get that part, I'll just die!"

"Or at least wither a little," her father amended.

For a time the conversation was light. Sheila, content to lis-ten, answered an occasional question and neatly tossed the conversational ball back to someone else so she could observe the group.

Nothing, she mused, can equal generations of good breed-ing. These people were not exceptionally brilliant, wealthy, or important. Yet the complacency of their conversation and natural ease of their manners was something others might work years to attain and never quite achieve. The twins already had it, poor Francine never would. Nor, Sheila admitted wryly, even after eating dinner with two presidents, would she.

Nell came around with cups of steaming coffee followed by Becca with a tray of strawberry shortcakes. "I'm going home now," Nell said softly to Marion. "You all just leave the dishes and I'll get them in the morning."

"None for me, thanks," Francine told her. "Caffeine is so bad for you. I'll make a pot of herbal tea. Anybody else want some?" She smiled at Buddy, who shook his head. Heyward rose with alacrity to follow her.

"Heyward, I believe Sheila needs milk and sugar." Rhoda's voice cut like ice.

"I take it black, thanks." Sheila had no intention of playing this game—on either side.

Becca took the seat Francine had just left. "I need to go," she told Buddy so softly that Sheila could scarcely hear her. "I've got a test tomorrow."

"Grow up, Beck!" Rake commanded. Color rose in her twin's cheeks.

"In a minute, kitten," Buddy said, giving her arm a pat. She gave him a quick smile in return.

Annie shifted her chair so she could see through the dining room to the kitchen. Her bright eyes darted in that direction again and again, avid and sly.

"How are you feeling today?" Rhoda asked Dolly, gracefully balancing her coffee and waving away the sugar Marion offered her.

"Fine." Dolly avoided Marion's eye and took three lumps. "As I was telling Jamison this afternoon—" She broke off and twinkled at Sheila. "Did you see these two ladies just frost up? My poor Dr. Rogers does not enjoy their current favor. He wants to build a medical school annex on one of their historical sites."

"It's not *our* historical site," Marion said tartly. "The past belongs to all of us, and generations yet to come."

"As one of the generation yet to come, I prefer hos—" Rake's father gave her a sharp look, and she stopped abruptly.

Marion continued as if her interruptions were no more than the buzzing of a fly. "If Jamison Rogers and his ilk are permitted to do it, they'll destroy every vestige of the past."

"But he's not going to destroy this one," Rhoda drawled, lifting stenciled brows over knowing eyes. "I haven't had time to call you, Marion, but this morning I spoke to someone in Washington. He assures me that Jamison can be stopped. What we need—"

Marion pursed her lips and almost imperceptibly shook her head. Rhoda smiled without mirth. "I won't say more at present, but I assure you that Jamison Rogers's goose is cooked."

Buddy leaned toward Sheila. "Get those two talking about history, and the rest of us might as well leave." He stood, setting his empty plate on an end table. "I need to make a phone call, in case mayhem has broken out."

Rhoda lifted one eyebrow. "Oh? The restaurant not going quite as smoothly as it could? Poor Buddy. Restaurants need so much hands-on management, don't they?"

He left the room without replying. As he, too, headed toward the kitchen, Annie almost fell out of her chair trying to see what was going on.

Francine and Heyward came back very soon, carrying steaming mugs. They paused, checked for a moment by the lack of two seats together. Becca rose. "I really do have to go, Gram. I have an exam. Please excuse me?"

Francine took her chair as if by right, and Heyward dropped into the one beside it. Musical chairs, with Becca and Buddy out, Sheila thought with a trace of amusement.

Neither Rhoda nor Annie thought it funny. One gave her son a look of disgust while the other regarded the couple with a malevolent stare.

Even Dolly looked troubled as Becca bent to give her a kiss.

"I'll come, too." Rake rose and flashed a dazzling smile at the entire audience. "Need to get my beauty sleep, you know. Glad to meet you, Sheila." But her exit line was for Heyward. "I'll be seeing *you* around." She flashed Francine a smile of triumph and followed her sister out the front door.

The energy of the whole room seemed to leave with them. Rhoda and Marion started a conversation about an upcoming historical society meeting, occasionally joined by a mutter from Annie. Dolly motioned Sheila to move her chair closer and reached for an old photograph album on a nearby table. "Let's let them *talk* history," she said in a loud whisper, "and I'll show you some. This is Aunt Bella's album. I got it out before dinner for Francine. Let's see, now . . ."

She turned the pages and found a browning picture of three girls standing before an elephant. The two little ones beamed at the camera while the older one wore the bored look of early adolescence. "Recognize anyone?"

Sheila looked wonderingly at the smallest child, a little girl with wide dark eyes and a mop of curls. "She left home that small?"

Dolly nodded. "She was so tiny her first year we called her Midget." She pointed to the elephant. "And that's Shah. Marion was madder than a wet hen that Aunt Bella made her take us to the circus."

She flipped to another page. In one picture, Mary and Dolly sat beside a boy in knickers near a flowering bush. "That's Roy Luther. He was always a bit sweet on Mary." In another picture, faded with age, Mary and Dolly rode sedately in a cart pulled by a disdainful goat. "Gus fell from favor when he ate Aunt Bella's best sheets. Oh, look, Marion, I didn't know we had this! Remember that suit? You were so proud to get it!"

The tall athletic girl standing on a flight of steps did indeed look proud—of her suit or herself. The caption read "Marion enters College of Charleston, 1926."

Buddy strolled back in with a glass of something that looked suspiciously like Scotch. "If you're interested in history, have you seen the old family Bible, Sheila?" He pointed his head toward the far end of the room, where a round table stood in the bay window. It held a large mahogany case with a glass top.

She rose and followed him, aware of Francine's glare. Lightly resting her hands on the case, she obediently peered through the glass at an old Bible opened to show a picture of Jacob wrestling the angel. Buddy bent beside her, one hand lightly at her waist. She could almost feel Francine's eyes boring into her back.

"Don't you ever change this thing?" Buddy turned to ask Marion. "Old Jacob's been wrestling since I entered the family."

Marion looked up, her cup halfway to her mouth. "What, dear? Oh, no, I don't. I lost the key long ago." She turned back to her conversation with Rhoda.

"Shame." Buddy peered down at the Bible's yellowed pages. "Francine could probably use this Bible for her research, couldn't you, Francie?"

Francine gave him her immediate attention. "I certainly could, Buddy. There are some dates I need to clear up."

Buddy turned his back to the room and said *sotto voce*, "Dolly's got her working on a history of the family. For posterity." From his tone Sheila couldn't decide if he took the history seriously or considered it a waste of time. Again he raised his voice. "How old is this Bible, anyway, Aunt Em?"

His second interruption of her conversation provoked Marion into speaking sharply. "Eighteen thirty-four, Buddy. It was bought to record Great-grandfather Wainwright's birth. But there's nothing in that Bible we don't know already." With frigid politeness she again resumed her conversation.

"Nothing *she* doesn't know, anyway," he whispered with a conspiratorial grin. He looked around the room and shook his head in dismay. "The way she leaves valuable things lying around..."

Sheila knew what he meant. Marion Wimberly was an antique dealer who believed antiques were to be used, not merely displayed. Every item in the room was old and lovely, and each was put to some practical or ornamental use.

Buddy called a third time. "Marion, would this Bible be of any value?"

She regarded him steadily. "To your pocketbook? Or to your soul?"

His voice rippled with good humor. "The pocketbook is what I had in mind."

She shrugged. "It has some value, of course. It's in good condition."

"But selling one's family Bible would be tacky, don't you think?" Rhoda drawled.

Perhaps to smooth things over, Dolly wheeled herself to the table in the bay window. "You know, Marion, I wouldn't mind getting this case opened." She looked over her shoulder and frowned. "You don't have to look so put out. It *is* a part of our family history, after all."

Marion shook her head. "I'm not put out, Dolly. But it would be a lot of trouble for nothing. There's nothing there except births, deaths, and marriages we already know about."

"No dates altered to keep a son out of the War?" Heyward teased.

His mother frowned at him.

"Of course not," Marion replied stiffly. She turned back to Dolly. "I'll call a locksmith tomorrow." That closed the subject.

Dolly stretched up and said confidentially to Sheila, "Mary may have told you, we take the War very seriously in Charleston."

"Except," Buddy said in a mock whisper, "we usually refer to it as The Late Unpleasantness. Speaking of late," he said in a normal voice, checking his watch, "I need to check in before closing time."

He bent and kissed Dolly's cheek. "Good night, Mama-in-law. See you tomorrow." Then he reached over and gave Sheila an unexpected hug. "Have a good visit," he said warmly.

Sheila returned to her seat, aware that if Francine's looks could kill, she'd be lying in pieces all over the floor.

"I believe it's time we left, too." Rhoda rose gracefully and set her cup on a table. "Don't you, Heyward?"

Heyward showed no inclination to move.

Marion inclined her head toward Dolly. "Francine, I believe Mrs. Langdon is ready to go up. Will you take her, please?"

Francine rose with obvious reluctance. "See you later," she called deliberately over her shoulder to Heyward as she pushed Dolly to the elevator.

Sheila had forgotten how long it took Southerners to say good-bye. Annie made her farewells in the living room, the front hall, and on the porch, each time remembering one more trivial thing she'd forgotten to say. Finally she almost dragged Sheila to the heavy outside door near the sidewalk and gathered herself for what looked like it would be, finally, her farewell farewell.

Sheila wasn't paying much attention by this time. She was totally absorbed in breathing as deeply as she could of the combined scents of roses and honeysuckle. But Annie's last words jolted her. " . . . do something about that hussy. I don't know why Rhoda puts up with it." She stumped down the steps in righteous indignation.

Rhoda was still lingering with Marion by the screened door, but if she heard, she was too well bred to reply.

While she said her own gracious, if cold, final good-bye to Marion, Heyward joined Sheila on the steps. "I'm picking up Francine in an hour. We thought we'd get a drink or two. Would you like to join us?"

"Not tonight, thanks. I'm pretty tired."

That wasn't the real reason. With the look she'd seen in Francine's eye, she wouldn't have dared.

SEVEN

THURSDAY

SHEILA WOKE EARLY the next morning and lay drowsily under the canopy of her bed. At first she thought it was raining, but surely she also heard a lawn mower? She opened one eye. She had not bothered to pull her shade, and a palm frond was pattering against the rail beyond her open window. A moist breeze smelling of the sea flitted across her face. She opened both eyes, then blinked in the bright sunlight.

It was only quarter 'til seven. For a few minutes she was content to lie and watch shadows flutter on her wall. But songbirds called her to get up, and her room was full of the scent of fresh-mown grass and honeysuckle. She swung her long legs over the side of the bed and pulled on a cotton skirt and sweater, then sought the morning shade of the piazza.

Softly she lifted a heavy rocker and set it beside the rail so she could peer into the yard below. Now if she only had a cup of coffee and a newspaper!

A tall man with grizzled hair and skin the color of ebony was cutting the grass with no regard for the hour. As she watched, he completed his work, stowed his mower under the porch, and mounted the steps to the kitchen. She heard the screened door shut with a whoosh beneath her, then the rumble of two quiet voices.

Resting her chin on her palm and her elbow on the railing, she considered the tops of houses she could see. Most of them were white, some were gray or pastels weathered to a uniform softness. The only sign of human life was an orange garbage truck rumbling down the street. She breathed deeply of the tangy salt air and seemed to inhale peace itself.

She thought fleetingly about the accidents, but couldn't take them very seriously. A run of minor misfortune, that was all.

She was just wondering whether to leave this morning or treat herself to one full day in Charleston when suddenly the hush was shattered by a cry.

"I'll look outside," the man said, as Nell rushed up the inside stairs to the third floor.

Sheila hurried inside and after her far enough up the stairs to see Marion's door. Nell stood in the doorway pleating her apron with nervous fingers. Marion, even at this early hour, was impeccably dressed in a linen skirt of palest green and a matching silk blouse. A large ivory brooch was her only jewelry.

Nell spoke in a low, urgent voice. "Will came in for his breakfast after cutting the grass, and after I got it on his plate I started in washing the coffee things. I was missing one cup, so I went in toward the living room to see if somebody left it beside a chair, like. The sideboard was empty, plumb empty! The silver candelabra are gone!"

Marion stood for a moment as if too overcome to speak. Then she regained her poise and spoke briskly. "You did right to come up at once, Nell. Is anything else missing?"

Nell shook her head. "I didn't take time to look."

"Was the front door unlocked?"

"I haven't opened the front door yet this morning. Dr. Rogers come by early with some medicine for Miss Dolly, but I let him in through the kitchen. He left it on the hall table," she added.

"Was he alone in the dining room?" Marion demanded.

Nell shook her head in rebuke. "Now don't you start in on Dr. Rogers. He has no cause to steal your silver."

"None I can think of," Marion admitted.

"What's the matter with our house, Miss Marion? Seems like everything going wrong at once."

Marion put one hand gently on her arm. "Nell, you are not to worry. Until now, everything that has happened has been an accident. And this is clearly a matter for the police—unless someone from the family can explain it." Her voice carried an odd note. At that moment she looked down and saw Sheila on the stairs.

"I was on the porch," Sheila explained, "and heard Nell cry out. Is there anything I can do to help?"

Even in troubled times, Southern graciousness reigned. "Thank you, Sheila. You are kind to ask. I was just going down to investigate. Will you join me?"

She stopped to open Dolly's door a crack. "Sleeping like a log. That new medicine Jamison's been giving her really helps."

The downstairs wore the look of a house not yet put to rights. In the living room pillows were still crumpled on the couch, a napkin lay on one table. Nell's hasty look had not encompassed enough. A silver bowl and salver were missing from a living-room table, a vase from the mantelpiece. The case holding the family Bible had been smashed, and the Bible removed.

Sheila took Marion's arm and gently indicated the case. "I think Nell would have heard if that had been done while she was here."

Marion looked puzzled, then gave a curt, dismissive nod. "So that lets out Jamison Rogers," she admitted.

In the dining room, in addition to the silver candlesticks, a Revere bowl had been taken from a stand near the windows. "Laws a'mercy!" Nell marveled. "They took almost everything you had!"

As she spoke, the man Sheila had seen mowing came in the kitchen door. He was one of the tallest, thinnest men Sheila had ever seen, but what drew her to him was the look of gentle wisdom in his eyes. This morning they were troubled. "I didn't see a sign of anybody out there," he said to Marion.

"Thank you for looking, Will. Sheila, this is Will Bartlett, Nell's husband. He's retired from the post office."

Will shook her hand. "Glad to meet you. You be sure Miss Wimberly calls the police, now."

He and Nell returned to the kitchen and Sheila wandered into the living room where Marion was bending over the damaged Bible case. Whoever had broken it had not bothered to conceal the act—shards of glass lay all over the table and inside the case. Marion stroked the dark mahogany and, as her hand trembled slightly, she looked up and gave Sheila an almost apologetic smile. "It wasn't all that valuable, of course, but it was one of the few old things we had that truly belonged to our family.'' She touched the brooch at her neck and took a deep breath. ''Well, I'd better call the police. In the meantime, we'll have to leave this room as it is.''

Nell called from the kitchen, scandalized. ''I don't want the po-lice seeing my living room looking like . . .''

''Nonsense. They won't want anything dusted or touched. I'll call while you finish getting breakfast on the table.''

Nell bustled into the kitchen. Already Sheila smelled hot biscuits and bacon. As she followed Marion into the dining room Sheila asked curiously, ''When does Nell get here?''

''Around seven, usually. That way I can get breakfast and be at the shop before eight. They come earlier when Will plans to mow. He prefers to work when it's cool.''

''How does she get in?''

''She has her own key to the kitchen door. She wouldn't normally have been in the front hall until she took Dolly's breakfast up. Yours, too, if you'd wanted it.'' Her voice held just a trace of a question.

Sheila enlightened her. ''I'm an early riser, especially in a new place. I sat on the upstairs porch for a good while. But except for Will mowing, I didn't see anyone in the garden below.''

Marion opened a drawer in the heavy mahogany sideboard. ''I like early risers,'' she said approvingly. ''Would you lay the silver while I call the police?''

They were just seating themselves when a twin called from the porch, ''May I have a biscuit, Nell? Is Francine up yet?''

''Not yet,'' Nell replied. ''Seems like she gets later and later.''

''Oh, well, I guess she's not really needed until Gram gets up, is she?'' She joined her great-aunt and Sheila at the table, munching a biscuit. Nell followed her with a cup, saucer, and plate, and moved to get a silverware setting from the sideboard. Flinging long hair over one shoulder, the twin dropped a large brown envelope on the table. ''Daddy left me a note to bring Francine these on my way to school. It's some stories Mother wrote about the family for something or other.''

Sheila looked at her, puzzled. The hair was Becca's, but the royal blue and yellow sweater, yellow pants, and bright-red mouth were surely Rake's. And the chatter! It made Sheila tired just to contemplate that much energy.

Nell dished her some bacon, eggs, and grits and said, "Why'd you take that crimp out of your hair?"

Rake smoothed it down. "It's the new part I'm trying out for. The girl has long straight hair. It took me forever this morning." She reached for another biscuit, then giggled. "We have math together this afternoon. Won't the teacher have a time trying to figure out who's who?"

She ate three biscuits with honey and a cup of coffee, chattering all the while. At one point she asked, "Do you still want me to get tickets for Monday, Aunt Em?" Before Marion could respond, she explained to Sheila, "This is a different play, of course. I'm the maid. You are coming, aren't you, Aunt Em?"

Marion nodded. "Of course. I said I would, didn't I? Here, Sheila, try some of this scuppernong jelly. Nell makes it from our own grapes, and it is truly delicious."

Just then the phone rang. Nell answered. "She's having her breakfast." A pause. "I'll see." She turned to Marion. "It's that Mr. Adams again."

Marion threw down her napkin in disgust. "At this hour?" She rose and spoke icily into the phone. "I have told you, Mr. Adams, I am not the least bit interested in selling." A pause. "I frankly am not concerned with what this does to your plans. As long as I am alive, that land will not be sold for subdivision. Is that clear?" A moment later, while Sheila could still hear the man on the other end speaking rapidly like a mechanical toy, she hung up.

Rake finished her breakfast and started to the front door. Sheila was surprised that Marion hadn't mentioned the burglary, but the girl would have departed no wiser than when she came if she hadn't happened to look into the living room. "There's glass on your living-room floor!" She darted across the hall and bent to pick up a piece.

Marion's voice stopped her. "Stop! We had a break-in last night, and I don't want anything disturbed until the police arrive."

Rake turned, her eyes wide. "While you were asleep? Nobody heard anything?" Her two companions shook their heads in unison. Rake gave the living room one last look. "I can't believe you missed it."

"Might of missed getting their heads blown off," Nell pointed out, pouring a hot cup of coffee.

Rake shrugged. "At least it would have been something happening."

"We got *enough* happening around here as it is," Nell told her, one hand on her hip. "You want any more happenings, you let them happen at your house. We can do with a nice spell of boredom, thank you."

She bustled back to the kitchen. Rake followed her, nibbling a piece of bacon as she went. Sheila, seeking to change the subject, asked about the large brooch Marion wore—the face of a woman on an oval of ivory.

"Great-great-grandmother Maria." Marion touched it gently with one gnarled finger. "A cousin of Arthur Middleton, who signed the Declaration of Independence. She married Colleton Wimberly and they had one son, Wainwright."

"She bought the Bible," Sheila remembered.

Marion gave her an approving smile. "That's right. Wainwright's son Scott, born the year after the War, was our grandfather."

Sheila leaned closer to look. "She's lovely. People in Charleston have so much more awareness of their history than the rest of us."

Marion gave Sheila a gratified smile as she dabbed her mouth one last time with the big linen napkin, then laid it beside her plate. "Our own family isn't particularly impressive, but Charleston has had many influential persons in its time. Middleton, Rutledge, Boone, Colleton, Long—if you're interested in history, Charleston has much to offer."

"I was a history major in college, but that's been awhile." Sheila decided to do a bit of detecting. She indicated the bandage on Marion's left wrist. "Does your arm bother you much?"

Marion shook her head. "Not much."

Rake gave a snort from the kitchen door. "Aunt Em wouldn't complain if she were up to her neck in boiling oil." She turned to her great-aunt. "For heaven's sake, you could have been killed!'' She turned back to the kitchen and started a lively conversation with Nell.

"But I wasn't, thank goodness," Marion told Sheila dryly. She seemed disinclined to say more, but Sheila prodded her. "How did you happen to fall?"

Marion hesitated, then seemed to come to some decision. Lowering her voice so Nell and Rake couldn't hear, she spoke rapidly. "Because you are Mary's niece, and seem to be a young woman of sense, I want to tell you. But please don't tell Dolly or Nell. I don't want them alarmed." She passed one hand over the lower part of her face, as if gathering up her courage. "I came home Tuesday afternoon while Dolly was at the doctor's, to fetch something I had left. The house was empty—Nell has that afternoon off, and Francine was heaven only knows where. As I came down, I thought I heard someone behind me. When I turned to see who it was, I was pushed. I must have struck my head, because the next thing I knew Francine was bending over me with ammonia. Luckily my only injury was this sprained wrist.''

She rose and took a key from the old sideboard. "We are not Chicago, Sheila, but while you are here, you will need to take some basic precautions. Please keep the door locked when Nell is not at home, and if you leave, lock the door behind you.''

Sheila sipped her coffee and asked, very casually, "Who knows that the house is usually empty on Tuesdays?''

Rake entered just in time to answer. "Anybody in Charleston who wants to know. Are you telling Sheila about the other thief?''

Marion put on a look of surprise. "What other thief, Rachel?''

Rake grinned and dropped into a chair. "She only calls me Rachel if I've been bad,'' she informed Sheila before turning back to her aunt. "The one who pushed you down the stairs. Surely you don't think we believed that 'slipped and fell' story. Daddy told us you'd been pushed right after it happened. He said there's been a lot of thefts in the neighborhood.'' If so, it didn't seem to bother her. "Well, I've got to go or I'll be late for class. See you later.'' She departed like a whirlwind with a final slam of the screen door.

"Did you call the police at that time?" Sheila asked Marion when they'd had a moment to take a calming sip of coffee.

Marion shook her head. "No, and possibly that was unwise. The only thing missing was an envelope of cash I keep in my dresser drawer for paying petty bills, and there wasn't much in that, so I saw no reason to alarm Dolly. After last night, though, I may have to mention it to them." She sighed. "I've never really worried about theft here at the house. We have so little to interest a petty thief." Sheila looked around the dining room, full of antique furniture and valuable old silver, and agreed. Only a professional would know how to dispose of what he could take at the Wimberlys'.

Before Sheila could speak again, Francine appeared. This morning she wore a lavender jersey and navy slacks, with a jaunty scarf. She was yawning delicately behind one hand.

Nell brought a teapot enveloped in a quilted cozy, then returned to the kitchen without a word of welcome. As Francine ate, Marion asked, "Did you and Heyward come back into the house last evening?"

A dull flush rose in Francine's thin freckled cheeks. "Yes, why?"

"We had a break-in. Several items are missing."

Francine looked around. "The candelabra!" she exclaimed.

Marion nodded. "And most of the other silver that was in plain view."

"Well, I didn't notice any silver missing, and I locked the door when I left." Francine's face was sullen.

"If you're certain," Marion said the last word with emphasis, "perhaps the police can find some fingerprints. Please don't go into the living room or touch the sideboard until they come."

They lingered over their coffee for twenty minutes, Marion checking her watch several times. At last she rose with a sigh of exasperation. "Where can they be? I simply have to get to the shop soon. I have an appointment with a very important client, and need to conclude it in time to drive to an auction that's halfway to Summerville."

She went out onto the porch and scanned the street, then returned. "Nell, would you speak to the police for me? You know as well as I do what's missing."

"They aren't going to be crazy about talking to a housekeeper," Nell said bluntly. "Besides, I wasn't in the house all night."

"Sheila can tell them when we went to bed and that nobody heard a sound. If they have further questions, they can reach me at the shop after three. I should be back by then. But I simply *must* go."

Marion resembled a tethered horse that wanted desperately to run for home. Dolly had not exaggerated, Sheila decided. Marion's shop was indeed her life.

Nell still wasn't persuaded. "You remember I promised to help Will's sister set up at ten for her sorority tea, don't you?"

"I'd forgotten." As Marion replied she was already filling a thermos with coffee from the pot. "But surely the police will be done by then. Will you be back in time for lunch?"

"I'll be here to serve it. It's mostly ready now. Will you be back from the auction by then?"

"Unlikely. And if I am, I'll just get a bite downtown."

Marion came through the dining room to pick up her purse and a jacket that made her skirt a crisp linen suit.

"What are your plans for the morning?" she asked Sheila.

"I hadn't thought."

"Take a walk." It was more a command than a suggestion. "See the Old Market and the homes below Broad Street. And if you're in King Street, pop in at the shop. I won't be there, but Miss Simmons, my assistant, will be glad to show you around." She turned to go, then directed a piercing glance at Francine. "Please don't forget what I said about not entering the living room until the police arrive."

FRANCINE BIT INTO her biscuit as if it were Marion's hand. Sheila sipped her coffee and waited. Years as an embassy wife had taught her it was the waiting that did it—encouraged people to pour out frustrations, angers, and loves.

Francine, however, did not speak.

Finally the doorbell rang, and Nell went to answer it. Sheila expected her to merely show the police in, but instead she heard Nell reply, "They are at breakfast just now, Officer. I'll see if they can be disturbed."

The policeman followed her into the hall and stood there in plain view while Nell announced, "It's the po-lice, ready for you to show them the damages."

Sheila waited for Francine to rise, but the young woman reached for another biscuit and bit it with her sharp little teeth. Nell stood stolidly waiting, the officer waiting behind her. With a mental sigh, Sheila rose. "Of course, Nell." It was not the first time in her life she had been left holding a bag.

She introduced herself, and shook a plump pink hand.

"Officer Johnson, ma'am." He was a slightly overweight young man with a red face and very yellow thinning hair. As he followed her into the living room he slapped a notebook against his thigh.

Sheila indicated where the various pieces had been. He bent over the Bible case, peering down with a frown between his eyes. "Hmmm," he said. "Might get some prints off this." He then examined the front-door lock, the windows, and the grass outside. At last he came back in, shaking his head. "Between you and me, ma'am, there's not a real good chance of catching whoever did this, but since it's Miss Marion, I know the chief is going to want me to make a try. Let me use your phone, and I'll get a fingerprint man right out."

While he was on the phone, Heyward called from the screened door, "May I come in?" He entered with the smile of one who is confident of his welcome. "I was going to work and saw the police..." He waved toward the street where a black and white car sat in front of the hydrant.

Most men would give their eyeteeth to go to work in cutoffs, a jersey, and running shoes, but most men wouldn't look like Heyward in them. L.L. Bean ought to send a catalog photographer down to Charleston for a few days, Sheila thought wryly. They'd make a mint on anything Heyward modeled. Did he choose his career, she wondered, because he looked so wonderful in the clothes that went with it?

She interrupted her own thoughts to answer him. "We've had a burglary. Nobody was hurt."

"That's good." He wasn't really paying attention to her. His whole attention was caught by Francine, who was placidly eating as if nothing out of the ordinary was going on.

"How you doing, Francine? How you doing, Nell?" he called.

"Fine, Heyward." Francine's smile was dazzling. "Want some biscuit?" She held out hers, and he took a bite.

Nell gave him a sour smile. "Could be better, Heyward. But at least nobody got hurt. Tell your mama to lock her doors day and night. I don't know what this neighborhood is coming to. You want a cup of coffee?"

"Don't mind if I do."

He joined Francine at the table. Nell brought him a steaming cup, then jerked her thumb toward the door. "Don't everybody look, but here comes an outsized oriole."

Seen at a distance, Annie's black slacks, yellow pullover, and black scarf over her scraggly hair did give that impression. Did she dress that way deliberately, Sheila wondered, or did her long thin nose and beady eyes seem to transform any clothes she wore into feathers? She was still considering the question when Annie flung open the screen and hurried into the dining room.

"What's the matter? What's the matter?" Annie twittered. "Is anybody ill?"

"Everybody's fine," Nell assured her. "Somebody broke in and stole Miss Marion's candlesticks."

"Laws a'mercy!" Annie sidled over to the sideboard and peered at where they had once stood. "Did they take anything else?"

"All the silver they could see," Nell admitted grudgingly.

"And the family Bible," Sheila added. Nell's lips tightened and Sheila realized she hadn't planned to tell Annie about the Bible. Why not?

Annie seized on the subject. "Do! We were just talking about that Bible last night—remember, Sheila? Who would steal a Bible?"

"We don't rightly know yet," Nell answered instead, "but the po-lice got everything under control, so you can just go back home and not worry about a thing." She turned back to the kitchen.

"Didn't anybody see or hear anything?" Annie demanded.

Sheila shook her head. "We were asleep."

Annie pulled herself out a chair. "Well, I'll be getting back home, then, but first, could I just have a cup of coffee, Nell? And maybe a biscuit? It's such a shock."

Nell fetched another two plates and set one before Heyward, gave the other to Annie, then poured yet one more cup of coffee.

Feeling overfed herself, Sheila stepped out for a minute to see if the policeman needed anything. He was nosing around the bushes of the yard like a cocker spaniel. "Don't see a thing," he admitted. She returned to the dining room where Annie was just finishing her coffee.

Nell gave Sheila a look. Without thinking, Sheila took Annie's elbow, helped her up, and gently steered her home. Only when she was on her way back did she remember where she'd seen that look before. It was the same silent signal Aunt Mary used.

Someone rounded the corner behind her, running. She turned and collided with Buddy.

"Sorry," he said, breathing hard. "Rake called from school and said you'd had a break-in. Is everybody all right?" He looked as if he'd come straight from bed. His white shirt was only partly tucked into his tan jeans and he wore no socks with his boat shoes. His face still wore its early-morning stubble. He didn't look as stunning as Heyward, but still presentable.

"Everybody's fine," Sheila assured him. "The policeman is looking for clues and we're waiting for the fingerprint person."

"Is Dolly upset?"

She appreciated his priorities. Most engaged men would ask first about their fiancée, not their dead wife's mother.

"She's still asleep. It's really been a very quiet crime. Nobody heard a thing."

He stepped into the front hall and peered into the living room. "No vandalism, thank God."

She shook her head. "No, mostly just silver taken, and the family Bible."

His jaw dropped. "No kidding? Right after we talked about it last night?" She nodded. Shaking his head in disbelief, he went to join Francine and Heyward at the table. Nell brought yet another cup.

Sheila considered the two men curiously. Surely even Charleston manners must be stretched to the limit by this strange triangle. Yet Buddy and Heyward discussed the weather and baseball scores in what seemed to be perfect amity. After a few minutes, however, she began to understand. Francine was adept at making each man think he was the center of her attentions, and she was greatly assisted by their egos. Heyward would never believe Francine could be seriously interested in someone as old as Buddy when she could have him. Buddy, confident of the superiority of his more mature charms, was able to treat Heyward with indulgent equanimity.

Amused, Sheila went to meet the fingerprint man at the door.

He was small and very round, in a suit as gray as the fringe of hair surrounding his pink skull. He set to work, singing under his breath in a bass that would have made any barbershop trio complete.

The sideboard was a mass of fingerprints. "Everybody who's touched that thing since I polished it Monday." Nell nodded. On the Bible case, however, only one set of prints came up clear: a set of three fingers resting on the side of the frame away from the lock. "We'll see what we can do with these, ma'am." The little man's speaking voice was as lovely as his singing one.

Sheila stood upright after examining the prints closely. "I hate to suggest this, but you might want to fingerprint me, too."

He looked up from the case, surprised. She gave him what she hoped was a charming smile. "You see, last evening I was examining the Bible in this case, and I am very much afraid..." She let the sentence trail off and shrugged slightly. A wary look appeared in his eyes as he pulled out a card and an ink pad. His look deepened to absolute suspicion when Sheila's prints matched those on the case. "I was afraid of that." She sighed. "Whoever broke the case probably wore gloves."

"Could be," he said cryptically. He stood and left the room, and in a minute she saw him talking with Officer Johnson, occasionally jerking his pink scalp in her direction.

Officer Johnson came in looking grave. "I understand you suggested Mr. Healy take your prints, ma'am."

"That's right."

"Mind telling me why?"

"Because I was looking at the Bible in the case last night, and from where the prints he'd brought up lay, I thought they might be mine. They were."

Buddy stood at the door. "Having trouble, Sheila?"

She shook her head. "Just that the only prints on the case are mine. The thief must have worn gloves."

Officer Johnson shifted his considerable weight from one foot to the other, apparently at a loss how to proceed. "This lady is a guest of Miss Wimberly?"

"She sure is," Buddy's voice was pleasant, but it had steel in it. "I was showing her the Bible last night, and she must have left her prints there then."

The policeman sighed. "If you say so, Mr. Endicott, I'll take your word for it."

Buddy put one arm around Sheila's waist. "I say so, Officer." Sheila moved away—unobtrusively, she hoped.

The policeman was more concerned about his protocol. "I will still need to ask the lady to account for her movements between the time the last person left this room last night until the things were discovered missing this morning. Ma'am?"

Only by the greatest restraint could she avoid laughing aloud. "I can't, of course. I went up to bed when everyone left, and slept alone in my room. I woke this morning before seven and sat on the porch alone until I heard Nell, the housekeeper, run up the stairs to tell Marion about the break-in."

His second sigh seemed to come from his boots. "You planning to stay in town long?"

Buddy stepped forward. "Officer, I resent—"

"What's going on, Stanley?" Heyward lounged in the doorway.

The policeman turned. "Hey, Heyward. I'm just asking if Mrs. Travis plans to be in town long. Her prints turned up on the case, and it's the only set we've got."

"Stan and I went to high school together," Heyward explained to Buddy before giving the policeman a wide, lazy smile. "I don't think Mrs. Travis had anything to do with this, Stan, but she's going to be around for several days. Isn't that right, Sheila?" The eyes that met hers were dancing with merriment. She bit her lip to control her own vexation. So much for leaving this morning!

"I'll be here a day or two," she agreed. "And I promise not to leave without letting you know, Officer. If it would make you feel better, you can search my room." He hesitated, giving away his dilemma. He wanted to do his best by Marion, it was clear, but could not bring himself to openly suspect her house guest. Sheila decided to leave him to struggle alone.

He stood and thought, slapping his notebook against his thigh.

"If you've got everything you need, Stan, I'll walk you to your car," Heyward suggested. "See you later, Francine," he called.

Mr. Healy trotted after them, and Buddy brought up the rear. "See you all later," he called. Sheila appreciated being included, and wondered if Nell did, too.

She returned to the dining room. "I may be spending a night or two in the Charleston jail," she announced.

"That's one way to get Miss Mary down this way," Nell muttered from the sink, "but I can think of better ones."

Francine still seemed determined to pretend nothing had happened. She poured herself another cup of tea, took a sip, and made a face. "Nell," she called, "what kind of tea is this?"

"Herbal, Francine, just like usual."

"It's a little bitter today."

"I got busy and let it brew too long. You want me to make you another pot?"

"No, I just wanted to make sure it wasn't full of caffeine."

"It's not," Nell assured her. "You want another cup of coffee, Sheila?"

"I think I do, if you've got more in that bottomless pot."

Nell sighed. "In this household, we could use one, sure enough." She went out to sweep the porch, humming Mr. Healey's song.

Francine sat and regarded Sheila with narrowed eyes. "At least nobody accuses *you* of letting in the thief." She stood suddenly. "But I'm going to bust this place wide open. You wait and see." With that cryptic remark she left—slamming the screen door behind her.

EIGHT

SHEILA FINISHED her coffee and carried her cup to the kitchen. Nell came in from the porch and put a kettle on to boil. "Here comes the oriole again," she muttered.

Annie lumbered up the back steps holding a glass pint measuring cup. "Do you all have any milk, Nell? I was about to have my cereal, and find I'm plumb out. I'll bring you some when I get to the store later today."

Nell went to the refrigerator. "I can let you have about a cup. Dolly hasn't had her breakfast yet, and she may want cereal, too." As she poured the milk into Annie's measuring cup, Annie poured herself a cup of coffee and liberally added milk and sugar.

Leaning against the counter, she addressed herself to Sheila. "You gonna be staying long with Dolly?"

Sheila shook her head. "Just a few days."

"It's getting hot." With that profound remark, Annie sipped her coffee and watched Nell wiping off the counters.

Sheila refilled her own coffee cup and waited. Sure enough when the silence stretched almost to the breaking point, Annie spoke again. "Did the police find out anything?"

"Nothing we didn't already know," Nell replied, deftly pouring hot water over tea bags in a large pottery pitcher.

"Well, you just can't tell where the world's going any more." Annie sighed. "We're all lucky not to be murdered in our beds." She slewed her eyes at them. "I wonder if Marion and Dolly know what's going on in the back house at night?"

Nell gave a grunt that could have meant anything from "yes" to "shut up and go home" and began hulling strawberries as if she were gouging out eyes. Sheila sipped her coffee and waited.

"It's my business, too," Annie insisted. "It's my family, and my good name. But if they want to put up with the likes of that I guess I'm not supposed to say anything, either."

Nell threw the hulls down the sink and turned on the disposal. Annie raised her voice. "It's sin!" Her beady eyes bulged with self-righteousness. "Some man over there every night, slinking out at five-thirty in the morning."

"You're up mighty early," Nell's voice was noncommittal.

"I have to go to the bathroom," Annie defended herself.

"Bathroom's on the other side of your house." Nell covered the berries with plastic wrap and thrust them into the refrigerator.

Annie flounced to the door. She stormed out the door, forgetting her milk. Returning for it, she spat out one parting shot. "You tell Marion and see what she says. Somebody's got to stop her before she disgraces this family!"

Nell waited until she was out of earshot, then murmured, "Go wash your mouth out with soap, woman, and say your prayers."

She turned to Sheila with a sigh. "Don't tell Miss Mary how things are in this house, Sheila. Not till we get them sorted."

Sheila went thoughtfully to her room, turning over everything she had learned. Marion hadn't fallen, she was pushed. And the Yale lock hadn't been forced, which meant someone used a key—or Francine forgot to lock the door after she and Heyward left. Who had keys? Sheila sighed. Probably everybody she'd met so far. The Wimberlys seemed to live like one big extended family.

She started to brush her hair, and asked herself another question. Why didn't Francine take Heyward to her own house? Was someone else already there—Buddy, for instance? Sheila wondered if Heyward knew Francine considered herself engaged to the older man, and decided not. The two times Sheila had seen all three of them together, Francine had done a masterful job of keeping both men on her string. But she also doubted that Buddy could be working all day and spending nights at Francine's. He didn't look haggard. Besides, wouldn't his daughters notice if he were missing every morning? Rake, at least, would not take that lightly.

Sheila filed her questions for later reference, but couldn't see that they had anything to do with falling trees, television fires, or Dolly's medicine.

As she stepped away from her dresser, she glanced out the north window of her bedroom. "Aha!" she whispered. Francine stood in the shadow of one of Rhoda Bennett's stucco pillars, deep in conversation with Heyward.

As Sheila watched, he drew her to him and they exchanged a kiss a fiancé should never hear about. As if Sheila's thought had reminded her, Francine pulled away and gave him a playful slap. She said something Sheila could not hear, and Heyward pulled her to him again. She resisted, shaking her head. He tried to pin her within his arms, she stepped back and spoke with rapid movements of her hands. He pulled her to him roughly and shook her by the shoulders until she cried out, broke from him, and ran to the fountain.

"Francine!" he demanded, his voice hard and urgent.

A movement on the sidewalk caught Sheila's attention. One of the twins was straddling her bike out of sight behind a huge palm, taking in the whole scene. As Sheila watched, the twin turned the bike awkwardly, as if gripped by great emotion, and rode away. Her hair streamed behind her in the wind.

Francine walked back toward Heyward, stifling a huge yawn.

Sheila was waiting for further developments when a voice startled her. "Sheila!"

She whirled, feeling as if she were six, caught raiding the brown sugar jar.

Nell stood in the door, holding an armful of fresh towels. Disapproval registered in every line of the old woman's dusky face as she shook her head slowly and sorrowfully. "Looks like Miss Mary forgot to tell you a few things about Charleston."

Sheila stared at her, stupefied. Surely Nell couldn't have seen what she'd been looking at. "What do you mean, Nell?"

Nell disappeared into the bathroom with the towels. "In Charleston," she said with emphasis, "northside windows are to let air in, not to look out of. We call it northside manners. That gives everybody privacy in their own gardens and on their own porches."

Sheila noted with amusement that Nell eschewed both "veranda" and "piazza" and used plain "porch"—which she pronounced "poach." She thought of one of her father's favorite sayings: "That's calling a spade a dadgum shovel."

She was saved from having to answer by the phone, which rang by her bed. Nell answered. "Miss Wimberly's home." Her face brightened. "She sure is, Miss Mary. How you doing?" She waited, then said warmly, "Why don't you just pack a bag and come join us? We'd be delighted." She listened again. "Well, I know how that is, but we'd be purely delighted to see you. I'll talk to you later." She passed the phone to Sheila. "It's for you." As Sheila took the receiver, Nell left the room.

"How are things going, dear?"

"I was just getting a lecture from Nell when you called."

"On what?"

"Northside manners. You forgot to tell me the northside windows are purely for ornament. Nell caught me using one."

"Oh, Sheila." Aunt Mary could not have sounded more reproachful if her niece had been caught with a kilo of cocaine.

"Don't fuss," Sheila warned her, "or I won't tell you our latest developments."

If she'd hoped to catch Aunt Mary between her social conventions and her insatiable curiosity, she was disappointed. "Nonsense, dear. What's done is done, but I hope you've learned your lesson. Now, what's happened?"

Sheila settled herself on her bed and proceeded to relate all that had happened since the afternoon before.

Aunt Mary took a minute to think things through. "So Heyward and Francine were the last to leave last night?" she murmured. "And now they are quarreling. Does he need money, do you know?"

"I don't know, nor do I know how we could find out." Sheila remembered something. "He and his mother were having a heart-to-heart chat yesterday afternoon right after I arrived—she'd called him to come home, and he didn't seem terribly enthusiastic."

"She could have discovered he was overextended." Aunt Mary was always able to think of an economic motive for crime. "Maybe Charlie can find out something. Meanwhile, what are your plans for the morning?"

"I was getting ready to take a walk."

"A walk? Is something the matter with the car?"

"No, Aunt Mary, this is for exercise. People do walk for fun, you know."

"Some people swallow fire for fun, too," her aunt retorted, "but I did not send you to Charleston for amusement."

"I *am* on vacation," Sheila pointed out. "I'll look for clues as I walk."

Aunt Mary's sigh was deep and sorrowful. "Very well, dear. Go and amuse yourself. But so far your presence seems to have brought more trouble than help."

"I didn't—"

Aunt Mary didn't let her finish. "Call me, dear. I must run. I've got work to do."

Sheila hung up in exasperation. To her knowledge Aunt Mary had never done a lick of work in her life except write letters or read books. When she managed to conduct her many business affairs was a mystery to the whole family. So why was she, Sheila, once again filled with a compulsion to industry to show she could do more than Aunt Mary?

She went downstairs to have another look around. Nell was in the hall, adjusting a stylish hat in the mirror over the hall table. "Dolly's up, and I've given her her breakfast. She said give her half an hour, then run up to see her. I'll be back to give you your lunch." She picked up her purse and left.

Neither the living room nor the dining room revealed anything the police had not already seen. Where was the telltale thread, the small silver button that always got left in detective stories? She could almost hear Mike Flannagan's growl, "Leave the detecting to the real detectives, Sheila." For once, she agreed. She had no knowledge about how to proceed.

With far more questions than answers, Sheila flung herself into a rocker on the piazza. While she waited to see Dolly, she buried herself in the news of the world as reported by the *News & Courier* and managed, for a time, to forget the Wimberlys and their problems.

Dolly, when she finally called for Sheila to come up, was indignant rather than frightened. "Imagine entering a home while people are sleeping! Someone could have been hurt!" Her ruffles danced. "Of course, I'm surprised we haven't been robbed before, with everything Marion brings home from the shop. Was she very upset?''

"Not that she showed.''

Dolly pursed her lips. "That's Marion. She and Aunt Bella were alike in that—keeping their thoughts to themselves.''

"You both seem very fond of your aunt,'' Sheila murmured, hoping to divert Dolly from the crime.

She succeeded. Dolly's face broke into her usual sunny smile. "Of course. She raised us, you see. Mama died when I was three trying to have our baby brother, and Daddy died two weeks later in the war. Aunt Bella's letter telling him about Mama didn't get there before he was killed.'' She gave a sigh that was more romantic than mournful. "Here, can you help me pin up this hair?''

Sheila took a brush and began to stroke the soft curls. "I didn't know you had a brother.''

"We don't—he was stillborn. So all our lives, really, there was just Marion, me, and Aunt Bella. No girls ever had a better mother.'' Her eyes flashed. "I hope they catch the thief. It's disgraceful to steal a family's Bible!''

Her pretty, plump face was creased with indignation. Absently she reached one round arm up to tuck in a tendril of hair, loosening another in the process. This morning's gown was lavender and blue, daintily scattered with wildflowers. She should have been painted by Renoir, Sheila thought.

Aloud she asked, "Do you think this is another in your series of accidents?''

Dolly shook her head doubtfully. "I don't see how it could be, do you?''

Sheila shrugged. "I don't know what to think so far. There doesn't seem to be any pattern or order. I thought maybe I'd go talk with Mr. Luther this morning, if you don't mind me going out. Nell's gone to help with a sorority party or something...''

Dolly waved her toward the door. "I'll be fine. If I need anything, Francine is just a buzzer away, and I have a lot to do.''

"Working on the history?''

"Heavens no—I'm leaving all that up to Francine. I work with a literacy group, matching people who want to learn to read with tutors. Right now I'm real busy. We've been running an ad on television recently, and a good many people have called. You wouldn't believe how many adults there are in this country who can't read." She wheeled herself toward the telephone. "I'll be busy until lunchtime." She waved Sheila away. "After seeing Roy, why don't you walk downtown? It's just a few blocks, and we don't eat until twelve-thirty. On fine days I eat on the upstairs porch."

It wasn't just Nell that said "poach." Sheila concealed her smile. "I can see why." She had seen the round table that morning, at the street end of the porch screened by a trellis of wisteria. "I'll be here," she promised.

At the door she turned, remembering Marion's warning. "Does Francine have a key?"

Dolly was already dialing a number. "Of course. Everybody has keys. But you can leave the door open. We always do."

Today was different. Sheila carefully locked the front door behind her and pocketed the key.

IT WAS LATE MORNING. Only bees occupied the Bennett garden. Rhoda was attending the antique auction. Miramise, her cook, was doing the weekly shopping. In the Wimberly household, Dolly was busily making calls in her upstairs front room—a room with no windows on the north side.

After carefully looking both ways, someone opened the Bennett gate and walked across the lawn toward the Wimberly property, where Francine's house sat on the property line. When MacFadden Bennett had bought his lot and built his wall, he'd let the little house form part of it. One door of the little house, therefore, opened directly into Rhoda Bennett's garden. Usually it was kept locked, but today a gloved hand tapped lightly on it.

Francine answered with a wide yawn. "Sorry. I seem to be sleepy this morning."

The visitor smiled. The theft had been a real inspiration. In the chaos afterward, it had not been difficult to put sleeping pills into Francine's tea. Francine seemed to think the smile a greeting. "Come on in." She ushered her visitor in and indicated one end of the couch.

The visitor took a chair across the room instead and dropped a briefcase on the floor. "So we need to talk."

Francine nodded drowsily. "We sure do. You see, if I were to tell..." She sank to the couch and started talking. The visitor's face grew white with anger. Francine's lips curved in a sly smile. But her voice grew slower, more sluggish, and her eyelids drooped.

She fought to stay awake, rubbing one thin cheek furiously with her hand. "Sorry," she said again, and her voice was slurring. "Maybe we could talk later. I just can't seem to stay awa—" Her head fell back against the couch and she slept.

The visitor sat motionless. Until Francine's breath came deep and slow, the only movement in the room was made by a fat fly batting himself against the screen of the open window.

At last the visitor rose. With great care Francine was lifted and positioned.

Her bones were so small, it was easier than one might have thought to lift her shoulders and strike her head forcefully on one sharp corner of the wooden coffee table. The visitor removed one glove to check her pulse. When it fluttered, a snort of displeasure broke the silence. A sofa pillow was held firmly over the sharp little nose. Francine twitched once, then lay still.

The visitor gave a small sigh of relief. But now much had to be done.

At last the visitor picked up one object and looked about the room with a final nod of approval. Who would ever know Francine had not stepped onto a stool, fallen backward, and hit her head? One more accident in the Wimberly home.

NINE

Roy LUTHER WAS OUT of town for the day and the pharmacist on duty knew nothing about Dolly's medicine. Since neither Dolly nor Francine seemed to want her around for a few hours, Sheila decided to follow Marion's advice and see something of Charleston. After all, she told herself optimistically, she often thought better walking.

This morning, however, her mind seemed to be on vacation, too. She spent a pleasant hour rambling around Charleston's Old Market and watching skilled women with shining black skin weave sweet grass baskets. The designs, they informed Sheila, could be traced directly to Africa. One basket—a large one that would be perfect for magazines beside her favorite chair—caught her eye, but she had no intention of carrying it around all morning. "I'll come back," she promised them. They nodded with the bored acceptance of women who had heard that line before.

"But I will!" she vowed silently, stepping around tourists in canvas hats, windbreakers, sensible shoes, and sunglasses.

She strode up King Street, which seemed to be mostly antique shops. Since she'd forgotten to ask the name of Marion's shop, she couldn't "pop in" to see Miss Simmons, but doubted that Miss Simmons would greatly feel the loss.

A church bell tolled overhead. Eleven o'clock. When she breathed deeply, the smell of the sea was so thick she could taste it. If she closed her eyes she could almost be back in Japan. It was a shock to open them to a lazy Charleston morning instead of the bustle of Tokyo. She felt a sudden compulsion to *see* salt water once again.

"Sheila?" a voice asked behind her. She turned.

One of the twins stood just behind her, a smile curving her lips. "I thought that was you," she said with satisfaction.

"How can you tell me from all the other tourists?"

"You forgot your camera." They laughed together. As Sheila adapted her long stride to the girl's shorter one, the twin asked, "Were you going anywhere special?"

Sheila nodded. "I want to see salt water. Is that possible?"

"Of course. I'll take you to The Battery—you can see miles of water from there."

"Spoken like a true marine biologist?" Sheila asked. When the girl nodded, she grinned. "You just blew your cover."

They walked briskly over to Meeting Street and down past large churches with, unexpectedly, their own graveyards beside them. "This is Rainbow Row," Becca explained as she steered them down a street of lovely old houses painted in soft pastels. Sooner than Sheila would have believed possible they reached what looked like a large bay.

Becca waved one arm in a fair imitation of her sister. "Where the Ashley and Cooper rivers meet to form the Atlantic Ocean," she intoned in a deep voice. "At least," she added with a twinkle, "that's what we say in Charleston."

Charleston had thoughtfully preserved its waterfront for the public rather than for those owning large houses on the other side of a small park. Farther down the street, houses were closer to the water, but always a street and a sidewalk away.

While they walked, dodging occasional bicyclists and swooping gulls, Becca entertained Sheila with talk about sea creatures and the effects of tides on the coastal ecology. Sheila found herself both informed and charmed. "You know an awful lot for someone who's only been studying this a couple of years."

Becca shook her head. "I've been studying it since I was seven. It was Heyward, you see. I was skating by his house one day, and I fell. He was cutting the grass and came over to pick me up. My knee was a mess, and I was pretty upset, so he picked me up, washed my knee, and took me into the kitchen for ice cream. Then he showed me his aquarium and told me about the fish."

"Today a fishtank, tomorrow an ocean," Sheila murmured, watching three skillfully handled sailboats and wishing she were out there tugging a sheet tighter against the wind.

Becca's laugh startled her. "Heyward doesn't have a fish-tank—his aquarium takes up one whole wall of his room. His sister Grace had it built in for his twelfth birthday, even though his mother had a fit. It's a salt-water aquarium, and marvelous! Almost like being underwater. When Heyward first showed it to me—well, I got hooked."

"On the fish or on Heyward?" Sheila teased.

A flush stained Becca's cheek. "On both," she admitted, "but he's never known that. He thinks of me as a kid sister." Her smile was brave, but not particularly cheerful. Sheila decided to change the subject.

"Your grandmother said you had a television fire recently. What happened?"

Becca shrugged. "Not much. It just caught fire."

She should have asked Rake, Sheila thought ruefully, but then she might have gotten more than was precisely true. She tried again. "Who all was there?"

"Rake and Aunt Em and I. There was a special on South Carolina writers, and her television wasn't working. She asked if she could come over to watch it, and we decided to watch it with her."

"Did she call on the spur of the moment?"

Becca shook her head. "Aunt Em always plans ahead. She asked us Sunday, while we were all sitting around on the porch."

"Who was there, sitting around?"

Becca thought. "Well, Rake and I, and Dad, Francine, of course. Gram was taking her nap. I think Mrs. Bennett and Heyward were over that day, too. Lamar was down in the yard, patching Aunt Em's tire. I guess that's all, except Nell. She was in and out. And Annie came over for a little while—just about everybody, I guess."

So anybody could have known the television would be on that evening if they wanted to rig an accident. "How did the fire begin?"

"Well, awhile after the program started, we smelled smoke—at least Rake and I did. Aunt Em had the sniffles and couldn't smell anything. I checked the television, and there was smoke coming from inside. It was a wire or something. We unplugged it and by then there were some flames. While I went to get some water to throw on it, Rake panicked and called the fire department. By then it was a full-scale emergency.'' There was no rancor in her laugh, and somehow Sheila knew that Becca enjoyed Rake's dramatics almost as much as Rake herself.

"Did the fire department ever find out what started it?"

Becca flipped her hair back against a breeze that seemed determined to wipe her face with it. "Not that I know of. Daddy said it looked like a wire was frayed."

There seemed nothing more to ask about that. Like the sailors on the bay, Sheila decided to try another tack.

"I didn't realize Heyward had a sister."

"She's a half sister, really, and older than Rhoda. Her mother was a Rutledge, and Rhoda's a Calhoun. Aunt Em says Mr. Bennett picked wives so his children would have blue blood in their veins. Not that it matters." She wrinkled her nose, but her next words betrayed her. "Heyward's middle name is Calhoun."

"What happened to Mr. Bennett's first wife?"

"She died years ago. Then when he was nearly sixty, Mr. Bennett married Rhoda. She was just eighteen, and beautiful."

Sheila was long past sentimentality about eighteen-year-old brides. "And when did *he* die?"

"When Heyward was six. Before I was born." Becca sounded a little forlorn.

"And Rhoda's never remarried." Sheila had made it as a statement, and was surprised at the vehemence of Becca's scorn.

"Not with all she has to lose. Mr. Bennett left her half his money until she married again. Then it would go to Heyward."

Sheila knew what Aunt Mary would think about this conversation, but she continued it anyway. "And Heyward got the rest?"

"Not a penny!" Becca said hotly. "He was so little, you see. So his daddy gave Grace what was rightfully hers, and left the rest to Rhoda. She hasn't given Heyward a single thing. That's why he's had to scrape and save to get his sailing school started. His mama said . . .''

What Rhoda had said Sheila would have to wait to find out. A church bell startled her into looking at her watch. "It's noon! I'm going to be late for lunch!"

"We can make it," Becca assured her. "I think I'll come, too."

Sheila was glad of her company, especially since Becca knew the shortcuts. As they passed a row of modern brick town houses built in Colonial style, Becca flipped a hand toward one. "That's where we live. It's close to Gram, very easy to keep, and somebody else does the maintenance."

"Do you work for the realtor?" Sheila asked.

Becca laughed. "No, I'm quoting Daddy. We moved in there after Mother died, when the house got too much for him. It was Rake's and Daddy's idea—I'd really rather have a real house, but at least this one doesn't take up much of our time."

She indicated that they should turn the corner, and Sheila was surprised to find them just down the block from the Wimberlys'.

They arrived, breathless from walking fast, just as Nell was starting up the stairs with a tray laden with plates of chicken salad, fresh strawberries, hot rolls, and iced tea.

She took Becca's unexpected arrival in stride. "Fetch yourself a plate, napkin, fork, and glass of ice. And don't you eat all these strawberries before everybody else gets some."

Lunch was unexpectedly pleasant, with no reminders of the hectic breakfast. Francine did not appear. Becca apparently had not heard about the break-in, and Dolly did not mention it. Instead she was full of reminiscences.

"I'll never forget the day we climbed onto the roof of the little house," she said, taking a second roll. "Now don't tell Marion I had two—she gets so aggravated with me. But why prolong your life if you can't enjoy it?" She spread the roll liberally with butter and continued, "It was Mary, Nell, and me. We spent all morning on that old tin roof, pretending we were shooting Yankees in the alley. When it got to be near dinnertime, we discovered we were covered with rust from the roof, so Mary told Nell to fetch rags and water for us to scrub with.

'Nobody will see the rust on you because you already look rusty,' she told Nell." Dolly interrupted herself with a peal of laughter. "Nell was so put out with Mary that she took down the ladder and went inside. We called and called, but Marion had her nose stuck in a book and Nell's mama, Mama Lucille, thought we were still playing. When Aunt Bella got home from the shop, she nearly hided us all!"

"Nell's been around a long time," Sheila observed, savoring a sweet strawberry dipped in powdered sugar.

"Since before I have." Dolly popped a strawberry into her own mouth. "Her mother was Granddaddy's cook. We all grew up together until Nell ran off to Savannah to marry Benny Lee."

"Dumbest thing I ever did," Nell muttered, coming out to bring dishes of ice cream and a pot of coffee. Sheila, having managed only half a glass of sweet tea, could have kissed her.

"But you got Will in the end," Dolly consoled her.

"Sure did," Nell agreed with obvious satisfaction. "But why are you telling Sheila my life story?"

"I was thinking this morning about when we were all girls together—you, me, Mary. Remember when you left us on the roof? That's the closest Aunt Bella ever came to whipping Mary, I think."

"Uh-uh." Nell shook her head. "The closest was when she dared you to peek behind Marion's pictures to try to find a snapshot of that new beau. Remember him?"

Dolly's eyes crinkled with delight. "We never did find that picture! Who do you reckon he was?"

"You could always ask Marion." Nell went back downstairs.

"Feels like Nell's been here forever, but it hasn't really been all that long, has it?" Becca asked, attacking her ice cream.

Dolly shook her head. "Six or seven years. She and Will lived in Savannah until Mama Lucille retired, then Will insisted they move back here to care for her."

"Who was Aunt Em's cook?" Becca puckered her brow trying to remember.

"Nobody. Annie had moved in with Aunt Bella and Marion during World War II, and after Mama Lucille retired, she did

all the cooking. They didn't really need much cleaning done—
they were out most of the day. After Annie married the Judge,
she and Marion shared a cleaning woman. No, Nell didn't come
back until after your mother died"—she squeezed Becca's hand
fondly—"and I got so sick."

"Funny," Becca mused. "I can't really remember the house
without you and Nell."

"Nell took a lot of grief from Will's family about coming,"
Dolly recalled. "His sister—all the girls Nell grew up with, really—went to Avery Institute." She stopped to explain to
Sheila. "That's a good high school for black children that's
been here since I was a girl. Aunt Bella and Mama Lucille had
wanted Nell to go, too, but she met that no-count Benny
and..."

Sheila licked the ice cream slowly off her spoon and watched
a mockingbird perch itself nearby as if eavesdropping on what
they said. Did mockingbirds imitate people, she wondered,
when they were in the privacy of birddom? She missed some of
what Dolly was saying, but it went on and on.

"...teachers and nurses and business women—including
Will's sister. She had a fit when Nell said she was coming here
to cook and keep house. Nell came as a friend—we both know
that. But it hasn't been exactly easy for Will's family to accept. She would never have done it except in emergency."

No wonder Nell felt free to tell a guest about northside manners, Sheila mused. She had spoken not as a housekeeper, but
as a member of the family.

"See how good it was for me to start Francine on that history?" Dolly chuckled, licking the last of the powdered sugar
off her fingers. "Makes me remember some of it myself." She
looked around, puzzled. "Do you know, I had forgotten
Francine. Do you suppose Nell called her?"

"Nell called her," said the housekeeper, coming onto the
porch again with a tray to clear the dishes. Becca rose to help
her. "I called, then I knocked, but she didn't bother to answer."

"She said she was going to be working on the history this
morning," Dolly said. "I guess she'll come when she gets hungry."

"Always does," Nell replied.

Dolly pulled one wheel of her chair to turn it toward the door. "Now, if you'll excuse me, Sheila, I always have a siesta at this time of the afternoon."

"And I have math class." Becca expertly carried a stack of dishes downstairs—the heaviest ones, Sheila noted with approval.

Sheila helped carry the last dishes down, but Nell refused her help with washing them. "I'm used to my own ways. You go rest."

So she took a notebook from her room, climbed into a double rope hammock slung across the end of the upstairs porch just beyond her own door, and began to jot notes on the morning's robbery:

1. Who could enter with a key to steal the silver? Who could dispose of it at a profit? The twins she rejected, but Buddy, Heyward or Francine were all possibilities. So, she admitted reluctantly, was Nell.
2. Where in Charleston could you sell stolen silver? (Beside that she wrote "Police would know better than I")
3. What time did Francine and Heyward leave the house?
4.

She had drawn a blank. Charleston was delightful, but the mildness of the Wimberly household crime wave combined with the mildness of the afternoon to make her yawn. She let her pen and pad drop, lay back in the hammock and tried to think. The breeze gently rocked her, the bees lulled her, and in less than five minutes she was sound asleep.

"SHEILA? SHEILA!" it was Nell, calling from the porch below. Sheila woke with a start and, as she swung her long legs over the side of the hammock, glanced at her watch. After three? It must be the sea air—she never napped in the daytime!

She leaned over the railing and could see Nell's feet near the steps. "Yes?" she called down, hoping she wasn't violating railside manners in the process.

"Francine still hasn't come, and I need to go home for a while. When she comes in, tell her I'm leaving the chicken salad in the Frigidaire."

"I'll go tell her right now," Sheila replied. "I wanted to ask her a few questions anyway."

She knocked loudly on Francine's door, but got no response.

"Francine?" she called. "May I come in?"

She knocked once more. Still no response.

Sheila had less inhibitions—or manners—than Nell. Shoving aside the thick branches of a huge old azalea, she pushed her way to the window and peered in through the screen. Then she drew a sharp breath.

Francine was lying on the floor. Her head just touched the leg of the coffee table and one arm was thrown out as if to catch herself. Her eyes were shut as if she were napping. But her skin did not flinch as flies crawled on her face.

TEN

SHEILA PUSHED HER WAY back through the azalea and threw herself at the door. It was locked. For an instant she considered ripping the screen, but the azaleas would make climbing in extremely awkward. Fighting an urge to vomit into the empty planter by the steps, she dashed back to the kitchen where Nell was placidly finishing a glass of tea. "Do you have a key to Francine's house? And call an ambulance."

Nell paused, the glass halfway to her lips. "Ambulance? What's the matter?" She had already turned to a cupboard and handed Sheila one of the keys that hung there.

"Francine's hurt—maybe dead. I think she fell and hit her head."

The words made a silly rhyme that kept echoing in Sheila's mind as she hurried back to the little cottage: "Francine's hurt, maybe dead, I think she fell and hit her head."

The little house was warm, the smell of blood in the air. Sheila knelt beside Francine and reached for her wrist to seek a pulse. As soon as her fingertips touched flesh, however, she recoiled. Already the body was stiffening.

Her own body began to tremble, and a wave of unexpected pity swept over her. Even unpleasant people didn't deserve to die like this. She swallowed a lump of nausea and walked unsteadily back to where Nell was just hanging up the phone.

"Ambulance will be here in a minute." She took one look at Sheila's face and leaned heavily against the sink. "Dead?"

Sheila nodded. "I think we'd better call the police."

Nell's eyes widened. "Po-lice? Again?"

Sheila was already at the phone. With one hand over the mouthpiece she muttered, "Just to be on the safe side, in case it wasn't an accident."

Nell stared. "Wasn't a...? You mean you think somebody could have...? Oh, my God." It was a prayer, not an oath. As if her knees had suddenly turned to water, she sank onto a convenient stool.

Sheila hung up. "Do you think I should tell Dolly, or wait?"

"Don't tell her until Miss Marion comes." Nell pulled herself heavily to her feet. "Here, let me call her. Lawdy, lawdy." She whispered the last word over and over until Marion came on the line, then she spoke cautiously. "Miss Marion, I think you ought to come on home. We've had another accident, and Francine has been hurt." It took Sheila a moment to realize that Nell was shielding her employer. After all, Marion was nearly eighty.

Nell must be well over seventy herself, but it hadn't occurred to Sheila to break the news gently. Repentant, she reached for Nell's unfinished glass of tea and thrust it at her. Nell took it gratefully, drained it while Marion was speaking, and set it on the countertop. Then she handed the phone to Sheila. "She wants to speak to you." She went into the dining room and collapsed into a chair, head in her hands.

"What's happened?" Marion asked. "Is Francine seriously hurt?" Sheila hesitated, and Marion continued. "Am I really needed? I just got back from the auction, and unless it's important—"

Aunt Mary might object, but Sheila interrupted the old woman anyway. "It's very important, Marion. Francine's dead. I just found her."

Marion's voice changed slightly. "Found her where?"

"In her living room, lying on the floor. I think she must have fallen and hit her head."

"She may just be hurt."

"No, I'm certain. She's dead. We've called the ambulance and police, but I think you ought to be here to talk with them."

Marion sighed almost inaudibly. "Very well. I've left my car for a minor repair, but I can walk home in about ten minutes."

"I'll come get you. Tell me where."

Marion was waiting at the door, and came out at once when Sheila pulled up to the curb. Only a slight tremor in her head betrayed her rigid self-control.

When they reached the house, a rescue vehicle was already parked by the hydrant, a police car behind it. Marion got out and started for the little house. "We might as well go on back. Please come, Sheila." Sheila appreciated what it must cost her to ask for help.

Two police officers were already busy on the floor, two rescue attendants waiting across the room. Marion paused in the doorway, swaying slightly. One of the officers got immediately to his feet. "You don't need to be here, Miss Wimberly. We'll see you in the house later."

"I am perfectly all right," Marion said formally. With more poise than Sheila could have mustered she entered the house and sat upright on a living-room chair.

Sheila, made of less stern stuff, remained at the door.

Francine lay as Sheila had found her, feet near a small stool by a tall bookshelf littered with a few books and papers.

In her first visit, she had hardly given the little house a glance. Now, while Marion watched and the two men knelt to check what had recently been Francine, she looked around.

The first floor of the tiny building was actually two rooms— a minuscule kitchen, more like a foyer, just inside the door and a living room to the left. Both rooms were tidy, but not very clean, and a limp geranium on the windowsill was yellowing from lack of water. A narrow staircase went up from the back of the kitchen, and in the back wall of the living room Sheila was surprised to see another outside door.

As if glad not to be looking at the dead woman, Marion's eyes followed Sheila's own. "That used to be the front door when Mama Lucille and Nell lived here. It opened out into what was our backyard then. When Aunt Bella sold that land to Mac Bennett, we sealed the door."

Sheila moved to try the brown ceramic knob. The door was certainly locked, but it gave slightly. Was this how Francine's midnight visitor had been getting in?

"She's dead, all right." The policeman spoke as if there had been some doubt. "Doesn't look like foul play, though—just a common household accident."

Marion looked from the stool to where Francine lay, and again she trembled slightly. "You think she just . . . fell?"

The officer nodded. "Looks like it. Probably reached for the top shelf and fell, hitting her head on the corner of the table." On cue, everyone in the room peered up at the top shelf, empty except for a large cloth bag.

In one movement Marion stood and mounted the stool.

"Stop!" the officer ordered. Marion hesitated, wobbled a little. He reached for her elbow. "Sorry I spoke so sharply, ma'am, but we don't want any more casualties around here."

Marion stepped down from the stool. "You are right, of course, Officer. I just wondered what was in that parcel. The bag is one, I believe, that our housekeeper uses to store silver in, and we had a theft of silver last night from our home."

He scratched his head. "And you think maybe this young woman took it?" Marion didn't nod, but he himself climbed onto the stool and brought down the bag. It clunked as he lowered it. He spread its contents out on the floor: the Wimberly silver and family Bible.

"Whew!" He shook his head and exchanged glances with his partner. "Looks like a case of divine retribution, if you ask me. This *is* the stuff that was stolen, I take it?"

Marion nodded.

"Officer Stanley Johnson has a complete list," Sheila offered.

The policeman seemed to notice her for the first time. "Stan? That'll be okay, then. He's very thorough."

The other officer started out the door. "I'll give him a call and see what he's got on the case. Why don't you go on inside, Miss Wimberly?"

"Well, if there's nothing we can do here, I need to see my sister. Perhaps, Sheila, if you . . ."

Sheila could recognize the inevitable as well as anyone else. "I'll stay."

As Marion left the room she walked as if every step was an effort. For once, Sheila thought, she felt her eighty years.

The second officer went into the yard for a smoke and the two paramedics, unleashed, squatted beside Francine. Reluctant to watch, Sheila restlessly prowled the two small rooms Francine had preferred ruffles and throw pillows to cleaning

Limp organdy curtains hung from the windows. Dusty prints hung on the walls. And three cobwebs hung from the ceiling.

The old furniture (old, not antique) was covered by pastel-blue bedspreads tucked and pinned to make it look soft and cozy, but they, too, were soiled. A pallid rubber plant languished on a stand beside the back door, and six or seven records stood beside a table holding an old stereo set. Sheila glanced through them and raised one eyebrow. Francine had a strong predilection for heavy metal. On the coffee table, an ornate china mug labeled "Francine" sat beside a sprawl of old books, letters, and papers.

Bored, and feeling faintly sick from the combined smell of blood and someone's Old Spice aftershave, she asked, "All right if I go outside for some fresh air?" They nodded, and she joined the policeman having his solitary smoke.

She found him, surprisingly, examining a huge red rose on a laden bush. "Pretty, aren't they?" He flicked his butt into the grass. "You feeling a little green about the gills?"

She nodded. "A bit."

"Here." He broke off the rose and handed it to her. "Smell this for a change."

She gratefully buried her nose in its deep fragrance.

"You live here, too?" He was staring at her curiously, as if trying to place her in the family.

"No, just visiting."

"There's lots to do in Charleston. Seen The Battery?"

She nodded.

"How about Boone Hall Plantation?" She shook her head. "Now that's one place you really ought to see."

She smiled. "You work for the Chamber of Commerce in your off hours?"

He grinned. "In Charleston, ma'am, every last man, woman, and child works for the Chamber of Commerce."

Sheila remembered the old man who'd given directions, the women weaving baskets, Becca's impromptu tour. "Now that you mention it . . ."

It felt good to laugh with him in the hot sunshine. But then she thought of Francine, who would never again laugh with a man in the sun. She shivered.

"There's not any chance that wasn't an accident, is there?" She inclined her head toward the little house.

He shrugged. "Not much. Maybe one in a thousand, if you want the odds. But if it's connected up with this morning's incident—do you think the young lady had a partner in crime?"

Sheila shook her head. "I don't know."

Before the officer could say more, his own partner came through the gate with a man who must surely be the coroner, accompanied by the same little fingerprint man Sheila had met before. He gave her a definitely suspicious look before bustling in to do his grisly work.

In a very short time the unsurprising unofficial verdict was in. Francine had stood on a stool, fallen, hit her head on the coffee table with enough force to kill her. There were no prints on the silver or the Bible. There were, however, identical sets of unidentified prints scattered throughout the little house.

Plump little Mr. Healy shook his head and said in his lovely bass voice, "Why ladies don't ask for help when they need it..."

"Do you need the silver and Bible as evidence?" Sheila asked. "If you don't, I know Miss Wimberly would appreciate having them back."

They exchanged looks, and the officer in charge shrugged. "We'll just make a note that she's got them."

Sheila placed the silver carefully back in the cloth bag and waited for them to depart, bearing Francine's body with them. Then, with care, she duplicated what the other woman's actions must have been. The stool, she noted, wobbled slightly on the carpet, but not much. And the shelf was in easy reach. Would it have been for someone six inches shorter? Was Francine forced to stand on her tiptoes—was that how she fell?

Sheila tried bending down six inches and reaching the shelf, but couldn't decide if the stool was wobbling because she was on her tiptoes or because of her awkward position. In either case, she was certainly in danger of repeating Francine's final feat.

"It *was* an accident," she told herself firmly. "You're only trying to make something difficult out of something simple." She took the silver with her and carefully shut up the little house. Tomorrow, she promised herself, she would just as carefully close her suitcase and go home. The Wimberlys were having a bad run of accidents, but that's precisely what they were. Back in the house, Nell fetched a cloth and dusted out the damaged case, then took the Bible from Sheila. "I think this time," she said, turning the pages, "we'll forget Jacob wrestling and have a Psalm of Comfort in Time of Trouble."

ELEVEN

IN LATE AFTERNOON, five women were on the upstairs porch. Marion was resting on a wicker chaise. Dolly sat in her wheelchair, her hands nervously playing with the ribbons of her wrapper. Sheila stood by the rail, thinking how peaceful the lawn looked in spite of everything that had happened. And Rhoda sat in a cloud of Chanel as if paying a social call.

Nell set a pitcher of iced tea with lemon and mint on the table and handed Sheila a glass she had brought up extra. "This is for you."

Sheila tasted it tentatively, then smiled. "Bless you, Nell."

Before the others could ask what was in it, Nell jerked her head toward the house next door. "I'm surprised we haven't seen Annie in all this excitement."

"It's her day for working at the library," Rhoda reminded her in a languid drawl.

When Dolly finished her tea, she brushed a hand across her face. "I can't get over it. God help me, I never did like that poor young woman very much, but to die alone like that...." She broke off uncertainly.

"Why don't you lie down again for a while?" her sister asked.

Dolly nodded. "I believe I will. Sheila, will you take me in?"

When she was settled in her bed, Dolly turned her head on her pillow and almost whispered in her weariness. "I can't keep from wondering if she was being punished. Do you think so? All along I've wondered if Francine was causing the accidents, and..."

Sheila gave her a reassuring pat. "I have more faith in divine compassion than divine retribution, don't you?"

Dolly struggled to push herself up on one elbow. "But she was at Boone Hall. She was the one who should have called in my prescription. She was at Buddy's the day the television caught fire, and she could have been here when Marion fell.''

The old woman was turning slightly gray, and her breath came unevenly. Sheila pushed her back onto her pillow. ''You rest and don't worry about it. By now Francine has answered for anything she had to answer for.''

''I guess so.'' Dolly gasped with pain. ''Ask Marion to call Jamison,'' she said weakly. Her hand fluttered toward the bedside table. ''And hand me a pill and a little water.''

Sheila gave her the medicine, then walked swiftly out to Marion on the porch. ''She's asking for her doctor.''

Nell pulled herself to her feet. ''I'll go down and call.''

Rhoda also rose. ''Well, I'd better be getting home. Heyward will be home soon wanting his supper.'' Her tone conveyed she still had to kill a chicken and dig potatoes. ''There's nothing to do here, is there, Marion?'' When Marion agreed, Rhoda said in her languid, flat voice, ''Call me if you need me.''

Nell telephoned the doctor and reported he'd be there in a few minutes. Nothing, Sheila thought, said more about the status of the Wimberlys than that they still expected—and got—house calls.

Thankfully, Marion also wanted a rest. Nell wanted to cook dinner. And Sheila wanted some time to herself. Not only did she need to think over the day, but she also had to steel herself to be firm on the phone tonight. No matter how badly Aunt Mary wanted to satiate her rampant curiosity, Sheila was coming home. After Francine's death, what house guest could in good conscience remain?

She wandered downstairs to the living room, trying to think clearly and succeeding only in not really thinking at all. At the table in the bay window she paused, surprised. She sought out Nell in the kitchen.

''Do you know what happened to the Bible? It's gone again.''

''Miss Marion took it. Some of the pages were loose, and she's going to get it rebound.'' Nell was rolling pastry, hadn't missed a stroke.

''Oh.'' Sheila perched on a stool.

In a minute Nell started talking, as if to herself. "I was thinking about that Bible this afternoon, and something funny that happened when Dolly and I were no bigger than that." She held her hand hip-high. "She got mad at me for something and said she was going to scratch my name out of the family Bible. I told her it wasn't in no family Bible, and she said it had to be, because I was family. So we snuck up to Miss Bella's room and took the Bible under the bed to see. We were too little to read— she couldn't have been more than four—but there were all these names with names written beside them, and Dolly said they were married folks, then there were two names at the bottom. She said, 'See, there you are, 'cause you're older than me,' and she drew a line through the name next to the bottom.

"About that time Mama Lucille found us. She jerked us out from under that bed feet first, and I got a whipping for being in that part of the house." She shook her head in dismay. "I realized this afternoon that Dolly must have scratched Marion out of the family!"

As Sheila joined in her laughter, she realized that when Nell spoke of Marion as a child, she used her familiar name. When, she wondered, had the black child been told to use a prefix of respect?

"You've been a part of this family a long time, haven't you?" she asked. She knew the answer, but felt Nell needed to talk.

Nell nodded and gave a heartfelt sigh. "Child, I sure have! All my life. I was born in that little house back there, with Miss Bella helping to bring me into the world. Miss Marion used to carry me around like a doll, they tell me. I don't remember that, of course." She shook her head with another sigh. "Miss Marion's had a lot on her these last few weeks. She sure has!"

"At least she got her things back," Sheila pointed out. "And the case shouldn't be hard to repair. Do you know who made it in the first place?"

Nell shook her head. "No, it was sometime after Miss Bella died, and we were living in Savannah then. I came up to help Mama Lucille at the time of the funeral, and I do know Miss Bella died with it beside her bed, because I picked it up to dust under it. Then when I came back to work a few years ago, it was in the case.''

Sheila sighed. "I can't think why anybody would steal it, can you?''

Nell snorted. "Of course. To confuse the issue. It was those candlesticks they were really after, you can take my word for it. I heard Miss Marion tell somebody once they are antebellum." She glanced into the dining room, as if to reassure herself that the candelabra were back in their rightful place.

"Maybe so. Do you have any more unsweet tea, Nell?''

Nell moved heavily to the refrigerator. "Sure do. I made you a quart.''

"How'd you get onto me?''

"Honey, anybody doesn't like my iced tea has to not like sugar or have something wrong with them. I make the best tea in Charleston. When I saw you didn't put sugar in your coffee either, I figured I'd make an experiment.''

"It succeeded," Sheila assured her.

Nell shook her head in dismay. "You'd do well to start drinking it sweet today. Sugar's good for shock, and the way things are going, we're all going to be needing lots of sugar.''

Sheila smiled, but declined the offer.

Later, on the upstairs porch, she drank her tea and munched a couple of cookies she hadn't tried to resist. How could it be only five o'clock? It seemed like a week since she'd sat in this very chair watching Nell's husband mow the grass. With a wry smile she decided that the Wimberly sisters were probably only in their thirties—it was just these long days that aged them so.

What were they really like, these Wimberlys? Well-bred, moderately well off, attached to their family and their hometown. But what about them was attracting all this trouble?

Sheila believed in coincidence, but coincidence has limits. This many accidents in two weeks... She leaned her head against the chair and, finally, was able to think instead of nap.

Carefully she reviewed the accidents in her mind, then she fetched her pad and wrote:

Wednesday	—twins' car hit by falling limb
Thursday	—Judge Black dies (natural?)
Sunday	—Marion gets nail in tire
Tuesday	—Buddy's television catches fire
Tuesday a week	—Marion gets pushed
Wednesday	—fan blade flies off (intended for Nell?)
???	—Dolly's medicine wrong lid

She considered the list. If Marion really had been pushed by a prowler, then until this morning, every single member of the family had had one true accident, everybody except Francine. And now Francine was dead.

Was that what it was all about? Were the other accidents staged so that Francine could be killed?

Not likely. None of the other accidents were in the least life-threatening, except possibly Marion's fall. Surely anyone planning to disguise Francine's death as one in a series of accidents would make at least some of them look more dangerous.

But had anyone actually *caused* the other accidents?

Take the tree, for instance. Had anyone checked to see if it had been sawn? And the television—was it checked to see if wires had been deliberately frayed?

She wrote down those questions, adding a note to be sure to see Roy Luther. Then she realized what she was doing. An hour ago she had been determined to go home tomorrow, certain that these were a series of unimportant accidents. Now she was all fired up to investigate them, certain deep inside her that someone, not something as blind as coincidence, was behind them. What had happened to change her mind?

She reached deep inside her and found the answer. It was something Nell had said—that Marion had "had a lot on her" these past two weeks. Marion, Sheila was suddenly certain, was the common thread in most of the accidents. Marion who wouldn't have smelled the fire until possibly too late, whose tire might have blown out at a dangerous rate of speed. Marion who was pushed. And it was Marion's silver that had been stolen. What if Dolly's medicine lid had been a mistake no one wanted to acknowledge? And if the fan had simply not been installed correctly? If those two were unrelated to everything else, then had Marion been singled out for acts of malice?

If so, by whom?

Sheila heaved a sigh nearly as deep as Nell's had been. Francine was the likely culprit, and Francine was dead. But what had Francine meant this morning? Had she known something, rather than been guilty herself? Did she confront someone, and...

Sheila shook herself vigorously. "You're getting too far afield, old girl," she said aloud. "We're investigating accidents here, not murder." And if Dolly was right, and Francine was responsible for the accidents, they could all breathe easier now that she was dead.

Her reverie was interrupted by a voice below. "Hey, Juliet? Why so somber?" A silver Jaguar convertible was parked by the fireplug, and a lanky figure carrying a doctor's satchel was standing below her in the yard. He gave her a quick wave and hurried up the steps to the porch.

In only an instant he stuck his head out the door of the upstairs porch. "Before I see Dolly, tell me what's going on. Marion said Dolly's had a shock. Is Francine with her?"

One abruptness deserved another. "Francine's dead. She fell and hit her head on her coffee table. Dolly's taking it hard."

His lips formed a soundless whistle. "Fell and hit her head on a table with enough force to kill her? That's a tricky fall."

"Sure was. And Dolly's pretty upset," she reminded him.

"Right. I'll see her now, but don't go away. I want to talk with you. Better still, see if Nell will send me up a glass of tea."

Nell was in the kitchen, making a pie. "It just don't seem right that she's dead," she said with no preamble. "If I wasn't a Christian, I'd say this house was jinxed."

"It's certainly had its share of accidents." Sheila leaned against the cabinet to watch Nell's plump brown hands deftly crisscross the pie with strips of paper-thin dough.

"Just this morning she's normal as can be, fussing about her tea. Remember? And off she goes to her house to work."

"Did she usually do that? Work in her house, I mean."

Nell shook her head. "She used to be with Dolly all morning. But then Dolly got this bee in her bonnet about Francine writing the family history." As she talked she rolled the leftover dough flat, dotted it with butter, sprinkled it with sugar, and made it into a long roll. Deftly cutting tiny pinwheels and putting them into a baking dish, she continued, "Mostly to get Francine out from underfoot, I thought. If so, it worked." She dotted more butter, sprinkled more sugar over the intriguing dish. "These past two weeks she's been spending mornings in her own house reading old books and letters. She even asked if it would be all right if she went out to visit Mama." She fetched the milk.

"Mama Lucille?" Sheila was startled. She was doing some rapid calculation when Nell did it for her.

"She is a hundred, but still percolating. Some days her mind's as clear as a bell and others she's back in her girlhood, but she loves visitors." Nell poured milk over the entire concoction and slipped it into the oven beside her pie without missing a beat in what she was saying. "If Miss Mary had come, I'd have taken you out."

"So Francine was really serious about this history."

Nell scraped her breadboard with a table knife. "I don't like to say things against the dead, but Francine wasn't serious about anything except menfolks. But I think working on the history made her feel important, like."

"Weren't she and Buddy...I mean, I thought..." Sheila was unashamedly fishing, and was rewarded.

Nell gave a second snort. "Buddy, and Heyward, and Dr. Rogers, too, if he'd have had her. One reason Francine liked this house, I always thought, was the number of unattached men around." Her voice was deep with disgust, and she scraped the dough emphatically. "Now you're more the doctor's type, if you don't mind my saying so."

Sheila shook her head. "Thanks, Nell, but I'm happy as I am."

Nell nodded wisely. "So's he. That's why you'd suit."

Sheila decided it was past time to state her errand. "I doubt that we'd suit, as you put it, but he did ask if we could have a glass of tea together when he's through with Dolly. Just give me a glass for him—I still have some."

Jamison Rogers joined her in a very few minutes. "She's back to sleep. Her pulse is rocky, which is to be expected, but she'll do. She doesn't need any more excitement for a few days, though."

"That's about all there seems to be around here."

He grinned. "Only since you came. It's pretty peaceful around here as a rule."

"Have you known the family long?"

"All my life. My dad was their doctor, too. One of the bannisters on the steps has teethmarks in it from one day when I was pretending to be a beaver while Dad took care of Miss Bella's flu."

Slouching in a rocker, he reached for his tea. He was not as handsome as Heyward, nor as pleasant as Buddy, but she found him more interesting than either. His frame was long and rangy, arms and legs as awkward as if they were connected by rubber bands through his torso. His face was long and thin, forbidding until transformed by a smile. His eyes were deep and black, hooded beneath his dark hair. And he reminded her of someone . . .

"Penny for your thoughts," he said, putting down his drained glass and reaching for the pitcher Nell had wisely sent up.

She held out her palm. "I was wondering if anyone ever told you you look like Abe Lincoln without the whiskers."

He slapped her hand lightly. "How dare you, ma'am? You are speaking to a man whose granddaddy refused to buy a car because it bore that Yankee's name." His face was solemn, but his eyes twinkled with fun. "You'll need to remember where you are. Now why don't you tell me *who* you are?"

On impulse she decided to confide in him. She badly needed some opinions from an outsider who knew this family well. She explained who she was and why she had come, then quickly she sketched the list of accidents. "Does any pattern jump out at you? Is there anything you know about the family that makes sense of this?''

He considered, chewing on his lower lip. Finally he shook his head. ''Sounds like a bad case of *accidentis pronis* to me.''

''Dolly thought Francine might be causing the accidents.''

He shook his head again. ''Somehow I can't see Francine climbing a tree to saw off a branch, or imitating Dolly on the phone. She was mean enough to push Marion, I suppose, if Marion had done something to anger her, and she could have loosened the fan blade, I suppose, if you're sure someone did. But I can't think why she would. She couldn't be sure nobody would be under it—it could have flown off anytime, and hurt somebody—even her. Nobody in their right mind would set such a time bomb—and whatever her faults, Francine was definitely in her right mind.''

Sheila smiled. ''Which is more than some people have said about you.''

''Oh?'' His thick black eyebrows went up like wings. ''What people—or dare I ask?''

''People who oppose your annex project.''

He ran his long fingers through his thick coarse hair. ''If insanity is the worst Marion has accused me of, I'm thankful. Rhoda Bennett considers me a monster.''

''All because of one project?''

He shook his head. ''No, Rhoda and I go way back. We've crossed swords over every progressive idea this city has had in the past twenty years. If that woman had her way, you'd still be wearing four-foot hoops and batting me with your fan.''

''Not me,'' Sheila assured him.

He studied her gravely over his glass. ''No, I don't believe you would, at that.'' He set down the glass and pulled himself to his feet. ''Well, I have to go. We'll talk more later.''

Sheila walked down with him. At his car he turned. ''A friend of mine works in the coroner's office. Would you feel easier if I—''

''What the hell's going on?'' The interruption sounded like the bellow of a wounded bull. A thickset young man continued to bellow as he stormed up the lot from the little house. ''Where's Miz Wimberly? Where's Francine?'' With filthy hands he shoved greasy blond hair out of his eyes and stood glaring at Sheila and Jamison. His cheeks flamed and his blue eyes bulged. "Where's Francine?" he repeated. "Where's my sister?"

He met Sheila's eyes and took a belligerent step forward. "If they've killed her," he said in a voice low with menace, "they'll have to answer to me!"

JAMISON AUTOMATICALLY turned and put one arm around Sheila's waist. Were Southern men trained to do that in their cribs? His introduction, too, struck her as formal for the situation.

"Sheila, may I present Lamar Jenkins, Francine's brother? Lamar, this is Sheila Travis, who is visiting Mrs. Langdon. You've guessed correctly, Lamar, that Francine is dead. But it wasn't murder. It was an accident."

"The hell it was!" When he lowered his head over his chest, his resemblance to a bull was almost complete. All he needed were two sharp horns. Aware of her red skirt, Sheila stepped back—and immediately attracted his wrath.

"What's going on?" he demanded again. "I come home from work and find the door locked, blood on the rug, gray powder everywhere, and no Francine." His eyes narrowed in menace. "How did she die?"

Jamison let Sheila tell him. "She stepped off a stool and hit her head on the coffee table. It could happen to any of us."

His eyes narrowed. "Not to Francine. She could climb like a cat. Besides, what would she want to climb on a stool for? She never used that stool. Never!"

Sheila studied him. "Did you know that several things were stolen from the Wimberly house last night?"

He grew wary and still. "What's that got to do with Francine?"

"They were found on the top shelf of Francine's bookshelf. The police think she was standing on the stool to put them up or take them down when she fell."

His face went a bright brick red. "Look, lady, I don't know who the hell you are, but you can't accuse my sister of stealing."

"She didn't say Francine stole anything," Jamison said sharply. "Maybe Francine found it and put it there until she could return it."

Sheila doubted it, but it calmed Lamar.

"Maybe so. Or maybe"—he paused and looked from one to the other suspiciously—"maybe somebody's framing her. Ever think about that, Doc? Ever think about it, lady? What if somebody was framing her, and bumped her off so it looked like she took it? What I want to know is what happened to the treasure?"

"The police returned it to Miss Wimberly," Sheila said stiffly.

"What's it got to do with her?" he demanded.

"It belonged to her," Sheila reminded him.

He looked baffled. "Belonged . . . ? Hell, lady, I ain't talking about nothing that was stolen. I'm talking about something Francine found, something she said was worth a mint of money. It was going to pay our way for the rest of our lives, she said. Now what happened to that, huh?"

Sheila and Jamison looked at him blankly. "What was it?" the doctor finally asked.

The young man shook his head. "Francine wouldn't tell me. Said it was her private find. But I can tell you one thing, if it ain't in the house somewhere, somebody killed her to get it. And they ain't gonna get away with it. That's all I got to say!" He turned on one heel and stomped down the sidewalk.

Jamison gave Sheila a wry smile. "After that exit, I'm afraid mine's going to look pretty tame."

"The tamer the better," she assured him.

He folded himself into the car and stowed his bag on the other seat. "I'll call you as soon as there's a coroner's report. And don't worry about Lamar. He's lazy and dishonest, and it's lucky Francine's death was an accident. If she'd been murdered, there are a lot of people who might put him at the top of the suspect list."

As SOON AS HIS CAR was out of sight, Sheila went to check out something she suspected. Hoping that Lamar's temper would keep him out of the vicinity for at least a little while, she fetched the key to the little house from the kitchen and hurried to it.

Swiftly she mounted the stairs and found what she thought she would. In one corner of Francine's bedroom was an air mattress and a filthy sleeping bag, with various items of soiled male clothes around it. One mystery, at least, was solved: She knew who Annie's mysterious visitor was—and why he'd been sneaking out at dawn. If her employers knew Francine's undesirable brother was sharing her house, they could have both been thrown out.

Afraid Lamar would return and catch her in the little house, she left everything as she'd found it and returned to her upstairs porch, considering what she'd already heard about this unpleasant young man.

Dolly had mentioned him before. It was Lamar who had repaired Buddy's television and changed Marion's flat tire. From the look of his clothes, he could stand a change for the better in his fortunes, and he was near enough to have pulled off last night's theft and scampered back to bed in a few minutes. He might have even used Francine's key to the main house, while she was out with Heyward. Had he taken the Bible as a blind, planned to burn it after he disposed of the silver? Perhaps Francine had found his cache, thought she'd hide it on the top shelf until she could return it secretly—or confront him with it. Yes, Lamar was a good candidate for last night's escapade. But what motive could he have had for causing the accidents?

Sheila decided to exchange thinking for a long, cool shower.

TWELVE

DINNER WAS A SLOW AFFAIR. Dolly took a tray in her room, and Marion made only a pretense of eating. Sheila was disgusted to find herself relishing Nell's potato puffs and broiled shrimp. Why did murder always make her hungry? Firmly she refused third helpings, but watched the leftovers disappear into the kitchen with regret.

She had not yet thought how to ask Marion if she had enemies when the old woman rose. "Sheila, I hate to leave you to your own devices this evening, but I must be alone. If Buddy calls, or the twins, would you tell them as quietly as possible what has occurred?"

Sheila didn't know if she was to speak in a quiet voice, or to imply that Francine's death was quiet news, but she did think Buddy ought to be informed pretty soon that his fiancée was dead.

When Marion had climbed the stairs, therefore, she sought Nell out in the kitchen.

"I've been wondering if someone ought to call Buddy at work and tell him about Francine."

Nell offered the shrimp platter while she considered. "He and Francine were getting pretty tight," she admitted.

"She told me they were engaged," Sheila replied, taking another shrimp.

"Humph." Nell turned toward the dishpan. "That's as may be. But seeing how's it happened here, looks like somebody ought to go tell him tonight. We don't want him reading it in the paper when he gets up tomorrow."

Sheila nodded, eating another shrimp. "That's what I thought."

"How you keep that skinny figure with all you eat?" Nell demanded. "You're just like your aunt. Eats anything she

wants and never gains an ounce, while I just look at food..."
Ruefully she patted her ample hips.

Sheila laughed and dropped four shrimp tails into the garbage can. "I'm fortifying myself, Nell. Seafood is my favorite eating. You don't want me to show up at Buddy's restaurant and get so hungry I forget my errand, do you?"

"Eat away." Nell held out the platter. "But you save one or two for Will now. Shrimp's his favorite, too."

Sheila pushed the platter aside. "Do you want a ride home, as long as I'm going out?"

Nell shook her head. "Will's probably at the curb already, as late as it is. If Mama Lucille wasn't home alone, I'd have him run me by Harbor Lights myself, but..."

"You go home. I could use a drive."

Half an hour later Sheila entered the dim restaurant and peered about her. A short waiter with a red coat and a very white shirt floated out of the gloom. "May I help you, madame?"

"I'm looking for Buddy Endicott. I'm a friend of his mother-in-law's and need to speak to him."

"Very well, madame. I'll send him a message. There's a half-hour wait for a table, if you'd care to sit in the bar."

"I'm not trying to get a quick table," Sheila assured him in what she hoped was a reasonable voice. "I just need to see Buddy as soon as possible."

He stood his ground. "Mr. Endicott is engaged at the moment. If you'll just wait in the bar..."

If he thinks I'm going to buy a drink in order to swell the coffers, he can think again, Sheila thought grimly. But when a waitress sailed by with a tall cool drink sporting a little blue anchor, she changed her mind. It had been a very long day.

Thus it was that Buddy found her, some twenty minutes later, feeling much better and not minding the wait half as much as she had thought she would.

"Sheila, what a delightful surprise!" If he, too, thought she had come by for a free meal, he gave no sign. He signaled the bartender, and a refill for her drink appeared as if by magic.

She started to wave it away, then thought better of it. She was going to need all the help she could get for this interview.

But before she drank too much, however, maybe she'd better give him the essentials. "I've come about Francine," she said quietly, taking a long pull on the straw. "She's dead."

Buddy stared at her blankly. "Dead? Francine? When? How?"

"Sometime this morning, they think. She seems to have fallen against her coffee table and struck her head."

Buddy fumbled in his pockets, then swiveled his head toward the bar and must have given some signal, for almost at once a pack of cigarettes appeared at his elbow. He lighted one with hands that were not quite steady. "How's Dolly taking it?"

"Pretty hard. We had Dr. Rogers out, and he left her a sedative. Marion seems cut up, too."

Buddy gave a short unpleasant laugh. "Don't let her fool you. Marion's a tough old bird. If it happened this morning, why didn't you call me before now?"

"We...I didn't find her until after three. She'd missed lunch, and Nell wanted to leave for a while. I went to call her, and..."

He reached out a hand of sympathy. "You found her?"

She nodded, then all of a sudden she started to shake. Her teeth chattered, and she was afraid at any moment she was going to bawl.

Deftly Buddy whisked a large napkin from a passing waiter and handed it to her. At last she took a deep breath. "Sorry. I'd been fine until then, but..."

"Probably shoring up everybody else." He smiled. "That's my job, remember? You should have called me as soon as you found her."

She shook her head. "I frankly didn't think about it. First we called the ambulance, then the police, then Marion. When Marion got home, she took charge."

"How did she look—Francine, I mean?" He lighted a second cigarette.

Sheila shrugged. "Not bad. Asleep, almost." Except for the flies. She didn't tell him about the flies. Just thinking about them sickened her. She took a stiff pull on her straw.

He looked about the restaurant. "Hey, you haven't seen the place, have you? Let me give you a guided tour."

It was a strange suggestion in the middle of that particular conversation, but before she knew what was what she was traipsing through kitchens, offices, and an empty banquet hall carrying her drink. By now the drinks were beginning to make her feel light-headed. She managed to walk steadily through three large rooms with diners scattered just far enough to provide seclusion and quiet, but when they got back to their table in the bar, she nearly collapsed into the booth. "It's lovely, Buddy. All of it." She meant it. She had expected something folksy, or overdone. Instead, the restaurant had both charm and warmth.

"We could do the same in Savannah if certain ladies would agree." Buddy's voice implied she knew all about it. Sheila decided she didn't *want* to know. She was still trying to figure out why she was getting a grand tour when she'd come to tell Buddy about the death of his beloved.

"I think I'd better have a cup of coffee before I drive home," she decided.

Buddy smiled. "I think maybe I'll drive you home instead. George can follow us and bring me back." He helped her to her feet and kept a solicitous arm at her waist all the way to the car.

"I'm not usually like this," she assured him at least twice.

"Of course not," he agreed. "It's been a day of shocks."

"You'll tell the girls?" she asked at the Wimberlys' door.

He nodded soberly. "I'll tell them in the morning. They aren't usually awake when I get home. Thanks for coming, Sheila."

BEFORE SHE WENT TO BED, she decided she had better call Aunt Mary—collect. What she'd have to put up with tonight would not be half what she'd have to put up with if she waited.

She splashed cold water on her face until she felt reasonably clearheaded, then put in the call.

"Miss Beaufort's asleep," Mildred objected.

"Nonsense. You and I both know she's reading a detective story and eating truffles," Sheila said sharply. "Tell her it's me and that something else has happened here."

When the sleepy voice came on the line she described the afternoon's events, ending with an abbreviated version of her visit to Harbor Lights.

Aunt Mary didn't respond at once. Sheila could picture the pert silver head cocked to one side in thought. "It *was* an accident, I suppose?" her aunt finally asked.

"I don't see how it could have been anything else, but it was certainly a freakish one."

Aunt Mary paid for at least a minute of silence. "I'm not sure you should have gone," she said at last.

"I don't think I'm in any danger."

"Of course not, dear. I was just thinking that an outsider sometimes precipitates a crisis."

"Aunt Mary, that's the third time you've suggested I'm causing things to happen," Sheila replied with some heat. "But I am in no way responsible. I'd scarcely spoken with Francine since I got here. I certainly didn't push her off the stool."

"And I suppose there was nothing you could have done to prevent it." Aunt Mary's tone suggested she could actually think of several things, if asked. "Now, Sheila, you'd better stop gallivanting around and pay attention to your reason for being there. This time there's been one accident too many."

"Aunt Mary—" Sheila began, but her aunt had no compunction about interrupting younger people.

"I must go now, Sheila." A delicate yawn came through the line. "You waited very late to call. Tomorrow, see if you can get me just after suppertime. Good night."

Sheila was surprised she didn't add "Be good, dear."

THIRTEEN

FRIDAY

SHEILA SLEPT FITFULLY and woke late to another warm, humid day that frizzed her hair and drained her energy. She ate breakfast alone, musing that the day promised to be as dull as any day in a house observing enforced mourning for someone scarcely missed.

Dolly chose to spend it in bed. Marion went to the shop to open up and give Miss Simmons a few instructions, then returned and disappeared into her workroom with a muttered "I might as well get on with some sanding."

After a brief visit with Dolly, Sheila spent the rest of the morning under Nell's direction, running errands and making such phone calls as were necessary in that dreary situation.

Francine's only relative (except Lamar, who seemed to have vanished) was an elderly aunt in Summerville. She declined Sheila's offer of transportation to Francine's funeral Monday, but called several times that morning to instruct them how things should be. Since Marion was hard at work and Nell seemed afflicted with sudden deafness, Sheila took all the calls after the first one.

"You put her in looking nice, hear?" she whined. "Don't you let her have a shoddy burying."

An hour later: "When you going to bring me her things? Don't you hold back on anything, now. I'm all she had, and all she had is rightfully mine."

"What about her brother?" Sheila asked.

"That no-count? Don't you give her nice things to him!"

Remembering the record assortment in Francine's living room, Sheila wondered what the old woman expected to get, but she dutifully went in search of Marion and offered to pack Francine's possessions and deliver them to the old woman.

She found Marion laboring over the sideboard. "Isn't this lovely walnut?" Marion ran her hand over the smooth surface with pride. Sheila nodded, although in its current raw state the wood looked drab and lifeless. Then she stated her errand and asked whether the aunt or the brother should be given possession.

"I'd give everything to her aunt." Marion wiped small beads of perspiration from her forehead with a wadded handkerchief. "The furniture and dishes are Annie's, and Nell can help you sort through the rest. If you would run everything out to Summerville, I'd be very grateful. It's only an hour, but I don't drive that far anymore."

Sheila sought out Nell, and between them they filled black leaf bags with clothes, shoes, and costume jewelry. While they were at it, they also boxed up the dirty sheets, Lamar's clothes (clean and dirty), and a pair of his heavy shoes.

In the downstairs, all Nell allotted Francine's aunt was the stereo and the records. "We can toss the plants, I think."

Sheila agreed. Neither of them would survive the drive.

When they were finished, and back in the kitchen with fresh cups of coffee, Nell moved to the phone. "Will?" she said when it was answered. "Can you come over here and take Francine's stuff up to her aunt in Summerville?"

"I'm going to do it," Sheila tried to mouth at her, but Nell ignored her until she'd completed her arrangements. Then she turned from the phone. "You're needed here, and Will will enjoy the drive."

Sheila would have enjoyed the drive, too.

AFTER LUNCH Sheila offered to clean up the kitchen and let Nell have some time off, but the old woman turned her down. "I'm gonna cheer up my spirits by baking a cake. You clear out of here for an hour, then come back for a slice of the best chocolate cake you ever tasted. It's Dolly's favorite."

"Is Dolly permitted chocolate cake?" Sheila was amazed.

Nell's brown eyes clouded. "Sheila, Dolly is so bad off that Dr. Rogers and I give her whatever she wants. If her heart don't get her soon, there's something else that will. I can't say more, because I promised him. But she's not going to be with us much longer, and I'm aiming to do all I can to make her happy."

Sheila was stunned. "But she's so, so cheerful, so alive."

Nell nodded. "Dolly has always seen the sunshine and not the clouds." She caught her lower lip between her teeth. "But the clouds are coming, Sheila. Everybody knows it. That's why I don't like her to be more worried than she has to with all"—she spread her hands wide and concluded, helplessly—"this mess."

Sheila gave her a quick hug. "I'm glad she has you, Nell."

The old woman returned her hug. "I'm glad she has you, too, child. Now you clear out of my road and let me get at my cake."

Saddened, Sheila decided to return to the little house and do what she could to clean it. "To save Nell the trouble" is what she told herself. But she had to admit she wanted to prowl those tiny rooms once more on her own. What had Lamar meant by a "treasure"? And where, in that minuscule house, could Francine have concealed it?

She straightened the house in a desultory fashion, plumping sad sofa cushions, adjusting a chair into its original depressions in the carpet, throwing away a few scraps of useless paper. The coffee table was still littered with papers, just as Francine had left them. Marion either had been too flustered to come back for them or considered them too unimportant to worry about. Probably the latter, Sheila decided, remembering the old woman's statement about the ordinariness of her family. Idly she looked through them. Francine's scrawled notes were interspersed with a couple of wills, a cookbook, a small packet of letters, and two diaries. Marion was right about them not being very impressive. The earliest date she found was 1887, and that was a dull letter signed "Bro."

She turned her attention to searching the rest of the house. At last, in the kitchen wastebasket, she found something of interest: a crumpled wad of paper across which Francine had written, in a scrawling flourish:

You and I have got to talk.
There is something which I need to ~~talk~~ discuss.

I have found something
I would like to see you at your earliest convenience.

Sheila hoped to find a later draft, but apparently Francine had been satisfied with her last sentence and written the note from it, leaving no telltale blotters or impressions in another sheet of paper.

She mounted the stairs and looked for a hiding place in the small bedroom with its sloping ceiling. She and Nell had already emptied the bureau and stripped the bed. Sheila was about to look for something taped beneath the bureau drawers when she heard a voice downstairs. "Do you need any help?"

Quickly she slid the piece of paper into her wide skirt pocket and descended the narrow stairs. Rhoda Bennett modeled a stunning gray linen pantsuit just inside the kitchen. "I was working in the yard and heard you in here," she said, letting her eyes roam the drab room. "I feel just terrible about all this"— her outstretched hands could equally indicate Francine's murder or the dinginess of the little house—"and know Dolly's not able to do much. So if there's something I could do..."

Sheila suspected her of rampant curiosity—or worse—but decided to take her at face value. "You could sort the papers. They don't need to be left spread all over."

Rhoda slid onto the couch and was already scanning the pages of an old journal when another voice spoke from the door. "What you all doing back here?" Annie stumped in, dressed in black from head to toe. Comparison with a crow was inevitable.

"Packing up Francine's things," Sheila responded.

Annie's eyes ran over the coffee table and darted to the bookshelves. "Those aren't Francine's things. Those are the property of the Wimberly family." She accented the name, as if to underline the fact that neither of the other two had claim to it.

"Marion has asked us to put things in order," Rhoda replied, raising her eyes from a paper she was reading. "How kind of you to wear mourning, Annie. I didn't realize you cared so for Francine."

Annie snorted. "I wear what I please when I please. And I got dressed today without thinking."

"As usual," Rhoda murmured, as if to herself. She resumed her reading.

Annie stumped over and read over her shoulder. "That's Aunt Bella's writing. Do you think Marion wants you to be reading Aunt Bella's private correspondence?"

Rhoda ignored her, laying the letter on the far side of the coffee table beyond Annie's range of vision and reaching for another.

Tension filled the room like cotton candy. "If anybody's going to do that, it ought to be me." Annie reached for the paper, but Rhoda deftly shifted her hands just before Annie grabbed it.

"You'll have to talk with Marion about that," Rhoda said coolly. "Now if you'll excuse me . . ."

Sheila couldn't help remembering that it was she, and not Marion, who had appointed Rhoda keeper of the documents, but, making a quick calculation, decided she'd prefer to tackle Annie. She knew Annie's weak spot, while Rhoda seemed unassailable.

"Let's go back to the kitchen," she suggested. "Nell said she was going to bake a chocolate cake."

"You go," Rhoda drawled. "I'm trying to lose a few pounds." She surveyed Annie's pudgy figure, smoothed her own sleek thigh, and returned to her reading.

Annie permitted herself to be enticed out of the little house and toward the feeder (Sheila couldn't help the image), but as they approached the porch steps she muttered, "One day somebody's going to give that woman what she has coming to her."

Nell gave them cake and tea and sent them out onto the porch. Their snack was interrupted by Buddy, letting himself in at the front door. "You poor boy," Annie cried, as if she hadn't been calling his fiancée a shameless hussy two days before.

Sheila searched his face as he greeted her, but could see no signs of grief. He hurried inside to check on his mother-in-law then, after a detour to pick up a plate of cake and a glass of tea, flopped into the rocker beside Sheila.

"Are you doing all right?" Annie asked, leaning across Sheila to make eye contact.

"Fine," Buddy answered absently. "Dolly looks pretty worn out." With one fingertip he drew a design in the frost on his glass.

Sheila nodded. "Dr. Rogers thinks she'll be all right, but has asked her to stay in bed a day or two."

"You gonna stick around?"

From his tone she couldn't tell if he thought that desirable or not, but having already made up her mind, she nodded. "Officer Johnson still counts me his prime suspect for the break-in," she reminded him.

Annie didn't seem to have heard her. "Maybe I should move back in, since the Judge is gone and all . . ."

Buddy shook his head. "That's mighty kind of you, Annie, but Sheila's in the spare room—remember? And I know Dolly wouldn't want you upsetting yourself on her account."

Sheila marveled at how he managed the old biddy. Annie leaned back in her chair content that at least she had offered the supreme sacrifice—and everyone knew it.

Buddy continued to inspect the frost on his glass.

Sheila waited, determined not to speak first. Finally Annie, unable to bear silence and having nothing to contribute, stood up. "Well, I guess I'll be getting back home. I left beans on the stove, but I saw the door of the little house open and thought somebody ought to check on it. You all call me if you need me, hear?"

Sheila nodded and Buddy said, "We sure will." Satisfied that she had done her duty, Annie stumped toward her own house, leaving her glass and plate for someone else to take in.

It was only a moment later that Buddy spoke, as if to himself. "Seems funny to think she's gone, doesn't it?" Sheila knew he didn't mean Annie. "I keep asking myself how I feel about it, and you know what? I just don't know." He paused, turned his head to look at Sheila. "We'd been talking a bit about marriage, Francine and me. Did you know that?"

She nodded. "Francine mentioned it."

He turned his gaze back to the frost forming on his glass. With one finger he drew a long line in it. "Nothing definite, you understand, but we'd sort of drifted into talking about it. Now that she's gone..." He made the long line into an "F." It immediately began to run in one large drop. He again spoke as if to himself. "...I find she is awfully easy to forget."

He paused, then turned with a smile. "Want to come down to the restaurant for dinner tonight?"

She hesitated.

"Nell can fix something light for Marion and Dolly," he pressed, "and make it easier on everybody."

Sheila's sense of humor won out. "It's one of the strangest dinner invitations I've ever had, but I'll come anyway—because it probably *will* make it easier on everybody."

He rubbed one cheek ruefully. "I didn't think how it would sound, asking you right after talking about marrying Francine."

"It had its awkward edges," she admitted.

He reached out and put one hand over hers. "Margaret used to say, Sheila, that I'd stop on the way to her funeral to check out the restaurant, and she was almost right. Marion and I are alike in that—our shops are our lives. I invited you because I wanted to show off how good my food is, but if tonight's not a good time..."

"No, it's a good time."

"Well, I'll have the girls, too, in case I get called away in the middle of the meal." He pulled himself to his feet. "How about if I send them around for you about seven? I can't leave the restaurant, but their yellow Beetle is back from the shop."

Sheila shuddered. "How about if I call for them in my aunt's car? My legs don't fold in the right places for Beetles."

He gave her hand a quick squeeze and stood up. "Your car it is. You know where we live?"

She nodded. "Becca showed me."

Taking his dishes to the sink, he saw Rhoda as she emerged from the little house.

"Doing a spot of cleaning?" he asked so genially that Sheila thought she must have imagined the edge to his voice.

"Helping out," Rhoda said icily. "Who's keeping the store?"

"It's a well-run business," he countered. "Just toddles on without me from time to time."

"Only," she said with emphasis, "because you are within calling range. Otherwise, things could fall apart and you'd never know it."

"But mine never do, do they?" he asked. Giving her a quick salute, he turned on his heel and walked rapidly away. Rhoda's eyes followed him until he was well down the sidewalk.

FOURTEEN

ONLY WHEN Buddy had turned the corner did Rhoda turn back to Sheila on the porch. "I'm not finished, but I have to get my hair done." She gave her perfect coiffure a pat. "I'll be back in an hour or so." She walked to the front door far more energetically than Sheila had ever seen her go before. Rhoda's interest in history must be genuine after all. So were her gardening instincts. She paused by the gate to automatically pinch off a dead rose.

Sheila remembered she hadn't told Nell she was going out to dinner. Nell took her absence in stride. Pausing in her dusting, she merely grunted. "I knew Buddy'd get some sense one day."

"Nell," Sheila chided her, "yesterday you were fixing me up with Dr. Rogers, now it's Buddy. You are an inveterate matchmaker."

"I never went to the war," Nell corrected her, "but I do like a bit of romance now and then. Not like Francine, mind—that woman had nothing in her head excepting men. But it gets dull around here with us three old women."

"You have the girls," Sheila reminded her.

Nell shook her head. "Rake's almost as bad as Francine—a new beau every week, and none of them brought around for us to meet. And Becca doesn't have a thought in her head except Heyward Bennett."

"Becca?" Sheila asked innocently. "I thought it was Rake who's invited Heyward to a dance."

"Mm-hmm," Nell said heavily, "and nearly brought Becca to tears. Them girls is as close as peas in a pod, but if Rake don't watch out she's gonna rip that pod wide open. She's always bossed Becca, and Becca's let her, unless it was something important. But if Rake starts in on Heyward, uhh-uh! In Becca's book, there's *nothing* as important as Mr. Bennett."

They were interrupted by the front door bell. Nell tromped down the porch to answer it and returned with Officer Stanley Johnson. "You talk to him," Nell instructed. "Miss Marion can't be bothered."

Sheila wasn't certain whether in Charleston one entertained the police on the piazza or the parlor, but mindful of Annie next door, she led the young officer into the living room and indicated a chair.

"How may I help you?" she asked.

He hesitated, as if uncertain how to go on. "It's about Miss Jenkins," he said, turning his hat around and around in his hands. "I have been assigned to this case because it related to the silver. Do you think she may have been the one to take it?"

"I have no idea. It was certainly found in her room."

"And all of it was there?"

She nodded.

He brought out a notebook and scratched his pen at the top of a page until it began to write. "There. But it could have been a plant, of course—someone who wanted us to think Miss Jenkins took the silver. Could you tell me who was around here yesterday morning—say from ten on?"

So they did have suspicions! But how could she learn what they were?

She began by answering his question. "Well, Nell left before ten, to go help someone set up a party, I believe. Marion had already gone to an auction. Francine said she would be working in her own house. And Dolly was on the telephone upstairs when I left—about quarter past ten, I suppose—for a walk."

"Then when you left, no one was on the property except Mrs. Langdon, upstairs, and Miss Jenkins, in the little house out back?"

"That's right. When I left, they were alone here."

"And Mrs. Langdon, now. Do I understand she's in a wheelchair? Could she have gotten to the little house?"

"No, nor could she have gotten into the house once she got there. There are two steps up," she reminded him.

"That's right." He sat heavily, uneasily. "Tell me about your walk. Where did you go?"

"To the Old Market, along King Street, down to The Battery—just a regular tourist's amble."

"Did you talk to anybody? Anybody who might remember?"

She didn't know if she was more amused or astonished. Surely she couldn't be his prime suspect for killing Francine as well as for stealing the family silver. What kind of guests did he think the Wimberlys invited home? Keeping her voice carefully under control she replied, "Possibly—I talked quite a while with some of the basket weavers, and later I ran into Rebecca Endicott and she took me to The Battery. We were together from just past eleven until we returned here for lunch."

He shifted in his chair, more uneasy than ever. "And could you tell me what your relationship was with the deceased?"

"What are you asking her all them questions for?" Nell demanded at the archway. "You thinking Francine was murdered or something?"

His hesitation gave him away. "Then you go find yourself another suspect," Nell told him bluntly. "Sheila just got here Wednesday, and she's been too busy to kill anybody. Yet," she added pointedly as she returned to her kitchen.

He looked so shaken that Sheila gave him a sympathetic smile. "I really didn't do it, Officer, but maybe if you'll tell me more about what you think happened..." She paused, waited for him to speak.

He cleared his throat and had the grace to look embarrassed. "Well, they've found what may have been the cause of the accident. She'd taken several sleeping pills, which could have made her dizzy when she climbed up on the stool."

Sheila had just begun to wonder why anyone would take sleeping pills in the morning, especially before reading dull wills and diaries, when his next words startled her.

"But the cause of death wasn't the pills, or even the fall. She died of asphyxiation."

"You mean she twisted her head and obstructed her windpipe?"

He shook his head. "We think maybe a pillow. The coroner found traces of lint in her mouth and nose. I need to have another look at the scene, if you don't mind."

"I certainly don't," Sheila stood. "Let's go right now." She thought of the sofa pillows she had recently plumped and repressed a shudder.

He stood, too, but held out a hand to restrain her. "If you don't mind, I'll go alone. I may need to remove some evidence, however, so if you could stay nearby..."

She nodded, and he lumbered down the porch.

In less than ten minutes he was back. "I think I've got it," he said with obvious satisfaction. He held out a pillow he'd carefully encased in a plastic bag. "They told me what to look for, and it was right there. Would you sign this, please, to release it?"

"Sure," she said with no enthusiasm. "So do you think she had an accident or didn't?"

"I think," he said portentously, "that she had an accident and knocked herself out, then somebody came along and finished her off. I will need to speak with Mrs. Langdon, to determine if she saw or heard anything."

"Mrs. Langdon is sleeping, under sedation," Nell informed him, again at the arch. She set down a tray bearing two glasses of lemonade and a plate of cookies. "But Mrs. Langdon can't see a thing from her room—the porch cuts off her view—and she was on the phone all morning for the literacy council. She told me when I returned that she had made over thirty calls in two hours."

Officer Johnson drank half of his lemonade before he spoke again. Then he daintily wiped his mouth with the tiny square of white linen Nell had put on the tray and asked Sheila, "Can you think of anyone who would benefit from Miss Jenkins's death?"

Sheila shook her head. "Unless it would be her brother, and I don't know where he could be."

He took Lamar's name and description, then closed his notebook. "We'll find him." He stood, gave her a grave nod and departed.

HE LEFT HER MUCH to think about, so she decided to stroll to the pharmacy before dinner. After she'd introduced herself as

Mary Beaufort's niece, she and the elderly pharmacist were soon chatting like intimate acquaintances.

"Dolly is still puzzled about that call to change her bottle cap," Sheila told him when they'd exchanged pleasantries. "She insists she didn't make the call, but I don't suppose you could have made a mistake like that."

The old pharmacist's eyes were bleary blue under bushy brows. "I could have, with the cold she had that day." With one hand he smoothed his thinning white hair, then turned his attention to his drooping mustache. "If she hadn't told me it was Dolly, I'd not have recognized her at all until she called me Buck—then I knew right away. Nobody but Dolly has called me Buck for years."

"But otherwise you wouldn't have known?"

"Not likely. Nobody sounds like themselves when they've got a code in the node." He cackled with laughter.

Sheila laughed with him, then asked her second question. "I wanted to ask you about the sleeping medicine she's taking, too. Aunt Mary has the same prescription," she lied shamelessly, "and says it makes her dizzy. Is that possible?"

He shook his head. "No, but you know how some women are, especially when they're getting older. Don't tell Mary I said that," he added parenthetically. "I don't say she's gotten like this, now—I haven't seen her for a while, but some women, whatever their symptoms, they blame their pills."

Sheila nodded sympathetically, and he warmed to the subject. "Those are sleeping pills, pure and simple. Gentle on the system, too. That's why they're safe for Dolly. But they don't make you dizzy. Tell Mary Beaufort she's like the rest of us—dizzy with age."

Sheila left him cackling at his own wit and retraced her steps toward the Wimberly house.

It was pleasant to stroll along the old sidewalk, humped here and there by demanding roots. Sheila breathed deeply of honeysuckle and sea air and found herself walking slower and slower. The sun dappled the sidewalk with bright patches. Big magnolia leaves reflected it back from their shiny surfaces. She bent to pick up some Spanish moss that had drifted from a huge oak and ran it through her fingers, enjoying the rough way

it curled around her hand. From Ashley and Rutledge streets
the swish of home-going traffic was a soft undertone to the
song of birds and the muted sounds of a radio coming from an
upstairs window. At this time of afternoon, as Charleston
drowsed its way toward suppertime, she found it impossible to
think about accidents and murder. Almost reluctantly she
turned the corner and passed Annie's house.

The peace of the afternoon was shattered by angry voices
coming from the rear of the Wimberly lot. Or, rather, one angry voice and one like ice.

As Sheila entered the gate, Rhoda was saying firmly "You
may not come in here without Marion Wimberly's permission." She stood inside the little house, one manicured hand
ready to close the door.

"My stuff is in there. They can't keep my stuff!" Lamar
stood about a yard from the door, his face beet red. He waved
one fist in the air, but Rhoda was not impressed.

"I don't know anything about your possessions," she em-
phasized the word, "but you'll have to talk with Miss Wimberly about them. She should be home soon."

Actually Marion's car was parked on the street, and Sheila
suspected that she was still busy in her workroom. If so, she
made no appearance. Sheila herself couldn't decide whether to
melt invisibly along the porch and into the house, or advance
into the fray.

Lamar turned and saw her. "Here, you! Lady! Come tell this
bitch I need my stuff!"

Sheila decided she'd better go to his aid before Rhoda killed
him with a look. She started speaking as she walked. "Your
things aren't there, Lamar. We didn't know where you were
and your aunt told us to bring everything to her in Summerville. We took it out this morning."

"You took my things?" If possible, his face had grown red-
der, and seemed to swell as he sputtered. "What about my records?"

One small mystery solved. Sheila gave him an apologetic
smile. "Sorry, Lamar. I should have suspected they were your.
But since we didn't know where to find you, we took it all, even
the records."

He took two steps toward her, his shoulders hunched menacingly. It took all her self-control not to back away. "I've a mind to call the police on you!" he bellowed.

Rhoda came out the screened door and her voice cut through his tirade. "That will be enough. Leave this property at once, or *we* will call the police and have you arrested for trespassing."

Lamar took one step back and blinked as if splashed by ice water. When he spoke again his voice was a whine. "I ain't trespassing, I come for my stuff." He swiped greasy hair from his eyes. "And what right've you got to say anything about trespassing! I ain't standing on your..."

The expletive was on his lips when Sheila hastily interposed. "Rhoda's been asked to sort through papers Francine was working on, Lamar. Now I really am sorry, but everything you left has been taken to your aunt's—your clothes, your records, even your extra shoes."

The catalog seemed, finally, to convince him. He backed up toward the gate, eyes glowering. "You shouldn't have done it without waiting to see if I'd come back."

"We didn't know where to find you. If you'll give me your address, though..."

He shook his head.

"Or your phone number?"

"No way, Lady. I don't tell nobody where I'm bunking. But I'll come by, in case you forgot anything. What about Francie's treasure! I'll bet you didn't find that, did you?"

She shook her head. "I looked, but I didn't find any treasure."

"Well, it's there!" he insisted. "She said we'd have it easy the rest of our lives. It's mine, and I'm going to search for it!" He took one step toward the door, then met Rhoda's cool gaze. "When that bitch goes home," he muttered.

Rhoda descended from the granite step onto the lawn. Her voice lashed like sleet. "There's not a thing in this house that belongs to you. Now go, and don't ever bother Miss Wimberly again."

Lamar went, but at the gate he turned to give Rhoda a long look of pure hatred.

RHODA WORKED ALONE for nearly an hour, then rose and walked gracefully into the yard, hoping to find Marion still in her shop.

Marion looked up from the sideboard she was rubbing with mineral spirits. "Hello. Isn't this going to be lovely?"

"It certainly will." Rhoda ran a practiced hand over the walnut surface. "But I need to talk to you. I've been working at Francine's, and I've found something I don't understand."

Marion bent her head to her work. "Treasure?" she asked wryly. "I heard Lamar earlier, but you seemed to have him in hand."

"I don't think this is what Lamar's talking about," Rhoda drawled, "but I can't be sure. You see . . ."

Marion stood erect and rubbed her back to ease it. "Not now," she said firmly. "I've been through quite enough for now, Rhoda. I don't even have the energy to be curious."

"Tomorrow morning, then?"

Marion nodded. "Shall I come to you?"

"Let me meet you in the little house. About ten?"

"Fine." Marion returned to her work, and Rhoda drifted in her usual style to her own house.

But before ten the following morning, Rhoda Bennett would die.

FIFTEEN

FRIDAY NIGHT

THAT EVENING Sheila found herself wined and dined in elegance, with waiters paying the kind of attention you only get when you are the guest of the owner. In spite of the weekend crowd, Buddy had reserved a table overlooking the water, and insisted that she eat a house specialty—roast oysters. As she wrestled with the huge glove and sharp knife necessary to wrest her meal from its shells, Sheila cast covetous eyes at the twins' crabmeat salads.

Rake chattered steadily about school, about the theater production she was to be in and the new part she'd just gotten, about nothing, while Becca asked questions to let Sheila share in the conversation whenever Rake paused for breath. Nobody mentioned Francine.

At eight Buddy came to the table and seated himself in the extra chair. A man in a red coat appeared immediately. "May I disturb you for a moment, sir? I've been looking for you for nearly an hour."

"I was in the banquet room, planning next week's setup. What do you need?"

The man bent near Buddy's ear and Buddy listened, made a decision, and sent him on his way, satisfied. Sheila watched with interest. In the restaurant Buddy acted with far more authority than she had seen in him before.

"I can leave in half an hour," he said, surveying the crowd with a practiced eye. A waiter glided up. "Just coffee, Pete, thanks." When the waiter left he confided, "Seeing food all night takes away my appetite. How was your own dinner?"

Sheila cast a baleful glance at her tray of empty shells and the oysters she still hadn't conquered. "Difficult."

He laughed and reached for the glove. "Here, I'll shuck and you eat." Once she was eating at a decent rate, Sheila admitted that the oysters were delicious. Again she congratulated Buddy on his restaurant.

He made a sour face. "Tell it to Marion. All I need is a little capital, and there's the perfect spot in Savannah—" He broke off midsentence and shook his head. "No point in boring you."

Sheila stared at him in surprise. "I'd have thought a successful restaurant would make more than a small antique shop."

He laughed shortly. "Oh, it does. But I don't own all the restaurant—Rhoda owns half of it. And Marion's money isn't all in the shop, it's in land. Old Granddaddy Scott Wimberly—her granddaddy, not my wife's—bought a lot of pine scrub in what is fast becoming suburban Charleston."

Sheila was enough her aunt's niece to feel squeamish about discussing her hostess's financial situation. "Do I deduce that Rhoda isn't interested in expansion?"

He nodded sourly.

She began to understand the animosity between the two. "Why did you go into partnership with Rhoda in the first place? If it's not too personal, that is."

Buddy gave a short laugh that was more of a bark. "It's no personal at all. I didn't. MacFadden, her husband, was a friend of my daddy's, and when I wanted to start out, Mac came in with me. The understanding was that when I could, I'd buy him out. But poor Mac died before I was ready, and the Ice Maiden doesn't give up anything she gets her hands on. Just ask Heyward."

"She's obnoxious," Rake declared, always her father's champion.

Becca spoke softly. "Of course if Daddy didn't have two daughters to educate at once, he'd have enough for the restaurant."

Buddy reached over and ruffled her hair. "But I'd rather have you two with all the trouble you are than another restaurant." Abruptly he changed the subject, swinging his eyes to meet Sheila's. "Would you like to catch a movie when I'm done?"

Rake's eyes brightened, but he dashed her hopes. "Just Sheila, kittens. I'm not up to squiring three tonight."

Sheila hoped her face didn't register pure shock, but it was the first time she'd been asked out by a man whose fiancée was awaiting burial. "I...I don't..." She hadn't formulated a decent refusal when Becca came to her rescue.

"How about a midnight sail? The moon is full."

"Good old Becca, keeper of tides and phases," Rake teased her. "But could we, Daddy—all of us?"

Buddy looked from the twins to Sheila. "I've been wanting to get on a sailboat since I got here," she admitted.

"Then a sail it is. You girls take Sheila to change, and I'll meet you at the boat in forty-five minutes."

True to his word, he was there before them, already taking the cover off the mainsail. "Welcome aboard *The End*," he called gaily.

"The boat," Rake added, pointing to the name printed in gold on the back.

"Rake named her," said Becca, gracefully jumping from dock to deck. "We were having a family argument about a name, and Rake finally said 'I'll be glad when we get to the end.' We all decided that was a great name. End for Endicott."

"Silly, but appropriate, don't you think?" Rake leaped as gracefully as her twin and turned to offer Sheila a hand.

As she clambered aboard more sedately, Sheila felt eons older than those two gazelles.

"Ahoy, there, Endicotts!" Becca gave a small gulp as Heyward Bennett strolled down the dock and smiled down at them. "Taking her out?" It took Sheila a minute to realize he was referring to the boat and not to her. By then Heyward had accepted Buddy's invitation to join them.

"I came down thinking I might go out alone—it's such a gorgeous night." As he came aboard Buddy cranked the motor and Becca cast off. They chugged out of the dock and into what Sheila presumed was a channel. Automatically she found herself falling into old patterns—helping Becca hoist the genoa while Heyward raised the mainsail and Rake vanished below, only to reappear in a moment with iced Cokes.

When Buddy cut the motor and they were gliding across the water without a sound, Sheila gave a small involuntary "Oh!" of pure joy.

"It's beautiful, isn't it?" Becca slid into the seat beside her.

Sheila nodded. "I always love the moment when the noise stops and it's just you and the wind."

Becca opened a Coke. "Give one to Heyward," Rake instructed.

"Want one?" Becca asked him.

"Sure." He took the seat next to her and held out his hand. Becca carefully did not touch him as she handed him the drink.

Sheila herself was tired of trying to fathom the complex relationships in this family. Night had nearly come, and beneath and around them the water was silky black, lapping the boat in greeting. She leaned against the rail and abandoned herself entirely to the pleasure of wind in her hair and the beauty of black sails against an enormous sky. On the eastern horizon the full moon was just beginning a spectacular entrance while Venus stared at them from above. Caressed by a friendly breeze, Sheila abandoned all thought.

But only for a moment. Becca moved to join Rake at the prow and Heyward slid across beside Sheila. "You really put a bee in my mama's bonnet," he murmured, stretching both arms along the rail behind her.

She shifted slightly to face him. "Oh? How's that?"

"Putting her to work sorting Francine's papers." His voice, she noticed, hesitated slightly over her name. Sheila was glad It was nice to find *somebody* who took notice that the woman was dead. But Heyward had paused only a second. He was already well into his next sentence. "...het up about some thing. She spent our entire dinnertime muttering and glaring a me as if I knew what she was talking about."

"You don't?"

He shook his head. "No, thank goodness. Whatever it is, i made her chomp her bit and gnash her teeth. Not a prett sight." Nor one Sheila could picture.

"Is it something she found among the family papers?" sh wondered aloud.

Heyward shook his head. "I don't think so, I think it has something to do with Francine's past. She never would say what happened to her folks or where she came from, and I think Mama has found some clue, because she said one time 'We've certainly all been fooled.' Then she lit into me about anything and everything, until I decided it was the better part of wisdom to come down to the boats. Maybe we'll find out tomorrow—Mama said she'll talk to Marion about it in the morning."

Buddy adjusted the tiller slightly and asked, "Is she seeing the light about your own situation?"

Heyward gave a short, humorless laugh. "My dear mama never sees any light unless it's glinting on her own gold, Buddy. You, of all people, ought to know that." He stood, stretched his hands high above his head and blew hard.

"What a night!"

Without any farewell he left Sheila and climbed up beside the twins.

"Prepare to come about," Buddy called. The three on the bow flattened themselves so the big sail could pass over them.

Sheila automatically started to make the sail fast, but was not quick enough for Heyward. "Tighten that sheet!" he shouted.

"She is!" Becca told him hotly. "You don't need to yell at her."

He raised one beautiful eyebrow. "Even the kitten has claws! It must be the moon. I've never seen so many temperamental women in one day in my life."

"Not me," Rake said lazily from the bow. "I'm feeling real copacetic tonight. Like my new word?"

Heyward gave her a dazzling smile. "I'd like it better if I knew what it meant."

Buddy called from the stern. "Take the tiller, Heyward, and let me talk to my guest." He moved to give the younger man his place and settled onto the cushions between Sheila and the stern.

She was afraid he would bring the conversation around to some of the puzzles—the stolen silver, or Francine's death. But Buddy seemed to have nothing more on his mind than being a charming host. Gladly she responded to his light, superficial banter.

It made the sail a nice time to remember in the horror of the days that followed.

SIXTEEN

SATURDAY

"WE NEED A FEW GROCERIES," Marion said the next morning, buttering her toast, "and I wondered, Sheila, if you'd be able to run to the Piggly-Wiggly. Nell cleans the upstairs on Saturdays, and I have a few things to do before I go to the shop at noon." She laid three bills beside Sheila's plate.

Accordingly, list in hand and direction in her head, Sheila set off at half-past eight to see exactly what a Piggly-Wiggly might be. She saw Heyward's car turn a corner two blocks from the house, but he missed her wave.

She set out confidently, but the one-way streets trapped her within minutes. It took half an hour of twists and turns, wishing she'd brought a map, before she found what turned out to be a very ordinary supermarket with a whimsical name. It was full of Saturday morning shoppers, and by the time she'd gone down every aisle at least twice finding everything on the list, she was over two hours getting back.

She was lifting the second bag of groceries from the Cadillac's capacious trunk when Buddy came up behind her. "Allow me, ma'am," he said in an exaggerated drawl.

"You just missed Dr. Jamison," Nell greeted her regretfully. "He looked in on Miss Dolly and asked for you."

"Ah, but she was just in time for me." Buddy set the groceries on a counter. "Did Marion leave her keys for me? I told her I'd get her oil changed."

Nell jerked her head toward the key hooks on a cupboard door. "Mind you get back in time for her to get to work by noon. She don't need to walk in this heat."

Sheila agreed. Just carrying in groceries had left her sticky.

Buddy departed, slamming the door behind him.

Nell and Sheila had just sat down at the small kitchen table for coffee and a chat when Marion came into the kitchen. "Rhoda hasn't called, has she?"

Nell shook her head. "Nobody called all morning."

Marion stood and rubbed her cheeks, which were flushed and damp. "I've been working all morning, and it's awfully hot out there," she said, as if to explain the perspiration and the smock she wore. "I really must get Buddy to put in a fan."

"Just be sure he gets a solid one," Nell warned. "Not like his last one."

Marion fetched herself a cup and stood indecisively beside the table. "I can't imagine what has happened. Rhoda asked me to meet her in the little house at ten. I left my door open so I could hear her, and put a note on the door for her to call me when she got there, but she hasn't come."

"Probably got caught up with something," Nell consoled her. "Have your coffee, then call her."

As the old woman took a seat at the table, Sheila saw that her hands were trembling, and her face, under the flush, looked strained and ill. Nell had seen it, too.

"You gonna get a stroke, working out there in this heat. You finish with Rhoda and get down to that cool shop for the rest of the day."

"My own idea exactly." Marion finished her coffee and reached for the phone. "Hello, Miramise? May I speak to Mrs. Bennett, please?" She paused. "In the garden?" She repeated the phrase in surprise. "Well, would you call her? Thanks so much."

Nell rested her ample forearms on the table and shook her head fondly. "Those two ought to just move in together and get it over with. Every day they have to consult on one thing or another."

Marion opened her mouth to reply, but she was forestalled by shrieks coming from next door. "Oh, Gawd, oh, Gawd a-mighty!"

Marion hurried onto the porch and toward the front door. Sheila, dispatching with northside manners, peered out the kitchen window and, finding her view blocked by a bony crepe myrtle, hurried to the dining-room window. Across high shrubs, it offered a partial view of the Bennett garden.

Miramise, the Bennetts' maid, was staring in horror at something Sheila could not see, something that lay in the bushes near the Wimberlys' wall.

"What's the matter?" Sheila called loudly.

Miramise raised huge round eyes. "Oh, lady, call the police!" she boomed. "Somebody done whacked Miz Rhoda daid!"

As soon as the police promised to come (probably deciding that they should make this block a precinct of its own), Sheila went upstairs to be with Dolly. To her surprise, she found her hostess placidly listening to a tape of Chopin études, unaware of the tragedy next door. It took her a moment to realize that, without northside windows, Dolly would have heard Miramise's screams only distantly, if at all.

Dolly's smile was cheerful, but she was still pale. Quiet as it had been, Francine's death had taken a toll on Dolly's heart. Sheila decided she had neither the skill nor the wisdom to break this latest news, so after chatting for a few minutes she excused herself and called Jamison Rogers.

He came immediately. "I gave her a mild sedative after I told her," he reported when he came to the kitchen sometime later. "She should rest most of today. This is far harder on her than Francine's death was."

"Harder on Miss Rhoda, too." The gruffness of Nell's voice betrayed her.

Jamison gave her a hug. "Harder on all of us."

He accepted a cup of coffee, then left for the Bennett yard. By now it was so full of policemen and related people that one more would probably not be noticed.

When Marion returned nearly an hour later, she reported that someone had indeed "whacked Miz Rhoda"—striking her from behind as she knelt weeding her precious flowers. There were no marks on the grass, and no weapon. But the police thought the murderer had used a large round stick—perhaps a baseball bat. It had been wielded with force and had killed her instantly.

The landscaping of the yard and the high wall had shielded her assailant from the view of anyone passing in the street—and, Sheila reflected ruefully, Nell's unvaried schedule and northside manners had shielded the assailant just as effectively from the Wimberly house.

Marion's face was even grayer beneath its tan and her wrinkles seemed carved with a scalpel. "You need to rest," Sheila told her.

Marion shook her head. "Heyward hasn't been found yet, and there's nobody at the house but Miramise. She's in no state to be left alone. I came over just long enough to see about Dolly."

Sheila knew the obvious response. I'm getting to be a corpse sitter, she reflected ruefully as she loped along the sidewalk. Heaven help her when Aunt Mary learned of this latest development.

At the big gray house, to her chagrin, she found a young policeman on duty. "Sorry, ma'am, but you can't go in here just now. There's been an accident."

"They's been a mur-der," a rich deep voice corrected him. A large, very black woman filled the doorway. "Now you get outta de doah and let de lady by." She stood back and shooed Sheila past the policeman's protests.

Still talking, she led the way into the house. "Miz Marion called you was coming. She say you'll stay till Mr. Heyward come, but I think you might need to stay a bit longer. He's not gonna be fit to see anybody for a while, and who's gonna answer de doah and de phone?"

Who indeed? thought Sheila with a mental sigh. As she followed Miramise into the kitchen, she composed a little speech she planned to give Aunt Mary concerning future vacations.

Miramise's voice was rich and heavy with country accents, and it rolled behind her as she walked. "I sho' hope de po-lice can find Mist' Heyward. He slep' on his boat last night after de big dust-up, and I ain't seed him since."

"Dust-up?" Sheila inquired.

Miramise poured them both tall glasses of sweet iced tea.

If she stayed long in Charleston, Sheila reflected, she could support one dentist single-mouthed. Miramise, meanwhile, like Ole Man River, was rolling along.

"De quar-rel. Las' night at supper. I doan 'member how it started, but I was s'prised Miz Rhoda let it go on so long. She liked peace and quiet with her meals."

Sheila, having an aunt who insisted on peace and quiet at her own meals, immediately comprehended Miramise's surprise. "What did they quarrel about?"

The maid rolled her big eyes. "Anything and everything. Mr. Heyward say all she ever think about is hiztry and fambly, and she say he never do. He say if you got one you doan need to think about it, and she say what's dat s'posed to mean. He say nothin' in p'ticular, but he rather *be* a fambly dan talk about it. Dat's on account of how he and his mama hadn't been much of a fambly since his daddy died," she added parenthetically. "And den Miz Rhoda, she say maybe he been plannin' to set up a fambly with dat trash next doah." Miramise had turned to the sink, but she turned quickly back to set the record straight. "Miz Rhoda meant dat nurse, you mind. Dey's no better fambly in dis town dan the Wimberlys."

Sheila nodded. "I understand."

Miramise rumbled on. "Den Mist' Heyward say she'd got no call to speak like dat of somebody who's done daid, and besides, he cain' set up no kind of fambly on the money he makin' right now, and she say he know whut he can do 'bout dat. I think she meant for him to go to lawyer school—she had her heart just plumb set on him being a lawyer like his daddy. So den Mr. Heyward say he's doing whut he wants to do, and dat when de time comes he'll set up fambly wid whoever he damn well please. Den he slam straight out the doah. Miz Rhoda 'us so mad she was trembly. Dat's the last I seed of him," she concluded anticlimactically.

"He went sailing with us last night—Buddy, the girls, and me," Sheila told her. "And he seemed fine. He did say that his mother had been upset about some paper she had found."

Miramise rolled her eyes in a knowing way. "Um-hmmm! *Now* I 'member! Dat's whut started de whole thing. She was talkin' 'bout some exception she couldn't rightly believe."

"Exception?" Sheila asked.

Miramise shrugged. "Somepin' like dat. She said people ought to be who dey really is, not somebody else. Udderwise how 'us histerical searchers gonna get it right? Dat's when Mr. Heyward made his first remark and drew her fire in his direction." Miramise nodded wisely. "Um-hmmm, he'd a done better to leave her be las' night. Anybody with half sense coulda tole him she was in high feathers 'bout sumpin'. She tole me she was gonna talk wi' Miz Marion first thing today. But doan look like she's gonna get dat chance."

"She didn't say what she planned to talk about?"

Miramise's round face registered astonishment. "Miz Bennett talk over her bizness with a maid? You didn't know her very well."

"How long have you worked here?" Miramise was not showing a longtime servant's grief.

The maid folded her arms and leaned against the sink. "I come nine years ago next month, and let me tell you, Miz Rhoda was one hard lady to work for. It's a plumb miracle I stayed. She wanted everythin' done just *so*"—she squared her hands expressively—"and when she called, you had to *hop*. Um-HMMM!" She paused, then said less theatrically, "But de pay's good, and she doan bother me none. I does my work and keeps out of her road." She surveyed the large comfortable kitchen and shook her head. "I bet I doan get another place as good. Good pay and reg'lar work is hard to come by."

Just then Officer Johnson came into the kitchen, and through the porch window Sheila saw men carrying a draped stretcher. He didn't even glance at Sheila as he said to the housekeeper, "I need to get a statement from you."

She rolled her eyes at him. "I doan know nuthin', Off'cer. I was in my kitchen right here the whole mornin', cleanin' up from brefust and gettin' ready for lunch. 'Ceptin' when I went upstairs to iron a dress. I couldn' see de yard all day."

Sheila moved to look out the porch window, expecting to have the same good view of the lawn Nell enjoyed. But Rhoda's landscaping insured that the kitchen, indeed, had no view at all except on the forbidden northern side.

Officer Johnson flipped open a notebook and took out his pen. "You last saw the deceased when?"

"Right after brefust."

"And that was when?"

"Eight-fifteen. Everybody in town knows Miz Rhoda finish brefust at eight-fifteen every mornin' of the week."

"Did she seem normal?"

"Cose she seem normal. You think a woman 'spects to get whacked on the haid?"

Officer Johnson had the sense not to reply. "What did she do then?"

"She come in here with orders for lunch, say she was gonna work in the yard. That warn't news. She was allus workin' in the yard if she warn't downtown at some histerical meeting. Then she say she's goan out to dinner tonight, and I can have the evenin' off, but to press her tortoise blue dress. So, soon as I finishes my dishes, I goes upstairs and presses that dress, den I comes back down here to work on lunch. I was just makin' a fruit salad"—she flapped a huge hand toward the sink, where strawberries, a pineapple, and melons still sat—"when Miz Marion called. I say she's in de yard and Miz Marion say go call her. So I goes to call her, and . . ." For the first time she faltered, perhaps remembering what she had seen. "You knows de rest," she finished lamely.

"You didn't see or hear anyone or anything strange the entire morning?"

"No, sir, I didn't. I done tole you all I know."

The officer turned to Sheila and, as she had feared, recognition dawned. "What are you doing here?"

"Marion Wimberly sent me over to help out."

"You didn't see anything, hear anything from over there?"

She shook her head. "I left for the grocery store about half-past eight, got lost and caught in crowds, and didn't get back until nearly eleven."

"Where did you go, for heaven's sake?" he demanded.

"The Piggly-Wiggly." It was hard to say with a straight face.

His own face registered amazement. "It took you two hours to get to the Big Pig from here? Lady, that's a ten-minute drive."

"Not the way I did it," she assured him.

He shut his notebook with a click. "Well, we can go into that more later. For now, I have made a note that since your arrival there has been a theft, a fatal accident, and a murder on this block. I'm not saying you had anything to do with any of these things, mind, but I'd just as soon you don't ever come to visit me." He wiped his ruddy face with one hand and reopened his notebook. "What's your official residence?"

"Chicago, but for two weeks I'm visiting my aunt in Atlanta."

"Atlanta?"

She flushed. "I mean, I was visiting my aunt there when she suggested I come visit her friend, Dolly Langdon, here."

He looked up bewildered. "So your residence is where?"

She sighed. "Oh, just put the Wimberly house next door."

He wrote laboriously.

"May I ask you a question?" she said when he was done.

"Sure."

"What killed her?"

"A heavy blow to the left side of her head."

"The left?"

He nodded.

"Do you know what the weapon was?" she persisted.

His look said far louder than words that he found her thirst for knowledge ghoulish and unbecoming in a lady. "I'm sorry, ma'am," he said stiffly, "but I can't say."

"Can't, or won't?" she pressed. "Have they found the weapon?"

"No," he admitted, "but they're still looking. And I assure you of one thing, ma'am. We're going to find it, and who used it. No one can kill Heyward's mother—" He stopped and cleared his throat to pretend his voice hadn't been about to break. "He's going to have to answer to me!" He strode off, slapping his notebook against one thick thigh.

SEVENTEEN

HEYWARD ARRIVED soon afterward. Pale, he was nevertheless as courteous as ever. He accepted Sheila's condolences with a small smile. "We didn't exactly part on the best of terms."

"You told me you quarreled last night. Did it continue this morning?"

"I didn't see her this morning. After our sail I slept on my boat. That's where they found me just now."

"But—" Sheila stopped. She wasn't ready yet to ask Heyward why she'd seen him two blocks from home earlier today.

He poured himself a stiff drink of brandy and gave her a wan smile. "You run on home now, Sheila. I'll take care of things around here."

She left the house, but did not go straight home. First she crossed the lawn and circled the fountain to where Rhoda Bennett had lain. The grass was trampled, of course, but Sheila still examined it closely. She looked under the bushes and determined that Rhoda's fierce desire for privacy had insured that except for the Wimberly dining room and Marion's workroom, there was no place anyone could have stood and seen the murder committed. But who would have the audacity to kill a woman in her own front yard and leave by her front gate, carrying the murder weapon?

Damp with the heat and strain, Sheila returned home to find Marion pacing the living-room floor, worry written on every line of her face. "I don't know what to do, Sheila," she confided. She sat on a straight chair and motioned Sheila to the sofa.

"You look like you could use a rest," Sheila said softly.

Marion gave her a grateful look. "I am bone weary, Sheila. First the two incidents of Thursday, and now—this." She gestured toward the north wall of the room. For only an instant her lips quivered. After all, Sheila remembered, Rhoda had been a neighbor for almost thirty years. Immediately Marion's iron control took over. "I don't know what to do about Dolly for these next few days. As you know, she is not well. She simply must not bear much confusion and worry. And Nell can't do her own work and take care of Dolly." She gave Sheila a long, direct look. "As much as I hate to ask, could you stay with her for a few more days?"

"I'm not a nurse," Sheila cautioned her.

"Oh, as unreliable as he is in other ways, Jamison takes excellent care of her health. What she needs is somebody to be here, shield her and distract her mind. She depended more on Francine than she realized, I think, for company as well as for errands and care, and Rhoda was . . . a longtime friend."

"I'll be glad to do what I can," Sheila heard herself saying. With a twinge of conscience she wondered whether she'd have made the same offer if a mystery were not included in the bargain.

Marion's relief was visible. "I'd be very grateful. I thought of closing the shop. But this is a busy season for visitors, and I hesitate to do it."

"Can't your assistant handle things for a few days?"

"No. She's not capable of handling it for more than half a day at a time."

Not capable or not permitted? Sheila suspected that Marion kept a tight rein on those who worked for her. That was confirmed when Sheila repeated that she'd be glad to help, for as tired as she was, Marion decided to go to the shop for what remained of the day, taking a sandwich with her for lunch.

Dolly was still sleeping, and Sheila was glad when Nell suggested she have a lunch tray on the upstairs porch.

After lunch, Sheila dialed a familiar number. "Why, Sheila, that place is worse than Chicago!" In spite of visits to the Windy City, Aunt Mary persisted in her belief that gangsters lurked behind every streetlight. "I only knew Mrs. Bennett slightly, but I knew her late husband fairly well. How did you say it was done?"

"She was hit over the head—possibly with a baseball bat."

"Nonsense, dear. Nobody goes around carrying a baseball bat. What do they think was the motive?"

Sheila hesitated. "If by 'they' you mean the police, Aunt Mary, then they think it was a vagrant. Rhoda's manner with stray men was rather imperious." She described the scene with Lamar. "It's possible he did it. He was certainly angry enough yesterday. Otherwise, I'm afraid it has something to do with things over here."

"Why is that, dear?"

"Well, Lamar keeps insisting that Francine had a 'treasure,' and from something I found, I think she was either blackmailing somebody or about to." She told about the scrap of paper she'd found in Francine's trash.

"But what would Rhoda Bennett have to do with that, Sheila?" Aunt Mary was unconvinced.

Sheila explained about Rhoda's reported "find" and what Heyward and Miramise had reported about Rhoda's mental state when she returned from the little house. "Obviously Francine did not kill her," Aunt Mary mused, "but Lamar could have, if what Rhoda found dealt with his past, too. Perhaps it's a family disgrace."

"As far as I'm concerned, the family *is* a disgrace," Sheila declared, "but Lamar's treasure wasn't among the papers that I saw. Rhoda may have had a look around on her own, however, and if she found it, it could prove a motive for both murders."

"Are you certain there have been two murders, dear?"

Sheila nodded before realizing her aunt couldn't see her. "Yes, the police said yesterday that Francine's true cause of death was asphyxiation. She was smothered with a sofa pillow sometime after she fell, possibly while unconscious."

"Oh." Even Aunt Mary was shocked. She thought for a moment. "The only problem I see with connecting the two is that Francine's death was carefully made to look like an accident, while Rhoda's seems an impulsive act of the moment. Do you know if she spoke with anyone this morning?"

Sheila sighed. "I don't *know* that she did, but I'm afraid she did. I saw Heyward driving away earlier this morning, while he swears he was on his boat all night until the police came for him."

"Did you actually see him, or just his car?"

Sheila considered the matter, closing her eyes to picture it again. At last she shook her head. "I don't know," she admitted, "and maybe it wasn't even his car, now that I think about it."

"What's he like?"

"Except for a lamentable taste in women, he's very likable."

"Likable young men have been known to do murder before," Aunt Mary reminded her. "Did he care enough for Francine to kill her rather than permit her to marry Buddy?"

"I have no idea." Sheila hoped not. "I'm still pulling for Lamar. I think he was our thief in the night, and that when Francine confronted him about it, he knocked her across the room and then killed her."

"You might steer the police in that direction," Aunt Mary agreed. "For one thing, it will keep them from thinking about Heyward until you've had time to investigate him a bit further, and for another, it might do your hot-tempered young friend a bit of good to taste what can happen to him if he doesn't mend his ways."

"By all that, I take it you don't think he's our culprit."

"No, Sheila, I'm afraid I don't, as convenient as it would be for everyone. Lamar doesn't tie in with any of the accidents, for one thing, and he's too obvious. This situation seems far more devious than he sounds capable of being. Aside from Heyward and Lamar, who are the other possible suspects?"

Sheila gave a short, mirthless laugh. "Everybody in the family, except Dolly, I suppose. Buddy was engaged to Francine and having trouble with Rhoda over business..."

"...business, dear?"

"Rhoda owned half his restaurant and wouldn't agree to buy a second in Savannah. They were extremely cool whenever they met."

"Disagreeing with business partners is not the same as murdering them," pointed out one who frequently disagreed with her own.

"Of course not. I'm just saying that several people around here might have had good motives to put Rhoda out of the picture. Rake might have done it because she was angry for her father's sake, or Becca might have done it for Heyward..."

"I beg your pardon?"

Sheila explained.

"Does she strike you as an unbalanced young woman?"

"No, if anything she seems eminently balanced. I'm not serious about any of these, Aunt Mary—but I suppose even Nell or Marion might have done it, although I can't think of a motive for them. I did think of one possible motive for the accidents, however. They all seem directed toward Marion."

"It isn't Marion who is dead," Aunt Mary pointed out reasonably.

"I know." Sheila thrust one hand through her thick hair, making it stand out from her scalp. "Is it possible, Aunt Mary, that none of these things are related? Or that Francine really did cause all the other accidents and her death is unrelated to them? Should we think of Rhoda's death as isolated from the rest, and just try to solve it, forgetting the accidents?"

Aunt Mary was silent for a moment, then sighed. "It really is very complicated, isn't it?"

"It certainly is," Sheila agreed.

Aunt Mary was silent again, so long that Sheila thought they might have been disconnected. She was just about to try a tentative "hello" when Aunt Mary spoke in her usual forthright fashion.

"Well, dear, I am counting on you to straighten it all out rather quickly. We have tickets to the ballet next Friday, you recall." A doorbell was heard behind her. "Oh, that must be Charlie bringing some papers I asked for yesterday. I'll have to ring off now, but you go find that weapon, and I'll give this a great deal of thought. Good-bye now." Before Sheila could so much as breathe into the receiver, she was gone.

SHEILA WAS SURPRISED to find herself a little forlorn. This was not the first time she had been involved in a mystery—only last spring she had discovered who left a woman's body in the basement of the institute for international studies where she worked. But in the past, Aunt Mary had always managed to be around whenever the mysteries were—or was it the other way

around? Sheila's father often said of his eccentric elder sister
"Trouble follows that woman like fleas a dog."

Now she missed having Aunt Mary around to rehash ever
development of the case, and found it both wearing and un
certain to keep her aunt informed via long distance. Had sh
given Aunt Mary every fact she needed to put her intricat
thought processes to work?

Sheila considered what she herself might best be doing. Sh
could certainly call the police and suggest that they pick u
Lamar for questioning, although her evidence against him wa
slim. She hoped, however, that she could get in touch with th
young homicide officer from Thursday afternoon, and not hav
to deal again with poor Officer Johnson.

She went down to the kitchen, where Nell was stirring some
thing in a large bowl. "Nell, would Marion or Dolly be likel
to have a work address for Lamar, do you think?"

Nell nodded. "It ought to be in Miss Marion's address book
She likes to keep up with relatives of her employees. Check he
desk upstairs, on the table beside her bed. She was makin
some calls this morning about Mrs. Bennett. I hope it was hir
who did it, and you can take a few days just to enjoy yoursel
around here."

Sheila must have shown some surprise in her face, becaus
Nell reached out and gave her a quick pat. "Dolly told me wh
you're here, child. I hope you can figure things out. We've ha
too many surprises lately." She turned back to her bowl, leav
ing Sheila to climb to the third floor and Marion's domain.

The office was like Marion herself—austere, elegant, an
aloof. Marion had chosen to use the sunny front room for he
bedroom, possibly because she worked here mostly at night, s
the sunlight streaming through the single dormer reached onl
a part of her office. To brighten it, she had chosen pale-ivor
walls and carpet, floral drapes, and a gold cover for the dee
slipper chair and ottoman next to the bookshelf. But the hea
of the room was obviously the gray filing cabinet and sma
Queen Anne desk, bare except for a neat stack of papers.

Although she looked in each desk drawer, she found no d
rectory. She did find, however, in the bottom drawer, Ma

ion's will. Feeling as guilty as if she had read it, she shut the drawer and hurried across the hall to the bedroom, which rivaled the office for austerity. Not a magazine, not a stray pair of slippers, not a rumple in the ice-blue spread indicated that anyone ever took off clothes and collapsed on that high mahogany bed to read. Three ornaments decorated the mantel—a Dresden ballerina in a yellow bodice with a porcelain lace skirt, an ancient Chinese vase, and a photograph of Marion's parents in street clothes. Beside the bed, sharing a small table with the telephone, was the directory she sought.

She wrote Lamar's work number down on the back of her hand and hurried back downstairs to call the police.

Officer Johnson was out and she could not recall the name of the other man on the case. To her chagrin, she found herself leaving her name and number for Stanley Johnson to call when he came in.

Downstairs beneath her room, she heard a familiar voice lifted in whining complaint. " . . . don't know what the place is coming to, I really don't. Seems like every day or two now there's something else. I don't know how much more Dolly's heart can take, but . . ."

Nell was moving about the kitchen with heavy tread, making an occasional grunt in response. Sheila was tempted to take off her shoes and climb onto her bed for a long nap, but as Annie's voice went on and on, she decided she ought to at least help Nell out.

Annie leaned (perched?) against the counter in cardinal red, drinking a glass of tea. "Hello, Sheila, are you still here?"

No one, Sheila reflected ruefully, could make you feel quite as welcome as Annie.

"Yes, Marion has asked me to stay for a day or two longer." She forced her lips into what she thought of as an embassy smile. "I take it you've heard about Rhoda?"

"I'll say I did!" The shock of remembering was enough to divert Annie momentarily from her tea. "I heard Miramise shrieking even over my TV, and as soon as a commercial came on I rushed right out to see what was going on."

Sheila was so intent on a picture of Annie avidly watching children's cartoons that she almost missed her big announcement.

"I know who did it, of course!"

Sheila looked at her blankly. "You do?"

EIGHTEEN

SHEILA FOUND DOLLY propped on pillows with her hair askew.

"Hand me a comb, Sheila, and my mirror. You'll have to pin me up in back—I can't manage." As Sheila did what she could to repair the damage, Dolly asked, "Has Marion gone to the shop?" When Sheila nodded, she swung her legs slowly off the bed. "Help me to my chair, please, and we'll sit on the porch."

Dolly did not immediately begin to talk. The effort to get into the chair and onto the porch had sapped her energy, and she was content to gaze over the lovely garden and neighborhood for several minutes.

Finally Sheila prompted her gently. "You wanted to talk?"

Dolly brushed a tendril of hair away and nodded. "I've never been particularly bright, Sheila, but Mary will tell you I've always had good instincts. My instinct this time tells me Rhoda Bennett's death was pure evil."

She paused and gave Sheila a searching look. "Do you believe in evil?"

Sheila nodded. "I've seen too much of it not to believe."

"Thank God. So many people don't, nowadays. Then they seem to think that their not believing makes it go away."

The sweet smell of honeysuckle, the buzz of bees, and the heat made evil seem very far away—until Dolly's next sentence. "It's someone we know, isn't it?"

Sheila hesitated just for a fraction of a second before answering. "The police think it might have been a tramp. I'm wondering about Lamar Jenkins, myself."

"Why?"

Sheila explained about Lamar's reported "treasure" and his anger with Rhoda the previous afternoon.

Dolly considered the idea. "I may be a wicked old woman, but I hope that's what it was, Sheila. She could have provoked him into it. Rhoda could be the most aggravating woman alive when she tried. But oh, do you know what I keep thinking? It's driving me plumb crazy. I keep wondering if I hadn't had my tape on, if I might have heard her call for help!"

Sheila shook her head. "I don't think she was able to call, Dolly. She was killed with one neat, surprising blow."

Dolly pursed her lips and looked across the housetops. Her voice was detached, almost dreamy, and Sheila wondered if she'd had another sedative recently. "I've seen many bad things in my life, Sheila. Always I've been able to look at them later and see some good that came out of them. When Alva died, I thought my world had ended, but I got to come be near my children here. When Margaret died..." Her voice faltered, then grew strong again. "You expect to bury your parents, Sheila. You never expect to bury your child. But since then, I have grown so much closer to the girls. They used to come in once a week or so, and now they are here almost every day. Good does come after bad things. I just hope I live long enough to see good come out of this horrible day."

Sheila nodded. "I hope so, too, Dolly."

Dolly gave her a wan smile. "For one thing, it's good to have you here to go through it with us."

Sheila's lips twitched mischievously. "Your local police think I may have caused it all. I've been warned not to come as their house guest."

Dolly's eyes resumed some of their old sparkle. "Don't let Mary catch them saying that." She picked up a fan from her lap and waved it lazily before her. "If it's not Lamar, who do you think it could be?"

Sheila was trying to think how to answer when Dolly surprised her. "You think it might be Heyward. Why?"

"He and Rhoda had a terrific quarrel last night, and Miramise says she'd been putting pressure on him to give up the sailing school for law."

Dolly sat in silence for a long time, her blue eyes searching the equally blue sky. "It's possible," she said finally, "but you need to know, Sheila, that I love that boy like a grandson—both for his own sake and for Becca's. She's crazy about him."

"Well, there are other possibilities, of course. Is there anyone in your family with a deep, dark secret past?"

Dolly's lips curved upward. "Not very deep, dark, or secret. Buddy was arrested in high school for stealing a car and driving under the influence of alcohol—it was right after his parents' divorce, and he was seeking attention, I always thought. He was on probation for a while, then it all blew over. But it's not as though it was ever a secret. Everybody knew it at the time. It was in the paper."

"Francine might not have known." She didn't realize she had said it aloud. Immediately her thoughts began to follow that trail. Could Francine have found an old newspaper and tried to blackmail Buddy into marrying her? If so, from what Sheila had seen, he was a willing victim. She couldn't imagine Buddy—sweet, charming Buddy—being threatened enough by a thirty-year-old police record to kill anyone.

Her thoughts were interrupted by a murmur from Dolly. "Poor child, she always hated gulls." She waved toward birds wheeling high overhead.

"Rhoda?" Sheila asked.

"No, Francine. She didn't have a very full life, did she?"

"From what I saw, she was filling her life rather nicely."

Dolly gave a gentle snort. "There was nothing in that. It's springtime, and the men are bored. I never worried about that girl the way Rhoda did. She nearly crowed when Buddy started squiring her instead of Heyward—but had to make certain everybody knew it wasn't anything the matter with Heyward, just the way his money is situated."

Becca had mentioned something about that. While Sheila was trying to remember, Dolly leaned forward to better share the tale. "Before Mac Bennett died, he made a very generous settlement on his daughter by a previous marriage. When he died, everything he had went to Rhoda for her lifetime or until she remarried, then it was all to go to Heyward. It seemed fair at the time—Heyward was just a little thing, and we all thought she would marry very soon. She didn't, though. Rhoda preferred Mac's money to every man she met. She kept her hands on the reins and doled out an allowance to Heyward that made him the laughingstock of his high school class."

Dolly's lips pursed into a disapproving rosebud at the memory. "Then when Heyward was ready for college, he wanted to go to the University of Miami to study oceanography. Rhoda insisted that he stay nearby and study law. He argued with her, and won, but she cut off his allowance—told me that college expenses were so high she couldn't afford to give him any spending money. Imagine that!" Dolly's plump chin quivered with indignation. "He had to work for every cent of his spending money, with her living like a queen!"

"And when he came of age?"

Dolly shook her head. "The will gave everything to Rhoda. Unless she chose to give it to Heyward, he'd be a poor man until she died." She stopped, stricken with the realization that she'd just given Heyward the best motive by far for murdering his mother.

Sheila tried to distract her. "Where did he get the money for his sailing school?"

Dolly ducked her head, then her chin came up defiantly. "Heyward's sailing school started out with one little boat, and I loaned him the money for it myself—with my daughter Margaret. Margaret loved to sail and raced quite a bit. In high school, Heyward crewed for her races. He told her once about his dream, and she decided to help him. I thought it was a splendid idea, so when he got home from college we took him out to lunch and made a deal." She touched the ruffle at her throat self-consciously. "You're probably thinking we were interfering fools..."

"I think you were dears," Sheila assured her. "Every kid ought to have someone who cares that much."

"Well, we didn't think it was fair for him to have nothing to start on, so we bought the boat. Margaret died soon after, and he and I arranged that what he paid back would go into the girls' college fund. After the first boat we bought another one, and finally we bought a place to dock them. It's been a good investment for me," she insisted. "Heyward is a very conscientious partner, comes by every so often to keep me informed about what's going on. But you won't tell Marion or Buddy will you? Especially Buddy—we didn't want him to know, since he and Rhoda were partners."

Sheila shook her head. "Did Rhoda know?"

"Gracious no! She was furious when he started the business. She wanted him to become a lawyer like his dad." She became very grave. "Sheila, you aren't *really* thinking Heyward Bennett killed his mother, are you? Because I am certain he never would have. She was a difficult person, but he just wouldn't." She shook her head firmly.

Sheila sighed. "I'm trying hard not to. As I told Aunt Mary, except for a lamentable taste in women, he's a very likable young man."

Dolly chuckled. "It's in the blood. Old Mac was a rake himself, before suddenly up and marrying Grace's mother—a stodgy young woman if you ever saw one. When she died, Mac squired every floozy in town, then shocked us all by marrying Rhoda, who was fresh out of high school. Just watch, Heyward will settle down some day."

They sat in peace, Sheila enjoying the creak of the cane rocker beneath her, Dolly occasionally brushing away a curl that the breeze had tweaked loose. "This is such a lovely house," Sheila murmured at last.

Dolly smiled with a complacent nod. "Granddaddy built this house. Timber was cheap, especially since Great-granddaddy had bought timber land every chance he got. 'Buy land,' Aunt Bella remembered him saying when she was a tiny girl. 'It's the only thing they can't make more of.'"

She leaned forward and pointed across the housetops to the southeast. "The boards were cut at a sawmill down near Colonial Lake—it's all houses now, of course. Granddaddy was just starting out in his daddy's business, and his parents gave him money for the house as a wedding present. He and Grandmother moved in in 1889. They had Brent, our daddy, and Aunt Bella, then Grandmother died when the children were in high school."

She peered down into the garden with pleasure. "In those days Harleston Village was not the most prestigious suburb—Marion wishes they had built south of Broad where the best families live. But I prefer Harleston Village for the same reason Granddaddy did—there's a family feel about it. The lots were larger, too. When I was a child, we owned the whole Bennett property for our backyard." She paused to remember.

"What was your father like?" Sheila asked. Dolly might profess not to care about history, but talking about it was calming her down, returning color to her cheeks.

Dolly's laugh rippled across the porch. "Daddy was a bit of a black sheep. He didn't give a rap about history—told Aunt Bella he'd rather make it than learn it. I always liked that, because it was one way I was like him." She tucked in another tendril of hair and smoothed her lap. "Daddy defied Granddaddy and went to Yale to become a lawyer rather than staying at the College of Charleston and going into the family business. 'Three generations of cotton factors, and you want to study law,' Granddaddy roared. He apparently did a lot of roaring."

She put up one hand and pretended to whisper. "The thing that made him the maddest, though was that Daddy wanted to go to a Yankee school. Granddaddy was so mad he refused to talk about him or even read his letters. But Aunt Bella wrote him often, and he must have treasured those letters. We still have some of them."

"I saw them at Francine's." Sheila almost said it, remembered just in time that she was trying to distract Dolly from events of the past two days. She said instead, "Do I remember that your parents got married while he was in school?"

Dolly nodded. "And I believe I told you it gave Granddaddy a stroke. Imagine that! He was so ill after that that Aunt Bella didn't even tell him until just before they came home that they had a little girl, Marion. Granddaddy was madder than ever—I guess because now he'd got him a granddaughter born north of the Mason-Dixon line." Dolly's blue eyes sparkled like diamonds.

"How'd your mother take her welcome?" Sheila wondered.

Dolly shook her head and brushed away a friendly fly. "I never knew. I suppose Aunt Bella made her welcome enough, and Mama Lucille. But she only lived here about four years—she was pregnant with me when they got home, and I was three when she died."

They heard the phone trill, but neither of them heard Nell trudge upstairs until she sighed suddenly behind them. "Such a year for dying. Your mama and the baby, Old Judge Black next door, Mama Lucille's sister, your daddy..." She set a tray on a small table between them. "It wasn't all the War, of course. There was that terrible flu epidemic, too. On the morning your mama died, I remember swinging on the front gate and watching three funerals pass down at the corner." She placed forks on three plates of chocolate cake before she said, "The phone's for you, Sheila."

It was Officer Johnson. "You wanted me, ma'am?"

"Yes." She filled him in on what Annie had seen early in the morning and told him about Lamar's brush with Rhoda the afternoon before. "It may not be anything," she admitted, "but I thought you'd want to know. And I have a phone number for him at work."

He thanked her and rang off, leaving the impression that if she was a busybody, at least she was a helpful one.

She returned to the porch, where Dolly was placidly eating cake and still talking about the past. "... tease her about her name." She turned to Sheila. "Marion was named for Francis Marion, who was—"

"The Swamp Fox." Sheila nodded, accepting a plate from Nell.

Dolly was surprised. "You know your American history?"

"I was a history major in college," Sheila informed her, "but in Charleston I'm shy about saying so. You all seem to live and breathe it, while I just read it in books."

"Not me," the old woman assured her, reaching for a glass of tea. "I had fun."

Nell brought Sheila a piece of cake and a glass of mercifully unsweet tea, then took her own plate and glass over to the nearby table and sat heavily in one of the wicker chairs.

As Sheila took another bite of the rich chocolate and savored it, Dolly turned to her in sudden inspiration. "I've just had a marvelous idea, Sheila. Why shouldn't you complete the history that Francine was doing for me? Nell and I could tell you what we remember, and you could get the rest out of those papers. It would give you a good reason for staying until all this"—she waved her hands vaguely, and Sheila supposed she meant to encompass everything from falling tree limbs to Rhoda's death—"is over."

Nell grunted. "Considerin' that three folks have died in less than three weeks, it may be over sooner than any of us think. Not too many of us left. But if you take my advice, Sheila, you'll clear out and take Dolly with you."

The idea had immediate charm for Sheila. "Aunt Mary would love it," she offered, "and her car is very comfortable to travel in. She's even got an elevator to her front door. Would you?"

She could see that Dolly was considering it, but then she shook her head. "I think I want to see this through, Sheila. I really don't think Rhoda's death is connected with the accidents we'd been having, and I don't like to leave Marion just now. I'd rather you stayed and wrote the history. Don't you think that's a marvelous idea?"

"Not particularly," she admitted, "but if you won't go, I'll stay—for a few more days, at least. And as long as I'm here, I'll work on your history, if it can be brief. I need to be back in Chicago Monday a week, remember."

Dolly reached over and gave her a little pat. "I'm sure you'll be done by then, dear. And that will give you something to do when you're not detecting. Why don't you get started just now, while I take another nap?"

In ten minutes Dolly was tucked up in bed, Nell was frying chicken, and Sheila was on her way to Francine's house. As Dolly had said, it was something to do when she wasn't detecting.

NINETEEN

An hour later Sheila leaned back on the lumpy couch and shoved long fingers through her hair in frustration. Marion was right. The Wimberlys were a very ordinary family. Only through Dolly's anecdotes and Bella's letters did it come alive.

Wearily she contemplated the documents. Scott Wimberly's diary was the dull account of a young man learning the cotton business, and if his wife Dorothea cooked by her cookbook Sheila was glad she'd missed dinner by several generations.

Brent Wimberly's will contained the amount of legal jargon new lawyers think essential, but translated into English it left everything he owned to "my beloved wife, Margaret, or, if she predecease me, to the issue of our marriage." Properly cautious for a man leaving a pregnant wife behind as he went to war.

But, Sheila smiled, Dolly wasn't quite as indifferent to history as she pretended—she'd named her daughter for her mother.

She turned to the next paper, Granddaddy Scott's will. Dated December 1, 1914, it was written in a large scrawl that failing health had tempered, but not destroyed.

I, Scott Wimberly, being sound in mind, if not in body, do hereby leave my estate as follows: To my son Brent, who has greatly displeased me in the matter of his education and has sorrowed me by his marriage, I nevertheless leave all real property I own, with the exception of the house in which he was born, and half the rest of my estate. The remaining half of the estate and the family home I leave to my daughter Bella, with a warning not to fritter away her money nor to let her husband get control of it should she marry, which seems unlikely. At her death, she can do what she likes with her money, but unless she marries and has children—in that order—the house shall go to Brent's child(ren), if he has any. If not, Bella can decide where it's to go, but I prefer that it stay in the family.

The will was signed in the same hand. Beneath, the signature of the witnesses seemed small, cramped, and protesting: William Black, Calhoun Rutledge.

On sudden thought, Sheila found Brent's will. It was typed on the letterhead of Black, Walsh, Bennett & Wimberly.

She carried it to the kitchen, where Nell was bent over putting something into the oven. "Nell, did you know Black, Walsh, Bennett and Wimberly?" Sheila asked the plump backside.

Nell turned and straightened, rubbing her back. "Sure, Sheila. Judge Will Black lived right over *there*"—she pointed through the screen door and across the porch—"all his life, until he died in 1918, and his son Alton Black, the next judge, lived there until he died a couple of weeks ago. Mama Lucille says it was old Judge Black got Brent Wimberly and Mac-Faddon Bennett both interested in law in the first place. When they each came back from law school, he took them in as junior partners."

"He was a judge, not a lawyer?" Sheila wondered aloud.

Nell shook her large head. "Not back then. He didn't become a judge until just a few months before he died, but everybody called him Judge Black ever since."

"And was MacFaddon Bennett Heyward's father?"

"Sure was. His daddy was about the same age as the second Judge—they both went into the firm in the twenties, but by then the old Judge and Brent Wimberly were dead."

Nell turned to the refrigerator. "You want a glass of tea?"

Sheila started to shake her head, then nodded. "You're about to make a tea drinker out of me, Nell. I've always been a coffee woman before."

"Coffee don't give the refreshment tea does." Nell busied herself with ice and glasses. "In hot weather, that is. When there's a chill in the air, I go for coffee myself." She dropped ice into a tall glass with a clunk and reached for a small pitcher.

"Was Francine the only one to drink herbal tea?" Sheila asked.

"She sure was. Wasn't it strange, her thinking the tea was bitter the morning before she died? If she'd have been poisoned, they'd have thought I did it." Nell started to peel potatoes.

Sheila mulled that over. What if Francine hadn't taken sleeping pills—what if they'd been put in her tea? With all the commotion from the theft, it would have been easy for just about anyone to do. What was it Nell had said about making the tea?

"When did you usually make her tea?" Sheila asked.

"Soon as I got Miss Marion's breakfast on the table," Nell replied. "She liked it kind of strong."

"And it sat where?"

Nell jerked her head toward a small yellow pot that sat on a distant counter. "Right there, where the pot is now. You think there really was something funny about that tea?"

Sheila shook her head. "I don't know, Nell. Francine seems to have taken some sleeping pills that morning, and I wondered if they were put in her tea."

"Not by me they weren't," Nell assured her.

"Of course not. But what if someone did put pills in her tea, to make her dizzy? No, that's not right. Mr. Luther says those pills don't make you dizzy, just sleepy."

"So somebody made her sleepy and pushed her off that stool? Sounds farfetched to me," Nell opined.

"To me, too. How did Judge Black die?"

Nell had returned to their earlier conversation. "Same flu that carried off so many others. Nineteen eighteen was a *bad* year for flu, and I don't mean that like my grandsons use the word."

"No, I mean the last Judge. Annie's husband."

"Oh, *him*." Nell spoke as if she'd just remembered his existence. "Well, he had a bad heart. It didn't do for him to get upset, but he got upset all the time, if you mark my meaning. About any and everything. Crochety old man—crochety young one, too. Used to tease Marion all the time that her name was really English. Got other kids doing it, too. She could lick most of them, but he was too big to whip. But you asked how he died." She leaned back against the counter and seemed to think it over. "You know, I don't really know. Miss Marion took Annie to their Women of the Church meeting, and since there wasn't much to do around here I went on home like I usually do for a while after lunch. The next day I heard he'd died that afternoon. I supposed it was his heart, but I didn't really ask. Now you aren't thinking..." It was too horrible for her to complete.

Sheila shook her head. "I don't think anything at this point. I was just wondering how often three houses in one block have someone die in them in one two-week period."

Nell pursed her lips and considered it. "Well, it's not often, I can say that, and I've known a lot of people die in my time."

"Do you think Annie would be willing to talk about it?"

Nell snorted. "Annie's willing to talk about anything at any time, but it's as much as your life is worth to go to her house. Getting in isn't hard, but getting out is like pulling your own back teeth without a mirror."

Sheila sat her glass on the counter and straightened her shoulders. "Well, wish me luck, and if I'm not back in an hour, call and tell me there's been an emergency."

"And have her come hightailing after you? Not on your life. But I'll call for something or other."

With her future thus assured, Sheila walked the short distance to Annie's house.

It was another balmy, lovely day. She was tempted to forget death and concentrate on soaring gulls and fluffy white clouds over palm trees. It took all the willpower she had to leave the bright sunshine of the sidewalk and ring Annie's bell, and when she had entered the gloomy front hall, she nearly bolted. Except when spying on others, Annie kept every curtain in the house closed, every shade down.

Three floor fans stirred the air in a desultory way, but the rooms were stuffy with the smells of old bodies infrequently washed and food left too long in garbage cans.

On her left Sheila could see a parlor filled with lovely old furniture and a dismal air of disuse. Annie led her instead into what was once a formal dining room but for many years had been where the old couple lived. A rumpled day bed in one corner indicated that Annie might sleep there now, too.

A mahogany dining table was shoved against one wall and piled high with catalogs, old law books, and mail. The Oriental rug was soiled to an almost uniform brown, and Sheila doubted that any carpet cleaner could reveal its former colors. Antiques were obviously unimportant to the mistress of the house. What occupied the place of honor was a large color television that completely filled one corner and obscured a covered fireplace. Set squarely in front of the television was a large and obviously new recliner chair in a particularly repulsive shade of orange plush. A second recliner in sensible brown leather sat with its back to the window, as if it had been pushed out of the way when the television was delivered and never returned to its original position.

Annie toddled over and turned the television down, but not off, then climbed into the orange recliner and waved Sheila to the other one. Since that chair faced not Annie, but the side of her chair, Sheila pulled one of the dining chairs over near the hearth.

"They arrest that Lamar yet?" she demanded.

"Not that I've heard. They'll probably want to talk with you first."

"I hope they lock him up forever. We're none of us safe in our houses anymore." As they talked, Annie's attention darted from Sheila to the television and back.

"You have a nice home," Sheila ventured.

"Not bad," Annie acknowledged. "It needs a little fixing up, but it was hard to get the Judge to make changes. I might do a few things now that the old buzzard has finally gone."

It wasn't precisely the opening Sheila had hoped for, but she took it anyway. "How did he die?"

Annie dragged herself from a particularly fascinating razor commercial. "Bad heart. He had it before we got married, even. I never expected him to live so long." Sheila had heard widows say that when counting their blessings. Annie was not one of them.

"Dolly said he seemed fine the night before," she tried.

Annie nodded sagely. "Seemed fine when I left, too. But you never can tell with tricky hearts. Take Dolly, now. She might drop off any minute, or live to be a hundred. You just can't tell." She settled back to enjoy a local used car dealer hawking his wares.

"What exactly happened?" Sheila persisted, feeling as if she were trying to wade uphill through a swampy stream.

Annie politely let the used car dealer finish before she spoke. "Couldn't get to his pills, I reckon. I found him lying there"— she pointed to a spot on the rug—"and they were over on the table. Don't know how they got there—I'd left them right beside his chair like always, with him snoring beside them."

"And you locked the door, of course," Sheila murmured, thinking aloud more than asking.

Annie nodded vigorously. "Of course—unless I forgot."

She returned to the flow of commercials, where a puppy was ecstatically making the right food choice. Sheila mulled over what she had heard. If Annie had locked the door, who could get in? She was about to ask, when Annie spoke again.

"Funny, heart attacks most often hit somebody when they're just waking up—did you know that? Lots of people die with them first thing in the morning. I read somewhere that your body has a lot of stress then, or something."

She paused. "I didn't know that," Sheila murmured, wondering if it was true.

"Yeah," Annie assured her. "The Judge moved his pills, then I guess sometime soon after he woke up from his nap he had the attack and couldn't get that far."

Sheila measured the distance with her eyes. The dining room was large, and the distance could have been fourteen feet or more, especially since the old man would have had to get out of his chair and go around it. "But why would he have moved the pills in the first place?" she wondered aloud.

"Folks get that old, they do funny things." Annie was now engrossed in a torrid movie that had interrupted the commercials.

"I guess young people do, too, sometimes," Sheila replied, feeling a need to protest in some minor way.

She was surprised, however, at the vehemence of Annie's reply. "They sure do. Take Rake, now. If she isn't careful, she's
going to break her grandmama's heart. Carrying on in that
theater and now trying to seduce poor Heyward. That miss is
going to get her comeuppance. You mark my words!" She
turned back to the screen where a sultry actress was earning her
own comeuppance.

Sheila had taken all the vituperation she could tolerate for
one day. She stood. "Well, I must be going. I just wanted to run
by and say hello." She had dredged the phrase from her childhood, when women came to visit Aunt Mary or, before that,
her maternal grandmother. It stimulated Annie to a predict-
able response.

"You don't have to be going yet." She started to hitch herself out of her chair. "I'll get us some Cokes."

Presuming that the squalor of the kitchen at least equaled
that of the dining room, Sheila had no intention of carrying the
visit to its usual, lengthy conclusion. "No, I really must run.
Don't get up." She waved the old woman back. "I can find my
way out. See you later."

She left with a feeling of pride. Her years of extricating herself from embassy duty calls had stood her in good stead.

IT WAS ONLY a short way to the Wimberly gate, but before she
reached it, Sheila had concluded two things. First, it was entirely possible that Judge Black, too, had been murdered. And
if so, it would be virtually impossible to prove, unless someone had seen the murderer going in or out. (And who, in this
city of exquisite good manners, would watch someone else's
front door—except Annie herself?)

Seeing Nell vigorously sweeping the upstairs porch, Sheila
called softly, in case Annie could hear, "I made my own es-
cape."

"I see you did." Nell gave her a big smile.

"Is Dolly still asleep? Can I go back to the little house for a
while?"

"Child, Dolly will sleep the whole blessed afternoon after
what the doctor gave her. You go right on. I'll call you for din-

ner if you don't get through till then.'' Nell turned back to her broom and Sheila returned to the Wimberly family papers.

By far the most interesting of them were letters Bella had written her brother during his northern sojourn, letters telling day-to-day details of living. Since Bella headed them by days of the week rather than by month and year, however, it was hard to put them into any sort of order. Sheila read one at random.

Friday night

Dear Brent,

It's terribly hot here. Lucille and I made scuppernong jam this morning and nearly melted into the pot. Tom came by later, and found me with my hair streaming into my face and my old blue dress on. He always does see me at my worst, it seems. I wish you would come home for a visit. Papa is still not well, and I think if he could just see all of you it would be easier for you to discuss things face to face. Perhaps you could explain better than I. He feels you have turned your back on the way we were raised. Did Marion ever get the dresses I sent for summer? It's hard to know her size and how hot it gets up there, but Lucille and I had a lot of fun choosing the fabric and making them up. How I long to meet her! Be sure to tell her often that she has an Aunt Bella who loves her already. Lots of love to all my Yankees, Bella.

A second had been written earlier, apparently.

Tuesday

Dear Brent,

The storm has finally passed. We lost two trees, including Mama's favorite magnolia, but none of us were hurt, thank God. The *News & Courier* said the winds were 95 miles per hour, and tides five feet higher than usual. Our new cook, Lucille, is a jewel. She insisted on staying with me during the storm, since Papa was in Columbia for the week, and she showed *such* courage. A chair blew into our yard, and when the calm time came, she rushed outside to bring it in. The winds returned, lifting her and the chair and carrying them three feet across the yard! She was trembling, but still holding the chair when she landed. She said she was afraid the chair would blow in a window if it stayed out there. I was sorry you could not come home for at least a visit during the summer, but I know the expense would have been terrible, and also Papa would not have let you have a pleasant stay. I work on him, telling him Yale is an excellent school, but he has not altered his opinion much as of yet. I pray for you daily. Your loving sister, Bella.

The third, and shortest letter, was worn, as if by much reading.

> Sunday afternoon
> Oh, Brent, how could you, without saying anything ahead of time? Papa is very upset, as you must have known he would be. He wouldn't even go to church this morning. Says he can't hold up his head. I have sat on the porch almost all day, rocking and trying hard to understand. I still love you, and hope you know that. But just now I am angry and very, very hurt. If you don't hear from us for a time, know that we are working on learning to accept things. Still your Bella.

Sheila read the letters through once more, trying to comprehend people who held onto prejudice for over fifty years. Poor Yankee bride!

But Bella had come to accept the marriage, if her father never did. She often sent love to Brent's "Yankees" in letters that depicted a strong, loving girl finding humor in life even while keeping house for her demanding father and missing her brother very much. Several times she referred to the mysterious "Tom" being home, or coming in for a visit, but apparently nothing ever came of the friendship. In fact, the hurricane was the most exciting event in Bella's placid—not to say dull—round of housework and church activities.

Sheila yawned and stirred restlessly. Her mind felt as if it were full of crawly things, part of them burrowing aimlessly through the Wimberly family history and part of them turning over facts from the Wimberlys' recent past—and Sheila was tired of both. What she needed was a long, rambling walk without conscious thought. If she didn't solve the mysteries subconsciously, perhaps she'd get an opening paragraph for Dolly's history.

She told Nell where she was going and set out at a slow lope. Her steps first took her south to Colonial Lake, glittering in the sun. For a few minutes she sat on a bench near one of the palms, but the sun in her eyes made her more sluggish than ever. With a yawn that was becoming habitual, she stood and turned east toward the oldest part of town.

Walking along King Street, letting her mind wander as she gazed into antique shops, she was startled to find herself outside Marion's shop. Marion herself was standing in the door, speaking to a short fat man in a gray suit. She beckoned for Sheila to come in. "Good day, Mr. Adams," she said with finality, and turned to Sheila. "Is Dolly all right?" Her voice was sharp with worry.

Sheila was chagrined to realize Marion thought she'd come about another emergency. "She's fine. She came out on the porch for a while, but she's slept most of the afternoon."

Marion nodded in her precise way. "Then would you like to see the shop?" It was more than an invitation.

It was easy to see that Marion's was one of the best in a city where antique shops are more common than grocery stores. Her furniture was carefully chosen and expertly displayed. Each table held the proper lamp or small glass ornament, each easy chair had a footstool before it. A tiny back room was walled in mirrors to reflect shelves and shelves of delicate figurines, china, and small silver pieces.

They finished up at a small Georgian desk that Marion used for business. "Everything is absolutely lovely," Sheila said, and meant it.

Marion's thin face wrinkled in pleasure. "It's been my life," she admitted. "I started working with Aunt Bella when I was barely ten, and it was just a dusty hole."

Looking about the bright, airy showroom with its polished cotton, carved mahogany, and delicate flowered porcelain,

Sheila found it impossible to picture the shop as a dusty hole. It was equally impossible to picture Marion Wimberly telling a lie.

Marion walked to a small armoire and took out a small glass paperweight. It was oval, filled with tiny blue and yellow glass flowers. "I want you to have this, Sheila, with my gratitude. Having you here has made this week much easier."

Embarrassed but delighted, Sheila pocketed the paperweight with thanks. She rambled down the street and turned into a tiny park with a miniature Washington monument in its center, took the paperweight out to once again admire the tiny flowers encased in solid glass. But even as she enjoyed it, she wondered if the paperweight would eventually remind her not of Marion's gratitude but of her own failure.

TWENTY

SUNDAY

SUNDAY WAS A welcome day of rest.

Marion and Sheila went to First Scots Presbyterian Church and sat with the twins in what seemed to be a family pew. After a chicken dinner, the Endicotts went home, Dolly took a nap, and Marion excused herself to go to her upstairs office.

"I don't like to do books on Sunday, but this has been an unusual week." Sheila heartily agreed with her.

Nell looked so tired that Sheila repeated her offer to help with dishes, and for once Nell accepted. It was while she was drying the big chicken platter that Sheila realized this might be a good day to visit Mama Lucille. Nell agreed with a smile. "It'll keep her from chattering to me for a while, and Will would appreciate not having to put his book down to come get me."

From childhood visits to the South, Sheila half expected an unpainted shanty sitting in the middle of a hard earth yard with one huge tree to give shade. Instead, they left the old part of Charleston and entered a newer section of brick homes surrounded by neat lawns, flowers, and, occasionally, gardens. Nell's home had blue shutters, a blue front door, and blue pansies bordering the walk. "Blue's Will's color," she said with a grin as she opened the door.

Will came to meet them when he heard Nell's key in the lock. "Sheila has come to visit Mama," Nell told him.

"That's just fine." He stepped back to usher them in. "She'd like that."

Nell disappeared into the back regions of the house and Will led Sheila into a living room cheerfully decorated in red, white, and—of course—blue. The effect was regal rather than patriotic. Deep-blue valances echoed the paler blue of the walls. A white velvet couch sat pristinely on the thick red carpet with white and gold coffee table before it. Two blue chairs across the room looked deep and comfortable, with big footstools and lamps placed just right for an evening with your favorite book. If there was a television, it was concealed by the white and gold cabinet in one corner. Catching a glimpse of herself in the large gilt-framed mirror over the mantelpiece, Sheila felt as if she had entered the room of a monarch.

But the only figure in the room looked more like a child.

Mama Lucille crouched, rather than sat, on a tiny cane rocker by the window where the afternoon rays of the sun could warm her tired old bones. The skin of her wizened face had faded to a pale gray-brown, and her hair was plaited into a myriad of tiny white rows against her head. As Will led Sheila toward her, the old woman turned her head and Sheila saw that her eyes had long ago clouded to a milky blue that would never see clearly again. She held out a gnarled claw as dry as paper, and when Will introduced them, she clutched Sheila as if afraid her guest would turn and run. "You Miz Mary's girl?" she inquired, showing blue gums.

"I'm her niece," Sheila said.

Will bent toward her. "She's hard of hearing. You'll have to talk louder." He brought a white velvet fireside chair for her.

"I'm her niece," Sheila repeated loudly, taking her seat.

"Is dat right? I'm surely glad to meet you, Miz Peace. Sit a spell and tell me about Miz Mary. I shore do remember her."

Will took the chair under a reading lamp and picked up a book that had been lying open on one footstool. From where she sat Sheila could see it was Plato's *Republic*.

The old woman fumbled for Sheila's hand again and held it the rest of their visit, rubbing and feeling it as if she could know Sheila better through her fingertips than through any of her other senses. "Yo shore are bigger than Miz Mary," she said, running her hand the length of Sheila's fingers.

"Yes, she's the tiny one in our family," Sheila shouted.

The old woman cackled with laughter. "She be dat all right. I mind when she'd come see us, she couldn't reach de cabnets where I keep de glasses. Had to haul a chair to hep her reach. Did she bring you?" She peered about the room as if she could see.

"No, she sent me to visit Dolly," Sheila bellowed, wondering if the neighbors could hear her. "She sends you her love."

"And I sends her mine. She's one fine lady, dat Miz Mary."

Sheila could think of nothing else to say immediately, but the old woman seemed content to sit and stroke the back of a younger hand. Then unexpectedly she raised her head, looked straight at Sheila with her milky eyes, and asked, "What trouble going on at Wimberlys'? Dat gal of mine won't tell me nuthin', but you'll tell, won't you?"

"Why do you think there's trouble?" Sheila found it embarrassing to roar at the old woman in front of Will, but he seemed engrossed in Plato.

"Law, chile, I kin feel it in my bones. I been a part of dat fambly since I was sixteen years old. I knowed Miz Bella's every mood, and I pretty near knowed Miz Marion's, 'cepting she holds things in so. But you's Miz Mary's chile. You's gonna tell me what's goin' on, ain't you?" Her voice was high and coaxing, and the cloudy eyes held Sheila's. Even though Sheila *knew* the old woman could not see, she could not shift her gaze.

As if hypnotized, she nodded. "We've been having a lot of accidents lately. Miss Marion had a fall." The title for Marion came unbidden to her lips.

Mama Lucille nodded her whole body. "I knowed it. I just knowed it. Be she all right?" Her voice lilted up at the end of a sentence.

"She's fine now."

"What else, chile?"

"Well, the nurse who looks after Miss Dolly had a fall, too, and hit her head."

"She de one who's daid?"

Sheila nodded again, wondering if Mama Lucille had been told about the death, or merely felt it "in her bones." Remembering that the old woman could not see her nod, she shouted, "Yes, her funeral is tomorrow."

She expected to have to tell the old woman about Rhoda Bennett, as well, but age had narrowed Mama Lucille's concern to her own. She abandoned Francine and returned to those she loved.

"Take good care of Miz Marion, you hear? She's one fine lady." Her voice dropped and she began to mumble. "Done made a place for hersef. I knowed she would soon as I lit eyes on her, coming off dat boat. Little biddy t'ing, white dress all ruffles and skinny legs sticking out. Mr. Brent was carryin' her. I puts out my arms, she wraps her arms 'round my neck, goes fast t'sleep. From den on, dat's my baby." The old woman rocked back and forth.

She began to croon under her breath a minor tune. Will looked over his book. "Give her a minute, she may come back."

Sheila smiled. "You seem to be using retirement well."

He gave a deprecating shrug. "I thought if I was going to read this again, I'd best get started."

"Do you like philosophy?"

He hesitated, then nodded. "I majored in it in college." Surprise must have flittered across her face, because he added with a smile wholly without rancor, "There weren't many places to use it unless I wanted to teach, which I didn't. It gave me something to think about while I delivered the mail."

Her eyes shifted to three pictures, two boys and one girl, on an end table. "Are those your children?"

Nell, entering in a comfortable shift and slippers, answered for him. "That's our grandchildren." Her voice was full of pride. She pointed to a wedding picture on the piano. "That's our daughter—she's married to a doctor in Atlanta." She picked up each picture and carried it over for approval. "This is her daughter, she's a lawyer in Nashville, and her oldest boy here is a math professor at Georgia Tech." She looked longer at the final picture, a young man with an engaging grin. "This is her youngest. He's . . ."

She paused, and Will completed it for her. "A philosopher like his granddaddy, still trying to find where to put himself. Right now he's a drummer in a rock band, but I tell them, just give him time. He's going to be all right."

Sheila looked from the photographs to the crone still clutching her hand while rocking and crooning to "her" white baby. So much history in only four generations.

Mama Lucille began to babble. "Pretty dress . . . dat yore weddin' dress?" She stroked Sheila's skirt.

"No, it's just a white dress." Sheila supposed she could distinguish the color.

Mama Lucille went on as if Sheila had not spoken. "Makes you look like a bride. You shore are pretty, child." Before Sheila could respond, the old woman began to rock and croon a tuneless lullaby.

"Mama Lucille," Will spoke firmly from across the room, "you stop singing and talk with Miss Mary's niece."

The crooning and rocking stopped, and she turned her head from side to side like a little brown bird. "Miz Mary? Miz Dolly's Miz Mary? Is she here? I shore do like Miz Mary. She always make me laugh."

"I am her niece," Sheila shouted, "and I came to say hello."

The toothless mouth curved in a baby's grin. "Why hello, chile. Glad to meet you. Yo shore is bigger than Miz Mary. She never was bigger than a drop in the bucket. You live 'round here?"

"No, I'm staying with the Wimberlys," Sheila roared back.

The tiny woman spoke in a suddenly lucid voice. "They's a fine fambly, a very fine fambly. I worked for them always. Miz Bella had her hands full, first with her daddy and then with them girls. She loved them, though—like dey was her own. Both of dem." She paused to nod for emphasis. "Neither one more than tother."

She rocked back and forth, back and forth, and this time Sheila saw the moment when her mind slipped a gear. "It's tolerably hot for August, ain't it? . . . I need to string my beans, Mr. Scott . . ." She paused and clucked to herself, then replied to someone only she could hear, "I won't spile it, baby, I'se just gonna wash and iron it for another day . . . go to sleep now . . . doan cry, baby . . . hush." She stopped rocking and her head came up as if listening. She sat for a moment perfectly still, then said in a consoling voice, "Ever'body knows dat. But don't let it bother you none. It jist don't matter atall." She began crooning, occasionally interspersed with a jumble of words. "I's comin, Miz Bella . . . now, Dolly, look what yo done spilled . . . I'm coming . . . I'm coming . . ."

Nell had left the room again. She came back to the door. "She'll probably be like that for the rest of the afternoon. Why don't you all come into the dining room for some coffee and cake?"

Sheila pulled her hand gently from the clawlike one that held it and was delighted to see coffee and pound cake with frozen peaches. "When do you have time to bake cakes at home?" she asked.

Nell pointed to Will. "That's the cake baker around here. Bakes a cake almost every week of the year, and never gains an ounce. While I come in and smell him doing it, I put on a pound."

"It's all in the genes." Will solemnly patted his Levi's.

When Sheila rose to leave, she had enjoyed the most pleasant hour she'd passed since coming to Charleston. "I'm glad you came," Nell said as she showed Sheila to the door. "Mama lives mostly in the past these days, but she really does enjoy visitors so."

"She has more past to live in than most of us do. And I'm glad I came, too." Sheila wished she could put into words what it meant to her to be treated as a friend by Nell and Will.

Nell reached out and squeezed her hand. "You drive safely, going home." She probably said it to her daughter, too.

On her way home, Sheila decided on impulse to drive out to Boone Hall to see where the string of accidents began. So entranced was she with the long drive of moss-hung live oaks and the tall plantation house, she almost forgot to check for missing limbs in the parking lot. What she sought was not hard to find, however. The parking lot had few trees, and only two old enough to be of any size.

She peered into their heights and saw what she had expected she would—the stump where a branch had split off and fallen of its own accord. That accident, at least, had had natural causes.

Later that evening Sheila called Aunt Mary and told her about her visit with Mama Lucille. "She's still lucid?" the older woman asked.

"Occasionally. She comes and goes. Talks about today and then suddenly is ironing dresses for little girls. She's clear enough to remember you, though—told me you weren't as big as a drop of water and stood on chairs to reach the glasses.''

Aunt Mary did not deign to reply.

THAT NIGHT Sheila dreamed that Francine, wearing a wedding dress, dove through a gap in the porch bannisters into Rhoda's fishpond. She sat up in the pond with a pineapple on her head and said distinctly, ''I've found a treasure!'' She laughed and laughed, until someone threw a pillow at her, embroidered with a seagull. She lay down in the water, saying scornfully ''But I hate seagulls. Everybody knows that.''

Sheila woke with a crick in her neck and a vague feeling that something had been very important, but all she could remember was the scorn in Francine's green eyes.

TWENTY-ONE

MONDAY

ONLY A FEW NURSES and friends joined Sheila and Marion at Francine's funeral the following morning. Sheila was surprised not to see Lamar or the grumpy aunt, and felt it would have been in good taste on Buddy's part to make an appearance. Had he so completely forgotten Francine that he didn't remember her funeral?

On the way home, to make conversation, Sheila remarked, "Dolly has asked me to work on the history of your family. I confess that I find it intimidating to be writing a history in Charleston, and hope she won't be disappointed."

Marion shook her head. "I think the entire project is nonsense, but if Francine could do it to Dolly's satisfaction, you certainly can."

Marion made an unexpected turn and pulled up to the curb in front of a pink stucco building on a cobblestone street. "If you are interested in history, Sheila, you might want to spend some time here. This is our famous Fireproof Building, designed by a Charlestonian, Robert Mills, who also designed the Washington Monument. It was built in 1828 to house archives. I believe it was the first fireproof building ever built. Now it is the home of the South Carolina Historical Society."

As Sheila murmured an appropriate reply, Marion pulled away from the curb and continued wryly, "There's very little here about the Wimberlys, I assure you. I hate to see you wasting your time on that project of Dolly's, and hope you won't give it more time than it's worth."

"I won't," Sheila assured her. "I am going to write a very brief history that nobody will probably ever read, but it will be worth my time if it makes Dolly happy."

"Dolly usually manages to make herself happy" was Marion's cryptic reply.

Marion stayed for lunch, which Nell served on the upstairs piazza. Dolly asked, casually, about the funeral and the other two replied, just as casually. Francine might have been the third cousin of a distant acquaintance, Sheila thought, for all the attention she gets now that she's gone.

As soon as she finished her last bite of lemon sponge, Marion placed her napkin neatly beside her plate and stood. "I simply must get back to work, and I may be late coming home. Remember, Sheila, that tonight you and I have the preview for Rake's new play."

Sheila's surprise must have showed on her face, for after Marion left Dolly patted her hand gently. "Miss Manners might not approve, dear, but after all, Rake is family, and Francine wasn't." Which, Sheila thought, summed it up nicely.

They remained on the porch, chatting in the desultory manner of the well fed who have nowhere to go. At last Dolly said, with a small yawn, "It's time for my siesta. Do you know if the police have arrested Lamar yet?" Sheila shook her head. "Then could you find out for me? I find I can think about other things very satisfactorily until I lie down and close my eyes, then I find my mind scuttling in all sorts of directions. If not Lamar, who? And why?"

Sheila nodded. "I have the same problem. Dolly, can you think of anyone—anyone whatsoever—who might want to harm Marion?"

Dolly's blue eyes flew open in astonishment. "Marion? Of course not! Everybody loves Marion." She hesitated. "She *is* a little tart sometimes, but that's just her way. We don't ever notice it. Why on earth do you ask?"

"Because most of the original accidents seemed to inconvenience her more than anyone else."

Dolly thought about it. "You could be right. If so, then Francine probably did cause the accidents. She and Marion never did get along. And you notice, since Francine died we haven't had a single new accident!"

In the face of such determined optimism, Sheila saw no point to bring up Rhoda's murder. Besides, Dolly might be right. The murders and the accidents could be totally unrelated. But if not? There was one possibility she had decided this morning she would not overlook—whatever Aunt Mary might say.

"Dolly, I want to ask you a very personal question, which you don't have to answer, of course. But if you don't mind terribly, tell me about your will—and Marion's."

Dolly waved her hands as if the question were of no importance whatever. "If you want to see mine, it's in my desk. But Marion's I will have to tell you about, for I don't know where she keeps it here. Bennett's have one, if I need it."

"Bennett's?"

"Our lawyer, dear. Heyward's father's firm."

"But it's still Bennett's?"

Dolly's laugh rippled infectiously across the porch. "It will probably be Bennett's till Doomsday. It was Black, Walsh, Bennett and Wimberly until I was thirteen, and both Daddy and Old Judge Black had been dead for ten years by then. Broad Street lawyers live long after they are buried in Charleston. Nobody's in any hurry to erase their memory."

She sent Sheila after the document and watched placidly while it was read. "It's not very interesting" was all she said. But it was certainly unexpected. She'd left a sizable amount to Nell, small sums of money and personal trinkets to the girls, then "everything of which I die possessed to my sister Marion."

Sheila looked up, puzzled. "But what if Marion dies first?"

"You sound like my lawyer," Dolly said. "If Marion dies first, then I'll make a new will. You probably think I should leave it all to Buddy, or the girls. But the twins will receive a comfortable sum each when they turn twenty-one—Alva left half his estate to Margaret, and she left it to them. As for what I have to leave, Marion will see that they get it when she goes— they are all the family we have. Why shouldn't she get to enjoy it for the time she has left? The girls won't need much for a few years. And if you're wondering what if I'm incapacitated before Marion dies, and *can't* make a new will, my nice lawyer thought of that first. He has a very legal letter in his files...oh, look! There's Roy Luther! Buck! Yoo-hoo!" She called down and the old man looked up and waved. "Come on up," Dolly invited him. "I have a chaperon, so it's respectable."

She turned to Sheila. "Run down and let him in. I've got a bone to pick with him."

The pharmacist greeted Dolly as one who'd known her since earliest childhood. "Didn't your aunt tell you it's rude to call to men on the street?"

She held out one plump hand and laughed. "Only strange ones, Buck. You're not that strange. Have you met Sheila Travis?"

The old man peered at her over his glasses and chewed his mustache. "I believe I did. Aren't you the one was asking me about mixing up Dolly's bottles?"

Sheila nodded, but Dolly spoke first. "You've made two mistakes this month, Buck. Seems like maybe you'd better retire."

"Two?" he eyed her suspiciously.

"You gave me the wrong lid, and you shorted me on those last sleeping pills."

The old man shook his head firmly. "If it was anybody but you, Dolly, I'd take exception. But you never could count."

"And I can count as well as you can," Dolly retorted with heat. "Better. That last bottle was very short. I hadn't opened it until last night, because Jamison gave me something much stronger, but before bed I wanted something light, so I opened the bottle, and—wait. Sheila, go fetch the bottle from beside my bed. The yellow tablets."

When Sheila handed her the plastic vial she passed it to the pharmacist. "There. Is that a hundred pills, Buck Luther?"

Even Sheila could see it wasn't. The bottle was less than half full.

"You've dropped them and forgotten it," he said tartly. "I sent you the full count."

Dolly gave him a sidelong glance under her lashes. "As high as you could count, I suppose," she teased him. "What are you doing up this way, Buck?"

"I went by to pay respects to Heyward, but he's out." He leaned back in his chair and stretched his legs out before him. "You know, Dolly, the way things are going on this street lately,

d consider moving if I were you. But,'' he added with both
gret and pride, ''it does look like our generation is going to
tlive both the older and the younger ones. Begging your
rdon,'' he added for Sheila's benefit.

JCK STAYED nearly an hour, and when he left Dolly was more
an ready for her nap. Sheila remained on the porch to think
out the will—and its ramifications. The girls might not need
oney just now, but Buddy Endicott did. Money to expand his
siness. Money for college. Sheila wasn't certain how much
lly had—whatever her husband had left her plus half of the
mberly house, presumably. She would have originally got-
half of Granddaddy Scott's real estate, too, although it
uld have been sold long ago. In any case, there was enough
make a difference in somebody's bank account, and if Mar-
died, Dolly would make another will.

On the other hand, if Dolly died first, what happened to the
ney?

She tiptoed to the door. Listening over the railing, she could
r Nell humming in the kitchen. Feeling more like a thief
n a privileged guest, she tiptoed to the top floor and that
tere office. Finding the will again was a matter of seconds,
l reading it a matter of minutes.

t was as organized as its author—and as unexpected as
ly's. Nell received a small bequest ''for years of friendship
 service.'' The twins received five thousand dollars each ''to
 them a start in life.'' Everything else, including income
n the sale of Scott Wimberly's real estate, was bequeathed
arious historical societies. The house she left to her favor-
istorical society ''to dispose of as they see fit.'' Behind that
ful wording, Sheila detected a hope that this house would
day be on a Charleston tour of historical homes.

o, Sheila thought, it is as simple as one-two-three. If Dolly
 first, most of the money goes out of the family. If Marion
 first, it stays.

olly was very ill. Was someone stacking the deck to be cer-
Marion predeceased her? Was there someone conscience-
enough to kill Francine and Rhoda so that Marion's death

would look like one of a series, rather than the primary int
tion? Or was there a reason to eliminate all three?

Only one person, it seemed to Sheila, could possibly bene
from all three deaths—and he would be likely to know h
these wills stood. But would he—could he—kill three wom
in cold blood and not turn a hair?

She was considering the matter when a voice on the land
startled her. "I'll be down in a minute, Nell—you think it'
the attic?" Buddy's footsteps pattered up toward the th
floor.

Sheila shoved the will back in its drawer and looked aro
wildly. Her first impulse was to hide, but immediately she
jected that as foolish. Instead, before he got to the top, she w
into the hall and called down, "Hi, I was looking for a ty
writer."

If startled, at least he came up the stairs as friendly and w
as ever. "Hello, beautiful," he said lightly without a trac
flirtation. "I was just thinking about you. How'd you lik
take a sail for two tomorrow morning?"

"I'm not certain just yet what my plans are," she hedg
She didn't tell him she'd been thinking about him, too. She
afraid he might ask what she'd thought.

"Let me carry it down for you," he offered, "as soon as
an old suitcase Marion said I could use to decorate for a
quet tonight."

He went to what Sheila had presumed was a closet door
stepped into a large attic room that must extend over her
room. She heard him sneeze, swear as he barked his
against something, then exclaim, "Aha!" He returned ca
ing a battered black suitcase covered with labels.

"It's a retirement party," he explained, "and they wa
travel decor. If you'll just carry this—" He handed it to he
lifted Marion's heavy electric typewriter as if it were
board. Gallantly he carried the machine to Sheila's room
set it on a small desk near the window. She asked herself a
followed him, "Am I alone with a man who has mur
twice, maybe three times, and plans to murder at least
more?"

"At your service." He smiled, holding the door for her. "Any time." She hoped that wasn't her answer.

They went downstairs to find the twins in the dining room, drinking glasses of tea (of course) and chatting with Nell. Nell had scarcely brought two more glasses when Annie arrived.

"It's hotter'n August out there," she said, wiping her red face with a wadded handkerchief. "You got any more tea, Nell?"

Nell was fetching her a glass when Heyward arrived, carrying a stack of file folders. It reminded Sheila of the morning after she'd arrived, when one after another all the family and neighbors gathered for the patient Nell to feed. Heyward set the folders on the table, carefully jiggling the top ones to be sure they didn't fall off. "Mom must have been secretary to half the clubs in town," he complained, "and I don't know what to do with all these. Some lady has already called wanting last month's minutes. Do you think Marion would take care of them for me?"

He was paler than usual, and his eyes were red as if he had not been sleeping well. While he waited for a response he brushed a lock of hair off his forehead as if it weighed too much to bear.

Nell competently moved the folders to a small corner table. "I'm sure she'll be glad to, Heyward." She fetched him a glass, too, and he sank into a chair at the end of the table.

"Do you know yet when your mother's funeral will be?" Buddy asked him.

He shook his head. "We're aiming for Thursday, but that will depend on the police. I've been at the funeral parlor most of the day, deciding things." His voice trembled a little when he said it, and Annie reached out to pat his hand. He drew his way.

Rebuffed, she turned her attention to Sheila. "How was Francine's funeral?"

"Rather pathetic, I thought," she said. "Just Marion and me."

Annie's eyes darted from one man to the other. "You didn't go, Buddy? Nor you, Heyward?"

Both men looked uneasy. "I had a meeting," Buddy said. As an attempt at sincere regret, it failed.

Rake flipped her ponytail and looked around the room. "Well, let's don't all pretend we're sorry Francine's gone. At least now she can't cause trouble."

Nobody spoke for a moment, then Marion asked from the door, "What do you mean, Rachel?"

They all turned in unison, surprised. "I decided to let Miss Simmons take over for the rest of the day." Marion moved to set her purse on the sideboard. "I have a bit of a headache, and think I'll lie down." She saw the stack of files. "What's this?"

When Heyward explained, she rested her hand on them and said, "I'll be glad to. Now Rake"—she gave Rake a frosty nod—"I arrived just in time to hear your unpleasant pronouncement about Francine's death. What kind of trouble did you expect her to cause?"

Rake had the grace to look embarrassed, but was determined to defend her position. "One person knows what I'm talking about. Nobody else need know now." She pushed back her chair and stood up. "And I, for one, am *glad* she's gone."

Sheila had looked quickly at the faces around her as Rake made her audacious claim, but she could read nothing from their expressions. Annie's eyes glittered, but whether from guilt or spite, who could say? Nell looked, predictably, troubled. Marion's eyes narrowed slightly. (Possibly, Sheila suspected, as Aunt Mary's would, because Rake was still exhibiting such bad manners.) Buddy's fist clenched beside his chair, but he said nothing. Heyward watched his own hand trace a figure eight on the polished table.

Becca was the only one to speak. "Rake, that's horrid. This time you've gone too far. I warn you—"

Rake flounced to the door. "Very well, my dear," she said in theatrical tones. "I shall take my leave." She blew the room a kiss, then said in a normal voice, "I need to get to the theater anyway."

No one spoke for a moment after she left, then Marion spoke crisply. "I have tickets for Sheila and myself for tonight. Do you want one, Becca?"

The girl shook her head. "I'll stay with Gram. I've got a phycology exam tomorrow."

"I'll be going, too." Annie lifted herself out of her chair. "It's almost time for my story."

When the screened door closed behind her, Heyward looked at Becca curiously. "What courses do you have this year?"

"Oceanography and phycology, in my major." She lowered her eyes and concentrated on an orange she was peeling.

"You're sticking with marine biology, then?"

She nodded, her hair shielding her face.

Buddy grinned. "She probably knows more than you do, old boy."

Heyward shifted his clear blue eyes from Buddy to Becca and back again. "She ought to—I've taught her everything I know."

He didn't say much more during his stay, but from time to time Sheila caught him look speculatively in Becca's direction. After one such time he shifted his eyes and caught Sheila looking at him. He smiled faintly, but at what she couldn't tell.

She wasn't wholly surprised, however, when he offered to walk Becca home so Buddy could go straight to the restaurant. Sheila only hoped the shy, reserved girl would open up and take advantage of her opportunity. Catching Nell's eye, she knew the other woman was thinking the same thing.

TWENTY-TWO

MONDAY NIGHT

SHEILA WORKED the rest of the afternoon on the Wimberl
family history. "It won't make the best-seller list," she warne
Dolly, "and the girls will probably die from boredom readin
it. But I'm about half through." She left her manuscript pile
neatly beside the typewriter when she and Marion left to go t
the theater.

The play was a Noel Coward, and far better than Sheila ha
expected. Rake, as the maid, only had three lines to say. But he
expressions, gestures, and reactions to the other characters d
lighted the audience, and she received a burst of applause of h
own at the end.

Flushed with excitement and still wearing her stage makeu
she bubbled about the play in the backseat all the way home
Marion's.

"I thought we'd have a small glass of champagne to cel
brate," Marion said. "I asked Nell to chill it for us." Rake
eyes danced at the unexpected treat.

Becca was studying at the dining-room table when they a
rived. Rake immediately spotted the two mugs beside he
"Who was here?"

Becca flushed slightly. "Heyward came over for a while. I
had some books he thought I could use. How was the play?

Self-centered she might usually be, but this time Rake w
not to be diverted. "What kind of books?"

"Oh, marine biology books." Her hand rested on them li
a caress.

"Well, you can study seaweed together, sister"—Rake be
over and tweaked her nose—"but don't forget he's going to
dance with *me*. And will I ever be stunning!" She struck a po

Becca's flushed deepened. "Don't be silly." She gathered her books into a pile and set them on the hall table while Marion came in with a chilled bottle, an ice bucket, several kinds of cheese, and a basket of crackers. Rake brought glasses, plates, and knives from the sideboard.

Marion had poured each glass but her own when suddenly she froze. "What's that?" She stared through the window and across the porch, her eyes narrowed and intent, her face slightly pale.

Rake, Becca, and Sheila spoke simultaneously. "What?"

Marion made a feeble gesture to calm them. "Probably nothing. I thought I saw someone in the yard." Absently she shoved the bottle into the ice bucket and went to the window.

Sheila crossed the hall in three long strides and flung open the front door. "Could you see who it was?"

Marion shook her head. "No, it was just a figure, flitting by the window as if making for the steps at the kitchen end of the porch. I am sorry to have alarmed you."

"I don't see anybody," Sheila said over her shoulder, "but I'm going to search the yard. Rake and Becca, you look up and down the porch, and Marion, you stay put."

She hurried out into the darkness, uncomfortably aware of the darkness behind each bush. She found nothing.

Rake soon joined her. "There's nobody on the porch. Aunt M and Becca are checking the street. What about in back?" Without waiting for a reply, she hurried toward the back fence with Sheila a few paces behind her. Behind them, a door jammed and Becca called something they could not distinguish. Sheila stood on a stump and peered into the neighbor's backyard, but saw nothing.

They returned to find Marion peering out the front gate and Becca waiting on the porch, a question in her eyes. Sheila shook her head. "If it was someone, he or she got away." She glanced at her watch. The search had taken over twenty minutes.

"The only damage is warm champagne," Rake mourned, topping hers with distaste. "And I'm dry as a bone."

"I'll get you some ice," Becca offered, starting to rise.

Marion waved Becca back. "I hadn't poured mine. It will be chilled." She filled her own glass and passed it across the table, taking Rake's for her own. "Sheila, will you have more? Or you, Becca?"

Sheila shook her head. "This is fine for me. To you, Rake." She raised her glass and the others followed suit.

For a few minutes the four of them discussed the play. Then Rake yawned hugely. Sheila, noting the size and number of Becca's books, offered to drive them home. They accepted with alacrity.

"Do you think there really was somebody outside the window?" Becca asked gravely as Sheila started the engine.

"I don't know, but your aunt certainly looked frightened."

"And it takes a lot to frighten Aunt Em." Becca fell silent.

Suddenly from the backseat came a horrible sound, first a gasp and then a retching that went on and on. Sheila turned, startled. Rake was curled into a ball in one corner of the seat, clutching her stomach and vomiting with all her might.

"WHERE'S THE NEAREST hospital?" Sheila shifted the gear.

Becca, draped over the back of the seat, turned briefly. "Do you think she needs a hospital? Maybe if we took her home..."

"The hospital," Sheila said firmly, and followed Becca's directions at twice the legal speed limit.

At the emergency entrance she called to a man near the door. "Quick! We've got someone here who may have been poisoned!" The man ran toward the car pushing a wheelchair, and helped Rake into it. She still clutched her stomach, eyes wide with terror. When she tried to speak, no words came.

Rake was whisked to a small room and the others directed to a registration desk. Numbly Becca answered the questions, one eye on the door behind which Rake had vanished.

"You'll need to sign here for permission to treat her." The woman behind the desk shoved a form toward Sheila.

"But I can't...I mean, I'm not..."

"You're her mother, aren't you?"

Sheila shook her head. "A friend. I was taking her home..."

"I'm her sister," Becca said unnecessarily. "Can I sign?"

"How old are you?" When Becca told her, she shook her head. "Needs to be a parent or guardian. They around?"

Becca seemed paralyzed. Sheila pushed her toward the phone and inserted a quarter, then when Becca had dialed the number, took the phone into her own hand.

Buddy, still at work, could hardly hear for the noise in the kitchen. "Did you say poisoned?" he demanded.

"Yes. We don't know how, but she's pretty bad. They need your signature. Can you come and sign? I'll tell you about it then."

As she hung up she realized Marion didn't know where they were, either. The phone rang four times before it was answered, and with dismay she heard Dolly's voice on the other end of the line.

"Is Marion there?" she asked.

"Sheila?" Dolly sounded pleasant, even half asleep. "I thought you were here, dear."

"No, I went to take the twins home, and we've...I've decided to stay with them tonight. Is that all right?"

"Of course, dear." Dolly yawned into the phone. "We'll see you in the morning."

"May I speak to Marion?" Sheila asked. But Dolly had already replaced the phone in its cradle.

THE REST OF THE night was a blur. Buddy arrived and signed the necessary papers, then paced the waiting room like a tiger. The only chairs were concentrated into one small room and set in rows facing a television that played endlessly, although no one watched it. Becca huddled in one chair, her eyes never leaving Rake's door. Sheila sat beside her and tried to go over every second of time since they had left the theater.

"Was Rake likely to have eaten anything at the theater?" she asked Becca. Becca just stared at her blankly.

Buddy had no idea, but suggested they could call a girl who shared Rake's dressing room. "Marsha Something—Becca will know."

Becca roused herself sufficiently to supply the name, and Sheila made the call. Marsha answered as if being wakened in the middle of the night were the norm, and sleepily assured Sheila that Rake hadn't eaten a thing before, during or after the performance. "I offered her a Snickers, but she said she was too keyed up."

Sheila hung up and returned to the hard seat beside Becca. "Are *you* feeling all right?" she asked Rake's twin.

Becca nodded miserably. Then tears filled her eyes and she shook her head. "I wished she was dead," she whispered. A huge tear slid down her cheek and she wiped it away listlessly.

Sheila regarded her steadily. "Because she's going with Heyward to the dance?"

"No." Becca sniffed and swallowed. "She wasn't going to the dance with Heyward. It was supposed to be me."

"You?" Sheila fumbled in her purse for a tissue and Becca blew her nose like a minor foghorn.

"Rake thought it would make him notice me. She invited him, then told me she had. She said I should dress up like her and flirt like she would, and then at the end of the evening I was to tell him it was me." Tears streamed down her cheeks. "I couldn't do that to Heyward, I just couldn't. He probably does like Rake more than me, but I can't trick him like that. Besides, I'm *not* like her. I just wish she'd stop trying to take care of me! Ever since we were little, she's done it. When I was bad, she even took my punishment sometimes. But I can't stand it anymore. Tonight when she started teasing me again, for a minute I wished she was dead!" Her voice broke, and tears rained into her lap.

Sheila handed her a tissue. "But you didn't put anything in her glass, or the food, did you?"

"Of course not! I didn't really mean it. But now I'm so scared. *She's* so scared. I can feel her, and she's terrified. Oh, Sheila!" She sobbed on the hard straight chair.

Buddy came from across the lobby and pulled her up, held her tight. "Hey, kitten, it's going to be all right."

As he held her, the door to Rake's room opened. They broke apart, and Sheila stood. A man walked unerringly to them and held out a hand to Buddy. "I'm Dr. Wilkinson." He was young—not much more than thirty—and very short. The little hair he had left grew in a fringe around his scalp and made a soft brown fuzz on top. Behind some glasses, his eyes seemed unnaturally large and grave.

"You've got a mighty sick girl, Mr. Endicott. I'm transferring her to intensive care, and, if you're a praying man, I suggest you begin. I'll see her again tomorrow, and we can tell better then how she's responding to treatment." He nodded briefly to Sheila.

Becca moved forward. "I'm her twin," she said softly.

He grinned, and his owl face became suddenly human. "I would never have guessed."

"Can we . . . I see her?"

He shook his head. "After she's settled in ICU you can see her for a short time each hour. But she'll be in transit for a while. If you want, there's a waiting room upstairs that's a little more comfortable. Marla can give you directions." He indicated the woman at the reception desk, then disappeared down the hall with a squeak of rubber soles on the linoleum floor.

Buddy and Becca chose to stay, of course, but Sheila had something else to do.

After promising to return early in the morning, she hurried home and went directly to the kitchen. Marion, unfortunately, had stacked the dishes and run water over them. She had also rinsed the bottle before putting it in the trashcan. Sheila appreciated her concern not to feed the little black roaches that claimed their own share of Charleston history, but wished Marion had been a bit less compulsive.

Feeling far from sleepy, she crept up the stairs to Marion's room and listened outside the door. From within came the deep breathing with occasional snores particular to the old. Sheila was surprised at the relief she felt.

Reluctantly she gathered supplies and went out to clean up Aunt Mary's car. The police, of course, would prefer that she leave it as it was. But the police wouldn't have to deal with Aunt Mary. Breathing deeply through her nose to avoid nausea, she took samples of the vomit that covered the backseat, then set to work.

She was just drying the upholstery when a soft drawl said behind her, "It's a funny time to be cleaning your car."

She whirled to face Heyward, wearing white pajamas with a blue robe over them exactly the color of his eyes. "What are you doing out?" she demanded.

He shrugged. "Couldn't sleep, so I was reading on our upstairs porch when you got home. Seemed like a funny time to be washing your car. I just thought I'd come see if everything was all right."

She hesitated, then nodded. "Everything's fine here." She stressed the last word. "But Rake Endicott's been taken to the hospital."

"*Rake?* What's the matter—stage fright?"

"Poisoning, most likely."

She watched closely for his reaction. His black brows drew together and he cocked his head to one side. "Rake?" he said again. "Who'd want to poison *Rake*?"

Sheila noticed that he didn't think for a moment that the girl had poisoned herself, or been poisoned accidentally. That was worth thinking about. But for now, she wanted to get to bed. As with most days since she'd gotten to Charleston, tomorrow would probably be very long.

She told Heyward where he could find Buddy and Becca, and bid him a brief good night. She carried the samples upstairs and put them in her desk drawer.

Before she slept, she crept up the stairs and listened again at Marion's door, assuring herself that the old woman was gently snoring. Dolly, too, seemed peacefully asleep.

Wearily Sheila returned to her own room and prepared for bed. Only as she was reaching to turn out the light did she see something she should have noticed at once: the manuscript that she had left neatly piled beside her typewriter was missing.

TWENTY-THREE

TUESDAY

SHEILA WOKE WHEN it was barely light. As she hadn't spoken with Aunt Mary since Sunday, she decided to brave her displeasure by calling before she was up. Instead of the husky voice, however, she got Mildred. "I'm sorry, but Miz Beaufort isn't home."

"Mildred? It's Sheila."

"Oh, Sheila." The maid dropped her formal voice. "Law, you sounded like somebody important. But I told the truth anyway. Your aunt isn't here, and she doesn't know when she'll be back."

"Where's she gone?" Sheila's curiosity was thoroughly aroused. Aunt Mary invariably slept late.

Mildred's voice assumed a deeper pitch of mystery. "I have particularly been told not to say. But if you have a message for her, I'll be glad to pass it on when she calls."

"Can't you give it to her later today?"

"No, child, she ain't coming back tonight. I don't know *how* long she'll be gone."

Sheila felt cold with dread. "She's not in the hospital, is she, Mildred?"

Mildred's rich laugh flowed over the wires. "Of course not. If she was, even if she said not to, I'd have called you right away. And your daddy, too. He gave me my orders several years ago. But right now, Miz Mary is fit as a fiddle and having herself a lark. Don't you worry about her. You just enjoy your vacation."

Sheila hung up without enlightening her about the joys of this particular vacation.

She wandered down to the kitchen and had the coffee made before Nell arrived. She also called the hospital. Rake was holding her own. Buddy and Becca were still there, but in the coffee shop having breakfast.

As gently as she could, Sheila told Nell what had happened. Nell's dusky face grew pale and gray. "Rake?" she almost whispered. "Someone tried to poison Rake?"

"Not tried," Sheila said grimly, "succeeded." She didn't think it was necessary to point out that Marion was a far more likely target. "And there's something else. I'd written about half of the Wimberly family history, and my manuscript seems to be missing. Did anyone come to see Dolly last night after we left?"

The maid shook her head and stuck out her lips. "Not before I left. She and Becca played a hand of canasta, then she watched television and Becca came back down here to study. She was still studying when I left."

Sheila sighed. "You don't suppose Dolly had Becca take it in to her to read?"

Nell had no idea. "I sure would like to take it home to Mama Lucille, though, when you're done. She'd like to hear everything she already knows written out like a story."

Nell carried plates toward the table. "I still can't take it in that somebody has poisoned that baby. How could they have done it? At the play, maybe?"

"I'm afraid it was here, Nell." She described the manhunt of the night before. "While we were all outside looking around, I heard a door slam at one point. I assumed it was Marion or Becca. But it could have been somebody else."

"It sure *was* somebody else," Nell growled. "Miss Marion never slammed a door in her life. And Becca? Uh-uh. She floats out and the door just floats shut behind her. Rake, now, every time she goes *out* the door she forgets and lets it slam. Maybe you got mixed up on which twin you was with."

Sheila shook her head. "Rake still had on her stage makeup. I couldn't have gotten them mixed up."

"Then it seems like somebody went in by the back door, waited in the kitchen until Miss Marion went outside, and put something in that bottle." Sheila hadn't thought about that possibility. It would have taken nerve, but no more nerve than it took to kill Rhoda in an open lawn on a spring morning. Especially, she thought with a shiver, if it was someone who could easily explain his presence if discovered.

Nell thumped silver on the table and bustled back into the kitchen to squeeze oranges.

Sheila wondered how long it would take Nell to ask the right question. It took her half a minute. "Why didn't everybody get poisoned, then? You all drank out of the same bottle, didn't you?"

Sheila sighed. "No, Marion had poured everybody's champagne but her own. Then when we got back in, Rake said hers was too warm, so Marion let her have what was in the bottle and took hers instead."

Nell propped herself against the counter and folded her plump arms. "Then whoever it was must have meant to poison Miss Marion."

Sheila nodded reluctantly. "I'm afraid so. If they were watching through the window they would have seen her pour our glasses, and they'd have known Marion would pour her own glass last..."

Nell nodded in affirmation. "Of course."

"...so all they had to do was get her attention at the right moment. They must have believed we'd all go back in and drink our champagne and then go up to bed."

"And Miss Marion would have died upstairs all by herself." Nell was clearly shaken. She pursed her thick lips and shook her head slowly like an automaton. "I can't think who'd want to poison Miss Marion, but it's as likely as anybody wanting to poison Rake. Who, Sheila?" Her voice was a husky whisper and horror stood in her eyes. "It's like a bad dream."

Sheila nodded.

Nell leaned heavily against the counter, her weight resting on her forearms, and stared against all custom out the northside window of the house. "Looks like you and me are going to have our hands full," she muttered. "Somebody's got to look after Dolly, somebody's got to stay with Rake and be sure Becca and Buddy don't wear themselves out, and somebody's got to keep an eye on Miss Marion to be certain somebody doesn't try something else. Not to mention somebody trying to make sure Heyward eats right with his mama gone." She heaved a huge sigh. "I don't know what we'd have done without you. I really don't."

Sheila gave her a wry smile. "Tell that to Aunt Mary. She keeps pointing out that things have gotten worse since I arrived."

Nell was able to give a small snort. "Well, that's true, right enough. But nobody's blaming you, and I'll tell Miss Mary so when she calls."

Sheila hoped it would be soon. At the back of her mind she was irritated. She had a few things to say herself. It was unlike Aunt Mary to take impulsive vacations, but it was unlike her not to let her family know where she would be. And it was most unfair for her to go off while she and Sheila were in the middle of a puzzle—especially when it was Aunt Mary's puzzle that she'd sent Sheila to solve.

MARION CAME DOWN to breakfast as usual, looking weary and a bit strained about the edges. "Just a sweet roll and coffee this morning, Nell. I need to get down to the shop early. The things from Thursday's auction are being delivered, and I need to shift things to make room for them." The thick veins stood out in her hands as she gripped her cup and took it to her lips.

Sheila wished she could postpone telling Marion about her niece, and was grateful when Nell did it for her.

"There's something you need to know," the old housekeeper said, setting a hot Sara Lee coffee cake on the table. "Rake got sick last night and Sheila had to take her to the hospital."

"What happened?" Marion demanded.

Sheila took her cue from Nell. "She got very ill on our way to her house, so Becca and I drove her straight there. They think it was something she ate—maybe the champagne. But she's going to be all right," she added in reassurance.

"You're certain?" Marion swayed in her chair, put one hand out to steady herself.

Sheila watched her with concern. After Francine's death Marion had seemed weary, but Rhoda's had left her drained with little energy for this attack. In less than a week, Marion had changed from a vigorous elderly woman to a haggard old one.

Sheila spoke gently. "The doctors say so. She'll spend a few days in the hospital, then she'll be fine."

Marion took a deep breath and nodded shortly. "Of course she will. Probably just too much excitement after last night's performance. Rake has a tendency to get overexcited."

Nell and Sheila exchanged looks, and behind Marion's head the housekeeper shook her own almost imperceptibly.

Marion sipped her coffee with very little show of concern. "I think it might not be wise to tell Dolly at this point."

"I agree with that," Nell said, moving back toward the kitchen. "She dotes on that child."

"Sees herself at that age," Marion said tartly. She finished her coffee and stood. "I simply must check in at the shop before I go to the hospital."

Sheila put out a hand to forestall her. "Why don't you let me go this morning? Buddy and Becca are there, and I'll call you with a report later in the morning."

Marion considered, then nodded with something of her old vigor. "I do need to be at the shop at least until noon." She turned to Nell. "I'll come home for lunch, and go see her after that. If that Mr. Adams calls, tell him I've said my last word on the subject." She turned to Sheila. "That man is pestering me to death wanting to buy some land. Won't take no for an answer."

When Marion had filled her Thermos and left, Nell dropped into the seat she had just vacated. "I hope pestering is all he's doing. You think we're wise to let her out of our sight?"

Sheila shook her head. "I wish I knew, Nell. But I think she'll be safer at the shop than anywhere else."

Nell pulled herself heavily to her feet. "Maybe we ought to all go to the shop and barricade ourselves in." Seeing the query in Sheila's eye, she added, "So far nothing has happened there."

RAKE'S CONDITION was unchanged. Sheila arrived to find the doctor with Buddy and Becca, suggesting they go home for rest.

"I'll stay for the morning, and call you immediately if there's any change," she offered. "Becca, would you mind sleeping in my bed, in case Dolly needs anything?"

Becca agreed almost without a sound. She still looked white and strained, and dark half circles had formed under her eyes. Buddy steered her gently by the elbow as they left.

Sheila curled up on the seat by the intensive care waiting room couch with a history of Charleston somebody had left.

"We don't want anybody to die without knowing their history," an old man said from across the room. He was small and thin, his clothes wrinkled as if he'd been there for a long time, and his round pink cheeks covered with a white stubble. His light-blue eyes were the saddest Sheila had ever seen, but he persisted doggedly with his jokes. "Other towns put out Bibles, Charleston puts out history books."

Sheila smiled and peered around. "There's probably a Bible around here somewhere, too."

He shook his head. "Nope, I looked. It would have been a comfort in the long hours. Everything looks so bleak in the night." He twisted knotty fingers together. They were a farmer's fingers, rough and stained with soil.

"Do you have someone in intensive care?" Sheila asked unnecessarily.

He nodded, his eyes sad. "Yes'm, the wife. She's not good."

Sheila assumed he was commenting on his wife's health, no her morals. "Has she been here long?"

He looked down at his hands, and they trembled slightly "About two weeks. Last time it was six. But I don't think I'll take her home with me this time." He fell silent, rubbing one hand with the other. Finally he raised his head. "You got that young girl in there? She yourn?"

Sheila shook her head. "A friend. That was her father and sister who just left."

He shook his head. "It don't seem right. Ellie, now, she'd *had* her life. I'll miss her, but her time may have come. Yes, her time may have come," he repeated, as if he got comfort from the phrase. "But a young one, now, she's got no cause to be in there. She ought to be out playing, or finding herself a husband."

He pulled himself to his feet, and Sheila realized how frail he was. He tottered to the door. "I think I'll get some breakfast, then I'll offer up a prayer for the girl. See you later."

Sheila settled in to read about the history of Charleston. She covered colonial days, antebellum days, and the Civil War before it was time to visit Rake—although "visit" was hardly the word, she thought, looking down at that white pale face with its closed eyes. Rake made no response when Sheila spoke. She'd turned to go when she remembered the old man's words. Lightly she laid a hand on Rake's shoulder and said a prayer of her own.

She returned to her seat and had just reached the Great Hurricane of 1911 when the old man wandered back in, hitched up his pants, and sat down. A toothpick wobbled in one corner of his mouth and he held it expertly between his side teeth as he spoke.

"Still reading, eh?"

She nodded. "I'm enjoying it very much. I like history."

His face said clearer than words "No accounting for taste."

"If you've been around here awhile you probably know almost everything in this book without reading it," she suggested.

He considered, and nodded. "Lived through most of it, I spect. I've been around here nearly eighty-nine years."

"Gracious! Do you remember this hurricane I'm reading about, the one of 1911?"

"Sure do, ma'am. That was a storm a body don't rightly forget. Me and Pa spent most of it trying to keep our durn fool cows from getting out the barn. It was old, you see, and the wind ripped the roof off and the door out. The beasts were frightened, like." He grinned, showing pink gums. "Me, too, if you want the truth of it. But Pa said the fool storm could have his cotton, but it couldn't have his cows. It didn't, either." He settled himself against the cushions in satisfaction.

"I don't suppose you know the Wimberly family, do you?"

"You mean old Scott Wimberly's family?" She nodded. He scanned the room with his eyes, found an ashtray, and flicked his toothpick into it. "I've lived on a Wimberly place all my life, ma'am. Same place. My daddy had it from Mr. Scott, then from Miss Bella, and I've had it from Miss Marion ever since he died in forty-nine.''

"I'm staying with them right now," Sheila told him. "But I didn't know Marion owned any farms."

He twisted his head in his collar to ease his Adam's apple. "She's got three farms and a passel of timber, plus more acres of scrub than a body can count. Mr. Scott bought up a lot of land 'round here when it was going cheap." He threw her a sage look. "Most folks didn't have much money back then, but being in cotton, Mr. Scott, he had some."

"And you knew his daughter, Bella?" Sheila had the feeling that what had been ancient history yesterday was coming alive.

He nodded. "Course I did. She and her brother—Brent his name was—usta come for the rent in a little buggy. She warn't much older than me. I gived her a mutt onct, and she named it Jacob after me." His laugh was light and raspy. "Grew up to be one smart dog, too, old Jake." He paused to ruminate, but seeing that Sheila was about to return to her book, he added, "I knew the little girl, too. A right pretty little thing—head plumb full of curls."

"You must mean Dolly."

"Yes, ma'am, Miss Dolly. That's her name. She left when she growed up, so I've had my dealings with Miss Marion." He looked down at his hands and rubbed them together, and continued to speak more to himself than to Sheila. "Some folk were a mite surprised Miss Bella left everything to Miss Marion, but I don't see it makes no difference. Miss Dolly had a family and everything, and Miss Marion did stay to look after Miss Bella all her life. Just gratitude, I call it."

Sheila wondered if two generations had thought Dolly cheated out of her inheritance. She could set at least a small part of the record straight. "I think they share it. Marion's lives in the house, and managed the property, but it belongs to them both."

He nodded slowly as if taking it all in—or wondering how she knew so much about the Wimberlys. Belatedly Sheila remembered that Aunt Mary had inherited her reluctance to discuss family finances from her Southern forebearers.

To her chagrin she felt her cheeks flush as she met the watery blue eyes across the room. "I've been asked by Dolly to write a history of their family," she explained, feeling foolishly defensive, "and I've read the wills. Their grandfather left the land to Brent, and Brent left it to them both. Bella inherited the house for her lifetime, and then it went to them, too."

"So that's how it was," he said with exaggerated politeness.

He sank into silence, and she returned to her book. In a few minutes he got up, peered up and down the hall, and came back. "Just looking to see if our doctor was out there. You have to catch him quick." He shook his head. "Some folks is almost too religious, to my way of thinking." Sheila was baffled. Would a doctor's religion keep him from taking time to see his patients' families?

The old man hitched up his pants and resumed his seat—and his former thread of conversation. "Take Mr. Scott, now. He come out to our place one Sattidy to talk about a new barn, and he was all worked up, carrying on about sin and hell until my daddy made me and my brother go back in the house. Next thing we heard, he'd had himself a stroke. No call to get that worked up about religion, if you ask me. I wasn't surprised when Miss Bella and Mr. Brent changed churches after he died." He stood up again to amble toward the door. "I think I'll visit Ellie for a few minutes now. She won't know me, but I like to be there."

Sheila returned to the hurricane of 1911 with more interest. The storm that ripped the roof off his daddy's barn must have been the same storm that carried Mama Lucille and a chair across Bella Wimberly's yard. Perhaps it was just as well someone had taken her first manuscript. She'd like to try her hand at writing one with more life in it—including, she smiled wryly, a dog named Jake.

She had reached the opening of Pinehaven Tuberculosis Sanatorium in 1924 when Buddy returned. "I couldn't sleep," he confessed, lowering himself into a chair near hers. "But I had a shower and a shave." She'd known the latter. He smelled wonderful. It was a shame to have to shake her head when he asked, "Any change?"

"Tell me again how it happened," he demanded.

She did, then asked, "And you were at the restaurant, right?"

He raised one brow. "Yes. But even if I weren't, do you think I'd poison one of my girls? I didn't even spank them, which they badly needed from time to time—especially Rake. Left it up to Margaret. It hurt me too much to hurt them." He flipped through a magazine, flung it down. "Oh, hell!" He crossed and recrossed his legs and finally stood, shoving his hands deep into his pockets. "I can't stand to be here and I can't stand not to be."

She reached out a hand to him. He took it and clung to it, then let it go and sat on the couch.

She asked, as much to distract him as anything, "Buddy, what if the poison wasn't meant for Rake, but for Marion?"

Either his surprise was genuine or he was as good at dramatics as his daughter.

She explained. "Marion's was the only glass not poured when we left the table."

He shook his head—too quickly? "Marion's a tartar at times, but nobody would seriously want to hurt her. Besides," he added cryptically, "she can't live forever."

It was too good an opening to pass up. With a mental apology to Aunt Mary, Sheila asked bluntly, "Do you know who benefits from her death?"

"Sure. She's made that very clear this past week. The afternoon you came I had made an appointment with her, to ask for a loan for the restaurant in Savannah. She said she had no ready cash, and I suggested she sell a bit of land. She turned me down flat. Didn't want to tie up her estate, as she put it."

"But won't you—or the girls—inherit most of it anyway? Who else is there?"

"You obviously don't know Marion very well. She's far more concerned with the big picture than the little one. The girls may come in for a bit, and Annie may get something, perhaps. But she's informed me in no uncertain terms that she's leaving most of it to various historical societies." He said it without rancor, almost with humor. She wondered if he knew the terms of Dolly's will, but couldn't bring herself to ask.

Instead she pretended to absorb the information, then asked idly, "Are any of them in need of money?"

He chuckled. "Wouldn't that be a terrific story? 'Crazed historical society goes on rampage and kills two members to speed up inheritance.' But frankly, Sheila, most of the people in those societies are perfectly sane, even about history. My mother, for instance, who is Charleston born and bred and has been a docent on almost every house tour in town. Only Marion and Rhoda have made a religion out of this city. If she weren't already dead, Rhoda would be my prime suspect for poisoning Marion."

She was surprised, and showed it. "But I thought they were such good friends."

"Only in front of company, my dear. They ran neck and neck for secretary of most of their organizations, on the theory that whoever keeps the records has the most power. But their rivalry has deep and furtive roots. If my good mama is correct, Marion fully expected MacFadden Bennett's second wife to be a Wimberly, not some chit fresh out of high school. In Rhoda's first years as Mrs. Bennett—also according to my sainted mama—Marion did her best to keep her out of the United Daughters of the Confederacy. But since Rhoda is a Calhoun (although a distantly related one), Marion finally had to concede. After that, Rhoda harped constantly on Marion's insistence that every name appear in every set of minutes and report. Marion insists it's for historical accuracy, to which the fair Rhoda once snapped, 'Ego, pure and simple!'"

He stood up. "But now Rhoda is dead and it is not Marion but Rake who has been poisoned. Isn't it about time we could see her again?" He wandered down the hall.

In a few minutes he wandered back. "About the same." He bent and picked up her book. "What are you reading? Oh." He thumbed through a few pages. "Look, here's the theater where you were last night." He took a seat beside her and laid the book in her lap.

"I didn't realize it was so old—or famous," she exclaimed, reading.

For the first time that morning his smile was genuine. "Everything in Charleston is that old and famous, Sheila. Even

Harbor Lights has been around for over ninety years—under a variety of names. It's my dream that in a hundred years someone will stroll in the front door and say, 'Now back in the nineteen hundreds this was owned by that famous restauranteer Everett Middleton Endicott.'"

"Middleton?" Her eyes widened. "As in the plantation?"

His eyes twinkled. "Of course. I told you, Sheila. Everything in Charleston is old and famous, even me. And in a hundred years I'll have a plaque on the wall of Harbor Lights saying 'Sheila Travis ate here.' I ordered it yesterday. Also one for the boat, which, by the way, we will save for another day."

His good humor was so tenuous that she wanted to help preserve it if she could—and keep his mind off Rake. "Don't forget a plaque for Washington Park. I sat there for nearly an hour one afternoon talking to pigeons."

"Too bad you missed Pitt," he said sadly. "He was always good for a chat."

"Pitt?"

"William Pitt, who had the good sense to promote the repeal of the Stamp Act of 1776. He used to stand on a brick pedestal—wearing a toga, of all things, and looking embarrassed to be caught without his top hat."

"What happened to him?"

"Acid rain. They moved him indoors."

"Pitt got pitted?"

He raised his eyes to heaven. "Lord, how lightly the woman takes the wonders of our fair city. What will she say next?"

"She'll say next that she loves your fair city. I came under protest this time, but next time I'll come by choice."

She had said too much. His brows lifted. "Protest?"

She nodded and tried to toss it off lightly. "I thought I'd rather stay in Atlanta, but Aunt Mary and Dolly insisted my life would not be complete until I'd seen Charleston. And now," she said, reaching for the book to end the conversation, "I know they were right."

"Well," he said, fumbling for a magazine from the basket beside his chair, "it has certainly been more exciting than usual since you arrived."

TWENTY-FOUR

SHEILA STAYED UNTIL Becca returned. As she was leaving the hospital, she saw a familiar rangy form in front of her and hailed it.

He turned. "Juliet! Left your balcony?"

"I climbed down to check out a poisoning."

When she enlightened him, he shaped his lips into a soundless whistle. "What on earth is going on in that neighborhood?"

She shook her head. "I wish I knew, Jamison. But those two old women—three, counting Nell—have had about as much as they can take. We haven't told Dolly yet about Rake."

"Good idea," he agreed, "although, strangely enough, Dolly's doing better than I would have expected. She's a tough old bird, you know—always looking on the bright side of things. Enjoys life more than just about anybody I know, which is probably why she's still around. How's Marion?"

"Looking like death warmed over. Rhoda's death was especially hard on her. You might need to give her something."

He shook his head. "She wouldn't let me touch her with a ten-foot pole."

"Not unless it had a white flag waving at the top of it," she agreed. "Did you hear, by the way, that Francine was suffocated by a pillow?"

His mouth again formed a whistle, through which he sucked one long note. "Have the police been informed about Rake?"

She shook her head. "Not unless the hospital does it automatically. I did take samples of what she threw up, though. Do you know how we'd go about getting them analyzed?"

"As a matter of fact, I do. Where are they?"

"In my desk drawer, in a lot of little Baggies."

"Lead the way. I'll follow."

He checked in on Dolly while she went upstairs. When she came back he tucked her bags into his satchel and stayed to chat for several minutes on the downstairs porch. Finally he looked at his watch. "Office hours start soon. How about dinner with me tonight?"

She shook her head. "Not tonight," she said reluctantly. "Right now I'm sticking as close to this house as possible. Maybe another time?"

"That's what they all say," he mourned, "all the beautiful detectives I run into. Perhaps if I committed a crime..."

A police car double-parked in the street and a burly female officer climbed out. "Dr. Jamison, is this your Jag parked beside the fire hydrant?"

"Have fun with your detective," Sheila murmured, deserting him without a trace of shame.

MARION DIDN'T COME HOME to lunch after all. "Called and said things were busy," Nell reported, giving Sheila a solitary tray on the downstairs porch. "Dolly's having hers in bed. I haven't told her about Rake, but she's still feeling a little weak from the excitement over the weekend."

"Me, too," Sheila agreed. Nell went back to her kitchen with a heartfelt "Um-hmmm!"

As Sheila ate Nell's delicious pasta salad, she decided to spend the afternoon rewriting Dolly's family history. She had done all she knew to do at this point about Rake's accident and Rhoda's murder, and with any luck she could finish in a few hours. At least now she had a framework of Charleston history on which to place the Wimberly family, and the old man's anecdotes would improve her rendition of Scott Wimberly and his daughter Bella.

Perhaps even Dorothea's cookbook would add some interest now that the people were coming clearer—the girls might get a laugh out of the recipe for acorn bread, for instance.

As she passed Dolly's door, Dolly called from her bedroom "Sheila? Is that you?" She sat up in bed, lunch tray beside her.

Sheila removed the tray to a nearby table, then sat by the bed for a brief visit. She could hear Nell's vacuum upstairs.

"I'm going to finish the history today—and maybe include some of your grandmother's recipes."

"Recipes?" Dolly asked.

"Dorothea Wimberly's cookbook was among the papers Marion gave Francine," Sheila told her. "I assumed she was..."

Dolly hitched herself up in bed and pushed her hair off her neck. "Why, yes, she was! I was named for her. Do you have it still?"

"In my room." She fetched it and laid it on the spread. Dolly picked it up and sat stroking the cover.

"They called them receipts in those days." She turned a few pages then handed it back to Sheila. She had picked the book up by its spine, and both of them were surprised when something fluttered out and slid to the floor. Sheila retrieved it with a smile. She recognized this skinny little girl frowning at the camera, one hand laid possessively on her white ruffled skirt. Marion as a child had been very like Marion as an old woman—even the thick bobbed hair was almost the same.

A smudged, floury fingerprint decorated one corner. She turned it over. In a spidery hand someone had written, "Marion at three."

Dolly took the picture and her face softened. "Poor baby looks terribly unhappy, doesn't she? She's always hated cameras." She pointed to the smudge. "Aunt Bella probably got it on baking day and stuck it in the cookbook. She was always doing things like that."

She put the picture into a drawer of her nightstand. "How's the history coming along?"

"It may be finally coming to life. I met an old man today who has known your family forever. Said he gave your Aunt Bella a dog she named after him—Jacob."

"I remember Jake!" Dolly exclaimed. "Go bring me that red album from the bottom shelf." When Sheila had fetched the album, Dolly leafed through the old photos until she pointed to one of a big spotted dog sitting mournfully in a tub while Marion gave him a bath. "He followed Aunt Bella everywhere. See? Here they are."

Sheila took the book and looked at the woman rather than at the dog. Bella had been of medium height, with a drab colorless face and an arrogant nose. Not a beauty by any standards. On the next page was a very old picture of a family—mother, father, boy standing with one hand on his mother's shoulder, little girl leaning against her father. "Who is this?"

Dolly peered across her covers. "That's Grandmama and Granddaddy, Aunt Bella and Daddy."

"You are very like your grandmother." Sheila couldn't help thinking how unfair it was that good looks should have gone from mother to son while Bella inherited her father's big nose.

She flipped other pages looking at faces that now seemed familiar. Marion at twelve in an antebellum dress. Dolly—predictably, in ruffles—peering at a bug on the sidewalk. A small Marion in a big chair clutched an infant who even then had a contagious smile.

Sheila pointed to a picture of Scott Wimberly in tails, glaring at the camera with the hauteur appropriate to one of his standing in the community. "That old man I met even knew your granddaddy."

"Do!" Dolly leaned back on her pillows and fanned herself with an envelope. "And remembers him?"

Sheila nodded. "Remembers him coming out one Sattidy," she exaggerated the old man's country tones, and Dolly laughed, "and going on and on about sin and hell. Was your grandfather an unusually religious man?"

Dolly considered, then shook her head. "Not that I knew of. He belonged to St. Michael's Episcopal, I think, but by the time I came along the family was Presbyterian. I think if anything, Granddaddy was more self-righteous than religious, at least from what I've heard. He died, remember, soon after I was born." She laid the envelope on the bedspread to brush a tendril of hair away from her cheek. Sheila was surprised to recognize the writing on the front.

"You've heard from Aunt Mary?"

Dolly picked up the envelope and fanned again. "Yes, dear."

"Did she say anything about a trip?"

Dolly didn't precisely answer. "She said not to worry about anything, that she's all right." She gave Sheila a sunny smile.

"And that's exactly what I've been thinking—that we don't need to worry anymore. I'm glad you are working on the history, Sheila. It begins to feel like everything is finally back to normal."

Sheila, thinking of Rake's still young form under the white sheet, wasn't quite so optimistic.

BACK IN HER own room, she typed up the nineteenth-century family history—mostly a collection of dates and names joined by meaningless phrases—in a matter of two paragraphs, for she knew absolutely nothing to turn those names into flesh and blood people. She then turned her attention to people she was beginning, in some sense, to know.

But now her increased knowledge made her ask questions she had not known to ask before. She reread Bella's letters, a frown puckering her brow, and chewed her lower lip as she considered possibilities. She started to type, slowly at first, and then faster as she warmed to her subject. When she had finished, she put the finished pages into a large envelope. "I need to go make some copies," she told Dolly.

She was gone less than an hour, but she found herself hurrying back to the house, afraid that something else might have happened. She found Nell mopping the kitchen floor, singing "Onward Christian Soldiers."

"You planning to go somewhere?" Sheila teased.

Nell gave her a broad smile. "No, just shoring up my spirits. Miss Mary is going to call you in about five—" The phone stopped her. "This will be her. I'll get it. You go on upstairs to your room and pick up when you're ready."

When she was settled on her bed, she picked up the line and waited for a pause in the conversation to ask "Aunt Mary, where *are* you?" With a click, Nell left the line.

"In my room, dear." The husky voice was unruffled as ever. "I understand you called me. Have you found out what's going on?"

"First things first. We've had another accident." Sheila filled her in on Rake's poisoning.

Aunt Mary took her time replying. "This is getting out of hand, Sheila. It's Tuesday, and you only have three days before you must return to Atlanta. Have you spoken to the police?''

Sheila sighed. "Several times, unfortunately. As I've already told you, I'm their preferred suspect. We haven't said anything about the poisoning yet, but Jamison has taken samples for analysis, so it's just a matter of time. Officer Johnson will love it that I was driving Rake when she started retching.''

"Do you think I should call Wyndham? He's very busy at this time of year..."

"Far too busy," Sheila hastily agreed. All she needed was her pompous brother-in-law from Mississippi having a clash of wills with Charleston's finest. "I'll be all right as soon as we clear it all up. Do you have any ideas?''

"Well, I've been giving some thought to our suspects. Do you know anything about that realtor person? His name, for instance?''

"Mr. Adams, I believe. Other than that I only know that he is very eager to buy some of Marion's land for a housing development, but she isn't interested in selling and I've discovered why. She's left everything she has to historical societies and wants to give them the property intact. From something I saw on her desk, I think Marion hopes they'll build a living village something like Old Sturbridge on this particular piece of property.

"All this means that Buddy could have a pretty strong motive for wanting to get rid of Marion. Dolly has left almost everything she has to Marion, on the assumption that *she* will leave it to the family. But she isn't. That means that Buddy and the twins will get very little unless Marion dies first.''

"Sheila," Aunt Mary's voice was distinctly chilly, "have you been prying?''

"No, Aunt Mary, I've been detecting. But sometimes they look very much the same. I've also been writing the family history that Francine was working on, in all my spare"—she gave the word a heavy emphasis—"time.''

As usual, sarcasm rolled off Aunt Mary like bowling balls down an alley. "Tell me about it" was all she said.

Sheila did, including the old man in the hospital waiting room and the anecdote Dolly had told about three little girls on a roof.

"I am certain Dolly wants you to limit yourself to basic facts, dear," Aunt Mary said with great dignity. "I certainly hope you won't hurt any feelings by what you put in."

"If you're back home, you can see for yourself," Sheila informed her. "I mailed you a copy half an hour ago."

"Well, why don't you let me read mine before you share it with the Wimberlys?"

"Fine with me," Sheila agreed.

"Now, to return to your purpose for being there, Sheila," Aunt Mary said crisply, "have you checked alibis for Thursday and Saturday mornings?

"I can tell by your silence that you haven't," she continued.

"No, not for Thursday," Sheila admitted. "But on Saturday, everybody but the twins was around. That's what makes the murder so unbelievable, Aunt Mary. Who would walk in off the sidewalk and strike someone down in broad daylight with so many people around?"

"Someone who seized an opportune moment or someone who was desperate," Aunt Mary replied. "What of the weapon? Have you found it yet?"

"No, the police—"

"Really, Sheila, you act as if you were on vacation down there. What do you do with all your time?"

"I *am* on vacation," Sheila reminded her, her own exasperation rising. "And as I have just told you, when not at the hospital or keeping company with dead bodies, I've been finishing the family history for Dolly. Besides, the police are far more capable than I am of checking alibis and looking for weapons. In fact, Aunt Mary, I have been absolutely no use around here, as you yourself have continued to point out. As soon as I can arrange for a nurse for Dolly, I am packing my bags and coming back to Atlanta!"

"Nonsense, dear. You just need to stop dilly-dallying around. After all, there aren't many potential victims left. Where is Marion just now, by the way?"

"She's at her shop, which seems to be the safest place for her. Nell and I are considering moving the whole household down there. It's the only place that seems to be excluded from whatever is going on." Against her will, Sheila heard herself asking "Do you have any ideas of what I should do next?"

"Not at the moment." Aunt Mary sounded as defeated as Sheila felt. She actually paid for two minutes of silence.

Finally Sheila said, with a sigh, "Well, we're costing you a fortune. Why don't I call you back tomorrow?"

"Don't worry about the expense, dear."

Sheila took the phone from her ear and looked into the receiver in amazement. "If you said what I thought you said, I think you need to call your doctor. Something is slipping."

"I am perfectly fine." Aunt Mary's tone was positively glacial. "Now you go see what else you can discover. Don't try to call me, because I plan to be out most of the day. I will call you tomorrow about this time."

"Well, if you get any bright ideas, call sooner. Would you like to say hello to Dolly?"

"No, I'll call Dolly another time. I just wanted to see how you were getting along. Now if I were you—"

"But you're not," Sheila said sweetly. "Have a good evening, Aunt Mary, and call me tomorrow."

It was rude to hang up without waiting for a good-bye, but there are times, Sheila told herself, when rudeness is justified.

She pulled an afghan up over her feet and settled more firmly against her pillows for a good, long think. But she'd had a short, fitful night and an early morning. Soon, once again, she succumbed to the lure of a Charleston siesta.

IT WAS A midafternoon, when people are dozing, watching soap operas, or resting on their piazzas. A car purred up to a well-kept brick house in a modern part of Charleston.

"It's open," a small cracked voice answered the bell. Mama Lucille's wizened face brightened as she recognized her visitor. "How you doin'?"

"I'm fine. Is Will here?" The visitor already knew the answer.

"No, he's gone to the liberry. Can you sit a spell?"

"No, I came to take you for a little ride, Mama Lucille." The visitor helped the old woman to her feet and gathered her shawl from the back of her chair. Together they walked slowly, carefully down the steps to the car. They drove away discussing the beauty of the day.

Will spent over an hour at the library, so it was not until after four that anyone knew that Mama Lucille had disappeared.

THE PHONE didn't bother Sheila, and she scarcely noticed when Nell came to the screened door of her room. She lifted her head from the pillow, however, as the old woman spoke. Her voice was tight with fear.

"Sheila? Mama Lucille is gone. Will came home from the library and found her missing."

"Could she have gone for a walk?"

Nell shook her head. "Not likely. She can scarcely stand alone. Mrs. Watkins across the street said a car came this afternoon and was there for a while, but she didn't see if Mama Lucille got in it or not."

Sheila stared at Nell, scarcely comprehending. "You mean you think someone has *kidnapped* her?"

"I don't know. But I do know I need to go home and start combing the neighborhood." She waited—for what? Sheila realized, all of a sudden.

"Go on home. I'll do dinner. What had you planned?"

"Roast. It's in the oven. You just need to make the rice and heat up the beans from yesterday. There's a congealed salad, too."

"Sounds like I can handle that." Sheila pulled a brush through her thick hair and joined Nell on the porch. "Just show me where things are. I'll take it from there."

TWENTY-FIVE

WHEN SHE HAD surveyed the kitchen and started the rice, Sheila
made herself a mug of coffee and flung herself into a chair o
the downstairs porch for five minutes of peace and quiet. A
usual, the air was thick with honeysuckle and a breeze brougl
just a tang of salt from the marsh. Somewhere down the bloc
a bird trilled for the joy of living, while a dog barked fa
enough in the distance not to be annoying. A lovely afte
noon, if one didn't have to think of kidnapping and murder.

But Sheila did. Who on earth would kidnap a helpless ol
woman—and why? What did Mama Lucille know that coul
make a difference? What did Sheila herself know, she aske
ruefully, that could make a difference?

She let her thoughts wander. Balancing her mug on the ba
ustrade, she found herself doing a mental walk-through of wh
someone must have done the night before. First, watch Ma
ion pour the champagne. Then pass the dining-room windov
on the garden level. That way Marion can only "think" she se
you—if indeed you want to be seen at all. Do you? Of cours
Otherwise, how can you get the people out of the house? S
how do you insure being seen without being recognizec
Probably by waving a hand to attract attention as you pass.

The tricky part is getting onto the porch and into the kitche
without being seen. How can you insure that? Deep in though
Sheila reached for her mug without looking, misjudged tl
distance, and knocked it into the azalea below.

"Damn!" In the quiet afternoon it sounded like a shou
Awkwardly she got on her knees and peered through the ba
nisters—or was it balusters? She seemed to remember some a
history professor in her dim collegiate past pointing out th
these round vaselike bannisters were called . . .

Sheila sat back on her heels, remembering her dream an
what she'd wanted to remember. The gap in the bannister
"I've found it, Aunt Mary," she murmured.

Abandoning her mug to the shrubbery, she went into the kitchen and found the key to Marion's workshop. Quickly bypassing pieces of furniture in various stages of restoration, she hurried to the farthest corner, where she'd noticed the stack of old bannisters her first afternoon when she was looking for the fan blade.

The one she sought was near the bottom of the pile, and it had been washed to a clean whiteness. But near one end Sheila found a stain she thought a police laboratory might be able to identify as Rhoda Bennett's blood.

Carefully holding it with a rag she found on a shelf, she gave it an experimental thrust through the air. It was certainly thick enough to deal a fatal blow.

"Who's there?" Marion Wimberly's voice quavered slightly outside the closed door. Sheila hurried out to join her.

"It's just me, Marion. By a fairly devious route, I just figured out what I think Rhoda may have been killed with." She waved the baluster slightly.

Marion took a step back, as well she might. "But those have been gathering dust in the workroom for years."

"Not this one," Sheila told her. "See, it's been washed, but I think this is blood." Marion shivered slightly as she saw the stain. Sheila finished quickly. "I think someone took it out long enough to kill Rhoda and was returning it last night when you saw him through the window."

Marion was very still, then she nodded. "You could be right. I usually lock this room"—she looked at the key in Sheila's hand and Sheila felt herself flush—"but sometimes I have been careless lately. Why don't you leave that . . . thing here, and we can call the police to come get it after dinner."

"Dinner!" Sheila had completely forgotten. "Oh, my goodness, Marion, I'm supposed to be cooking your dinner, and I just hope the roast isn't burned to a crisp!"

DINNER WAS A necessarily somber affair. Marion had had to be told of Mama Lucille's disappearance and that so far no trace of her had been found. Strangely, the old woman's disappearance seemed to frighten her as nothing else had done. "Where do you suppose she could be?" she asked several times. She pulled her roll to pieces on her plate without ever eating a bite of it.

Sheila began to envy Dolly, secure in her room with Beethoven on the tape recorder and no idea that anything out of the ordinary was going on. She hadn't even been told about Rake's illness, until her condition changed one way or the other.

After dinner three old friends of Dolly's came by for an evening of canasta. Marion, with apologies, returned to her shop, where the patient Miss Simmons was waiting for the final cataloguing of the new items from the auction. When dishes were done, Sheila decided to run over to the hospital to check or Rake.

At the intensive care waiting room Heyward Bennett gave her a weary smile. "Becca's gone to fetch her books. She'll be back in about half an hour."

"What are you doing here?" Sheila dropped her long frame into a vinyl chair that emitted a long *squissssh* as she sat.

"I've closed the school for the week, and couldn't stand sitting around the house, so I came to spell Buddy so he could go to the restaurant for a while. It's a good thing I did. Becca' pretty cut up about this."

"Aren't we all." Sheila wasn't asking a question. She picked up a magazine, but couldn't concentrate. There was so much she wanted to know about this young man.

"Heyward?" she began tentatively. He lowered his magazine and raised his brows. "I want to ask you two questions which you may choose not to answer. But I need to ask them okay?"

He shrugged. "Sure."

"Tell me what you and Francine were arguing about th morning before she died."

Heyward linked his fingers and flexed them, then said a courteously as anyone could say it, "I honestly can't see that it any business of yours."

"She's a detective, and Gram asked her to come to invest gate our accidents." Neither of them had heard Becca come in She stood at the door, holding a stack of books and two Coke She put one of the drinks on a white Formica tabletop wit unnecessary precision before she turned to Sheila. "But our accidents have nothing to do with Heyward."

"Probably not," Sheila agreed, "but since Heyward was one of the last people to talk with Francine before she died . . ."

"How do you know?" Above her drink, Becca's eyes were slits.

Sheila gave her an apologetic smile. "I hadn't heard of northside manners at that point, so I saw them from my bedroom window."

Becca didn't return the smile, but she looked very thoughtful. Finally she said, "I think Heyward has been through too much already. He doesn't need to be involved in our troubles."

Heyward held up one hand to stop her and leaned forward in his seat. "No, if this lady is indeed a detective—are you really, Sheila? You don't look like any detective I ever saw."

She raised one eyebrow. "Don't all the detectives you know have frizzy black hair?"

He shook his head. "Nor good legs, either."

"Cool it, Heyward," Becca said in a tone of authority.

He gave her a look of surprise, but said nothing more.

Sheila leaned toward him. "I'm not really a detective, but I've been able to help the police in a few cases, and Dolly thought I might be able to clear up the accidents."

"And Mother's death?" His blue eyes pierced hers.

She shook her head. "None of us expected that."

"Neither did Mother." The way he said it, it didn't sound flip.

Sheila let silence linger for a moment before she asked again, gently, "What *were* you and Francine quarreling about before she died?"

He took a long drink of Coke and set the can on the table. "It had nothing to do with the accidents."

"Of course not," Becca said stoutly.

"How do you know?" Heyward asked her.

Becca bit her lip, gave Sheila a speculative look. Sheila nodded, and Becca mumbled, "I was biking past and overheard you."

Heyward stared at her. "What did you do, hide in the bushes to listen?"

Becca's cheeks were a deep red as she bent her head in shame. "I didn't hide to listen," she muttered, "but I did stop when I heard her say Daddy's name." She raised her head to Sheila's and her eyes blazed. "I'll tell you what they were fighting about. I don't have any need to protect that woman. She told Heyward that Daddy was going to marry her unless Heyward could make her a better offer. She said she would rather marry Heyward, but she would marry a rich restaurant owner over a poor sailor. She said that unless Heyward could come up with some money—"

"Hey, that's enough." Now Heyward was angry too. "You have a right to be mad on account of your daddy. Francine did make it sound like she was marrying him for his money. But Francine is dead. D-E-A-D," he spelled it. "She's not going to marry your daddy or anybody else. The woman had a dreadful accident after that conversation, and—"

"The woman was murdered."

Sheila's statement froze them both. Becca's eyes widened in horror while Heyward knitted his brows in disbelief.

"Murdered?" Becca whispered.

Sheila nodded. "Smothered with a pillow off her couch, after she'd hit her head. Did she mention any appointments for that morning, Heyward?"

He seemed to be trying to think. "No. And she was so sleepy I wouldn't have been surprised if she'd spent the day in bed. While she was with me she was totally concerned with who was going to marry her—as Becca so ably reported." His voice was heavy with sarcasm.

Becca's eyes were pink with unshed tears, and they formed the only color in her face as she raised her eyes to meet his. "You make it sound so horrible," she whispered. "It wasn't! I was riding by and I heard you and Francine talking. I heard her say Daddy's name, and then, through the bushes, I saw her face. She had the nastiest look I ever saw. I couldn't stand it. I had to hear what she was saying to you."

"I hope you can remember it long enough to testify at my trial." Becca looked startled. "Or haven't you thought that far ahead yet? Think about it, honey—Francine has a quarrel with Heyward Bennett and Francine dies. My mother has a quarrel with Heyward Bennett and she dies, too. You didn't happen be around for that one, did you?'' She shook her head. Sheila had never seen anyone look so miserable.

"I saw you Saturday morning," she volunteered, "driving a couple of blocks from home."

He gave a short, unpleasant laugh. "No wonder you looked so surprised when I said I'd spent the night on my boat. I didn't see Mother, though—got all the way to the house and realized it wasn't going to do any good. She wasn't going to change her mind."

"About what?"

"About lending me enough money to buy a larger marina that's coming up for sale. Buddy told me about it, and it would be perfect for what I hope to do with the business—docking spaces to rent out, as well as space for the school. She got wind that I was looking at it and called me on the carpet." He pointed to Sheila with one long finger. "The afternoon you arrived, if I remember correctly."

She nodded. "You'd come home because she wanted to see you."

"See me? She wanted to skin me alive—just for looking! When I suggested that she might put up the money, she was livid. I asked again Friday, with no luck. Saturday I woke up feeling good..." His voice quivered, and Becca reached out to touch his arm. He shook her off and finished fiercely, "I thought I'd try again. But when I got to the house I got cold feet and just put the car in gear and drove back to the boat. That's the truth, believe it or not. But it's probably enough to get me convicted." He slumped back against the loveseat cushions and closed his eyes. He was, Sheila saw, very pale.

Becca's eyes flew to Sheila's. "But he wouldn't...he didn't..."

Sheila looked from one to the other. Heyward opened one eye and waited for her response. "I don't know, Becca."

"Well, *I* do!" Becca sat up very straight. Now her cheeks were pink with anger. "Heyward may be silly, but he's not a murderer."

"Thanks for that semivote of confidence," Heyward muttered.

Becca ignored him. "I mean, he's gone with a lot of tacky women. But that was just to spite his mother—make her take some notice of him. He never in his life did anybody any harm."

Heyward was icy in his courtesy. "So! Besides listening behind the bushes, you also keep a record of the women I date—and their Nielson ratings, ma'am?"

Becca's eyes flashed scorn. "They haven't had any ratings. For years I waited for you to find somebody worth giving you up for, but they were all trash, just trash. And Francine was the pits."

Heyward had heard only one phrase. "Give me up? Why?"

Becca was beyond shame. "Because I loved you, you fool. How could you not know it? Everybody else in town does. Practically all my life I've wished for you on the first star and told you good night on the moon. And all the time you've gone around with *trash*!" She seemed unconscious of the tears streaming down her cheeks.

Heyward stared at her without a word. Then he took a tissue from a box the hospital had thoughtfully provided and wiped her cheeks. "This is how we met," he told Sheila. "Here, blow," he commanded, handing Becca another tissue. Then he touched her hesitantly on the shoulder. "Do you still love me?"

She raised her head. Her face was red and blotchy—less lovely than Sheila had ever seen it. But when she nodded, Heyward shook his head in wonder. "Nobody has ever loved me like that. Nobody."

Becca sniffed furiously. "I do."

They met midway between their chairs, supported by nothing more visible than love.

Sheila rose and left, unnoticed. Heyward Bennett might be guilty of one—maybe even two murders. But this was not the time to discuss it.

TWENTY-SIX

SHE'D BEEN ASLEEP for nearly an hour when the phone rang. At first she left it for Marion, but when it had rung several times, she sleepily answered.

"Is this the Wimberly house?" The voice, light and nasal, could be either male or female.

"Yes." She steeled herself for obscenities.

"This is the hospital. Could you call Mrs. Travis, please?"

"This is Mrs. Travis."

"Miss Endicott is asking for you—says it's urgent. I hate to bother you so late, but she really is overexciting herself."

Sheila sighed. "I'll be right over."

She shoved one hand through her hair and pulled on a pair of slacks and a sweater. A glass of water almost cleared the cobwebs from her brain. What time was it? Half-past two.

With a nasty thought for young adults who have to have what they want when they want it, she tiptoed down the stairs and carefully locked the door behind her.

Although the moon was still bright, it was filtered by leaves and Spanish moss until the ground was a fairyland of shadows. So safe had she felt in the placid streets of Charleston that she had forgotten to lock her car when she'd come in earlier. She slid into the driver's seat and put the key into the ignition.

The car was suddenly full of a sickly sweet smell, and that was the last thing she remembered.

GRADUALLY SHE BECAME aware of her aching head, then of a dreadful taste in her mouth. She was lying on something quilted and thin, on a bare and very dusty concrete floor. Her back, hips, and elbows were stiff and bruised, as if she'd been dragged. Hugging herself for warmth, she forced herself into a sitting position and promptly sneezed. Then she tried to look around. She could not see a thing.

Since childhood, she had been cursed with an irrational terror of dark places. Wherever she was now, it was very dark. She turned her head in all directions, but not a sliver of light appeared. Now her shivers were from more than chill. She imagined small furry things approaching her from all sides, and strained her ears to catch their rustlings. She heard nothing.

"Help." She whimpered, drawing her feet close to her knees and hugging her legs and trying not to imagine roaches coming her way.

"Get up," she ordered herself, and forced her limbs to obey. Standing seemed worse—more of her was exposed to darkness. Fighting a desire to curl herself into a screaming ball on the floor, she began to feel the thick darkness that surrounded her. On three sides her tentative fingers felt nothing, but behind her they met a wall. Following the wall and placing her feet carefully to avoid stumbling, she went all the way around the space.

It seemed to be a room, about twelve by twelve, and empty. It had three doors, firmly locked, and two windows, containing not glass but boards. The latter she discovered by getting a large splinter firmly implanted in her right forefinger.

Sucking the wounded finger, she retreated to lean against one wall. She couldn't remember how she got there...

It seemed real enough, but she slapped herself in the hope that she was dreaming. A pain scissored through her head, and her mouth had a sweet taste she couldn't quite identify.

She began to remember the phone call. Had someone fooled her? Or was this just another unrelated incident? Her head began to buzz. She massaged her temples, trying to gather up her courage to explore the center of the room.

One step into the darkness was all she could manage. After all, she comforted herself, what difference did it make whether furry things found her in the middle of the room or against the wall?

She inched her way back around the room to a door that seemed more solid than the others. It rattled a little, but was securely locked. "I'll have to wait until daylight," she said aloud. Her voice sounded hollow, bringing new apprehensions. What if someone else was in this space with her? She strained to listen for breathing, heard nothing.

She was feeling dizzy, so she found the spread and sat on it, feet tucked beneath her and back against the wall.

How long she sat there she could not have said. She heard a truck changing gears, and the cry of an owl. She wanted to call out but was afraid her captor was somewhere outside, waiting. For what? Why hadn't he killed her and gotten it over with?

Cold, afraid, and dizzy, she slumped against the wall. She comforted herself with the notion that someone would come looking for her, but how would they ever find her? She had no idea how far she might be from Charleston, and knew that whoever had abducted her would have had to use her car to get back to town—or wherever they chose. Lamar, for instance, might be halfway to Washington by now. If the car was gone in the morning, what would the Wimberlys think? Would they be sufficiently alarmed to call the police? Not until they had checked with Aunt Mary, certainly—and where, oh where, was Aunt Mary?

At last she didn't care if an army was waiting outside for her to cry out—she could stand inaction no longer. "Help!" she shouted until she was hoarse. "Help! I'm locked in!"

She called until she could only whisper, then lay down, exhausted, and drew the spread about her. Chilled and terrified of the dark, she hugged her knees and wept.

PERHAPS AT LAST she slept. She heard the voice at first as in a dream, distant and coming closer. "Hello? Is somebody there?" It was a man's voice, light and hesitant.

Sheila jumped to her feet and began to pound on her side of the door. "Yes, I'm in here. Please get me out. Please."

"I'm doing my best." She heard sharp blows and mutterings, then a rasp as a padlock was removed. She moved away from the door. At last thin rays of moonlight entered through the open door. Sheila staggered out into the unexpected arms of Roy Luther.

He staggered under her weight. "There, now, you'll be fine." He patted her shoulder awkwardly.

Sheila drew back, took a deep breath, and gave him a tremulous smile. "I don't know how you got here, but I'm glad to see you."

"I thought you might be." Beneath his mustache his lips curved upward. "I'd have been here sooner, but I wasn't sure which cabin you were in and I couldn't seem to make you hear me. I've been knocking and listening at all the doors."

His arm swept a semicircle and for the first time Sheila looked about them. She shuddered with horror. They stood knee-deep in weeds on what had been the lawn of a tourist court. Long ago the expressway had shifted the traffic far away, and now it was a semicircle of forlorn stucco cottages, paint peeling and windows boarded, sitting in a patch of tall grass and sandspurs. Even the moonlight couldn't beautify this lonely place.

Mr. Luther took her by one elbow and steered her to an ancient blue Ford in mint condition. "Let's get you out of here."

She collapsed into the seat, choking back a sob of relief. "I might never have been found. How . . . ?" Her voice was only a rasp.

He chuckled. "I followed you from Dolly's. I'd begun to think something peculiar was going on in that house—most of it after you got there. While you were fetching Dolly's pills yesterday, she told me something that helped me decide to keep an eye on things. I don't need much sleep anymore, so these past two nights I've dozed in my car down the street, thinking I might see or hear something important." His eyes twinkled in the moonlight. "Been watching too much television, haven't I?"

She shook her head and shivered in spite of herself. "Not for me you haven't. So you saw me leave?"

"Yep. I woke up when I heard your car door slam, but that must have been the back door, because then in a few minutes I saw you come and get in the driver's seat. Next thing I knew someone got out of the backseat and got in the same door, so I figured you'd moved over."

Sheila shook her head. "I'd been chloroformed, I think. Who else was in the car?"

"I couldn't tell. It was too dark under the trees and I was down the block."

"What happened then?"

"You drove off. I followed you to the old motel and stayed down the road. I'm not very good at this," he said apologetically. "I was afraid of being seen, so I never got really close enough. The car stayed there for twenty minutes—at least I thought to check my watch—and then it passed me going back to town."

"Well, I'm glad you came to find me." She was beginning to feel again, and knew that every joint in her body ached.

He shook his head. "I didn't, not at first. You see"—again his voice was full of apology—"I thought you were still in the car. So I turned around and followed it. But I got caught by a train and lost it. In town I cruised around and finally saw your car sitting in an empty lot. It was empty. That's when I decided maybe I ought to hightail it back out to the motel to see if anybody got left out there. I really didn't expect to find anybody."

"You were no more surprised than I was," Sheila assured him. She reached over and gave his thin arm a fond squeeze. "I'll always be grateful."

"Well, you just rest now. We'll be back in town in a little while."

He didn't speak again until they were driving down Market Street. "If I were you, I'd go to a hotel tonight and go back tomorrow. Saves a lot of explaining."

"But I don't have my purse." She could imagine the kind of hotel that would accept her in her present state—dusty and wrinkled, hair standing on end, with no luggage and no money.

He chuckled quietly. "Oh, I can take care of that. If it were my niece, Mary'd do the same." He pulled into the parking zone of Charleston's most prestigious hotel. "Just wait a jiffy. I'll be right back."

In spite of herself, Sheila dozed, so she could not have said how long he was gone. When he returned he looked satisfied with himself. Gallantly he opened the door. "Here's your key. I told them you're an actress who hasn't taken time to remove her makeup. Just through that door and up to your room. I won't come with you, but I'll check on you in the morning."

She climbed out. "I can't tell you how grateful I am. Thanks again."

She crossed the lobby, attracting remarkably little attention, and let herself into her room. There she stopped short.

The room had two double beds, and someone was propped on one of them like a little queen.

"My, what a sight you look, dear." The husky voice trembled a little. "Come in and shut the door, and tell me all about it."

SHEILA STAGGERED to the vacant bed and collapsed onto it. "Aunt Mary, how did you get here?"

As she said it, she remembered another time she had asked that question—in Chicago in February, when she had come home to find Aunt Mary ensconced in her apartment drinking iced tea in spite of zero temperatures outside. Some of that iced tea would taste good right now. Sheila's throat was sore and swollen from calling for help. As if reading her thoughts, Aunt Mary slipped out of bed and brought her a glass of iced water.

"Aunt Mary, how did you get here?" she croaked again. The last time this happened, she and Aunt Mary worked together to solve a murder. Not that Aunt Mary did much work. Then, as now, she specialized in sitting and looking ornamental.

She was looking particularly ornamental tonight, dressed in a pink negligee heavily ruffled in silver lace to match her silver hair. She settled herself back against her pillows and with the shell-pink nails of one hand she stifled a yawn. "Now, dear, tell me what happened."

Sheila forced herself to go to the basin and wash her face and hands. She tried to force Aunt Mary's comb through her hair and gave up the attempt, returned to her bed and took off her slacks, shirt, and shoes, and slid between the sheets. "I could sleep a hundred years," she said thickly.

Aunt Mary sighed and reached for the lamp. "Very well, dear. I'll see you in the morning."

Sheila awoke to soft music and the smell of hot coffee. She wanted some so badly that she almost leaped out of bed—until she realized that every bone in her body felt like lead. She peered through her not-quite-open eyelids and saw Aunt Mary by the window, reading through a chink in the drapes and nibbling a bun. "Good morning!" she caroled when she saw Sheila was awake.

Sheila clutched her aching head. "It will be," she muttered.

Aunt Mary poured a cup of coffee and pattered over to the bed. "Drink this, dear. You'll feel much better."

Sheila struggled to sit up and took a sip. Aunt Mary was right. She felt better immediately. Perhaps it was the slug of whiskey someone had added to the original pot.

"I'm not going to tell you a thing," she warned huskily, "until you tell me how you came to be sitting in that bed in the middle of the night."

"It's my bed," Aunt Mary replied, "and at that hour anyone who isn't sleeping in her bed should reasonably be expected to be sitting in it."

Sheila felt close to throttling her little aunt. "What are you doing in Charleston, then?"

Aunt Mary's eyes widened. "Helping you, of course. You seemed to need a little assistance, and I felt I could be of more use here in a hotel than under the Wimberly roof."

"So where were you last night when I needed you?" Sheila demanded.

"I was busy here, dear, but at least I had asked Buck Luther to keep an eye on things. Dolly told him Monday I was here, and he came over and offered his help. *I* can't sit around in cars all night, and besides,"—she preened herself a little—"he wanted to do me a favor."

"Well, he certainly did me one." Sheila yawned. "I'm going back to sleep. See you later." She slid effortlessly into dreams.

When she woke again Aunt Mary had opened the drapes and turned up the music. "How long have you been here?" Sheila asked without preamble.

"Since Sunday. Charlie drove me to the airport after church."

"Does Mildred know where you are?"

"Of course I do." Like a jack-in-the-box, Mildred's head appeared through the connecting door. "Good morning, Sheila. I hope you're feeling better. May I order you some breakfast now?"

Sheila ordered a huge breakfast—after all, Aunt Mary was paying for it—then turned to her aunt. "When did *she* get here?"

"Last night. She's keeping Mama Lucille company."

"Mama Lucille?"

"Don't shout, dear, you'll disturb her. She's very frail, you know."

"So's Dolly—and possibly Nell. How could you..." She stopped. "But Dolly knew you were here. Otherwise she couldn't have told Mr. Luther."

Aunt Mary nodded. "I sent Dolly a note as soon as I arrived."

"What about the worry you've caused Nell?"

Aunt Mary shook her head. "I asked Will to tell Nell as soon as she got home. I'd begun to put some things together and feared Mama Lucille might be in some danger. They came over last night for a little chat, and have agreed to leave her here until this is all over. Now tell me what happened to *you* last night."

As Sheila described the evening's events, a deep line appeared between the silver brows. "That was really going too far!" she declared, eyes flashing.

Sheila heartily agreed.

"Have you got it all figured out?" she asked, flinging off the covers and going to rinse out her mouth. It felt like the bottom of a parrot's cage. On the other hand, she was alive.

Aunt Mary nodded. "I think so. Have you?"

"I think so, too. I had a lot of thinking time in the dark, and I believe I know what this is all about. The question is, what are we going to do about it?"

"The first thing you are going to do," her aunt said firmly, "is spend the morning in bed. Do you need a doctor?" Sheila shook her head. "Good, because the less people who know you are here the better. Now I'm going to have a nice talk with your Officer Johnson and write some letters. Then, when you feel better this afternoon, we'll work on a plan."

TWENTY-SEVEN

THURSDAY

AT THREE O'CLOCK on Thursday afternoon, Mary Beaufort put on a delicate pink linen dress and amethysts, tucked her tiny feet into patent leather pumps, and went, by appointment, to visit her longtime friends the Wimberlys.

Nell threw up her hands when she saw who was at the door. "Well, aren't you a sight for sore eyes! Did you ever find out what happened to Sheila?"

Mary shook her head. "I'm not worried. Sheila is quite able to take care of herself. But I am puzzled that she didn't leave a note. She usually has excellent manners. Could it have blown under the bed or chest?"

"Might have," Nell agreed. "I haven't gotten up there for a good sweeping yet." She handed Mary a piece of paper. "I found what you wanted," she said softly, "right where you thought it would be. But you be careful how you use it, now."

"I'm going to try," Mary assured her.

Nell ushered her guest into the living room, where there was quite a gathering already. Dolly had come downstairs for the occasion in her favorite pink and violet wrapper—a colorful complement to Aunt Mary's pink linen and Marion's gray silk suit.

Jamison had come by to check on Dolly. "I don't want you overdoing it," he warned.

"I feel better than I have in days," she had assured him. "Stay and visit awhile. I want you to get to know one of my dearest friends." She patted the chair beside her and, to the surprise of everyone (except Aunt Mary, who had arranged it), he accepted.

Annie had come straight from the funeral reception at Rhoda's. She watched the sleek white limousine pull up to the Wimberlys' door and could hardly wait to see who was arriving. She perched on the other end of the sofa looking like a plump crow in her funeral finery. "I never expected to wear it twice in a month," she had said three times now, smoothing her black skirt.

Becca, seated on a low chair in the corner behind her grandmother, gave Buddy a smile as he came in behind Nell and Mary, bearing a tray of glasses, plates, and a frosty pitcher. "Lemon meringue pie this afternoon," he announced. "The Big Pig had a special on lemons."

"Nell is just trying to embarrass us, isn't she, Mary?" Dolly said gaily by way of greeting. "Years ago," she explained to the others, "when we were about ten, Mary and I decided to make a bowl of meringue just to eat." She gave her friend a sidelong glance.

Mary returned the look with dignity. "It was at least a learning experience, Dolly. Now we both know you don't put egg yolk into meringue."

"But it took them a dozen eggs to learn," Nell completed the story, bringing in three pies piled high with fluffy meringue. "I thought Miss Bella and Mama Lucille were going to kill them both."

When introductions were over, Becca turned to Nell. "Did I hear that Mama Lucille has been missing?"

Nell nodded. "Gone for two days, then came toddling up the walk pretty as you please. I don't guess we'll ever know what happened."

Aunt Mary demurely stroked her skirt, as befits one who doesn't know what a conversation is about.

"I was certainly sorry to miss Sheila," she said. "I flew over especially to drive back with her, then just missed her. I can't understand her just leaving like that."

"I can't either," Buddy said. "We still had a sailing date..."

"And we were going to have dinner," Jamison added.

Dolly gave them a roguish smile. "No wonder she left!" She looked toward the bay window. "Has everyone left at the Bennetts'?"

Jamison nodded. "Almost. I looked in on my way here. Everything was under beautiful—and understandable—control. Grace throws such lovely parties."

Marion gave him a frosty glare. "Grace and Rhoda did not always see eye to eye," she acknowledged, "but it was a beautiful funeral. I will not have you spoiling it . . ."

"Here's Heyward," Becca warned them. She stood, but remained where she was.

He stood in the door, looking pale but very handsome in a black suit and white shirt. "May I come in?"

"Of course!" Dolly waved him to a seat.

"Avoiding washing dishes?" Buddy teased him.

"At least." Heyward flung himself down on the floor beside Becca's chair. He leaned against her knee as if he'd done it always, and without thinking she sat down and rested one hand on his shoulder. He flexed his fingers. "If I have to shake one more hand . . ."

"Your mother was highly respected," Marion reminded him. "They all came because they wanted to pay their last respects."

"I know." He sighed and leaned his head farther back. For the first time he noticed Mary Beaufort and leaped to his feet. "I'm sorry, ma'am. I didn't see there was a visitor." He put out his hand and she took it between both of hers.

"I won't ask you to shake, Heyward," she said in her deep old voice, "but let me say how sorry I am about your mother."

"Thank you, ma'am. You must be Sheila's aunt—you've got her smile."

"I've got her stubborn streak, too," Aunt Mary told him, "and that's why I've really come." She turned to Buddy. "How's your other daughter—the one who was poisoned?"

The room became absolutely still. Dolly's hands stopped playing with her satin sash and rose tentatively to brush away a nonexistent curl. Annie demanded, "Poisoned? Who's been poisoned?"

"Rake," Buddy admitted, "but she'd doing fine. She'll be home by Saturday."

"The poison was intended for you, Marion," Aunt Mary continued relentlessly, "but Rake drank your champagne?"

Marion made a gesture of impatience. "Really, Mary, I don't now why Sheila chose to discuss this with you, but please on't upset Dolly with it. It's all over now."

"Why wasn't I told?" Dolly demanded. "When was this?"

"Monday night, Gram," Becca told her, "right after the play. But she's going to be fine, really. Right now she's lying up in the hospital like a queen, giving orders to everybody—everybody but me." Her hand lightly stroked Heyward's hair back from his forehead. "I don't take orders from her anymore."

"Just me." He grinned.

"Not even you," she assured him. "I'm my own woman now."

"She's my woman now, too," he announced. "This isn't exactly the right time to do it, Buddy, but may I have your daughter's hand in marriage?"

"Take all of her," Buddy said above the murmurs that arose from the womenfolk. He waved his hand expansively. "Take them both, if you can afford them. They're expensive to keep, though."

"Then maybe I'll just take one." Heyward chuckled.

Dolly beamed at them like a fairy godmother who had made it happen all by herself. "Just what I would have hoped for both of you!" she exclaimed. "When's the wedding?"

"We haven't talked about that," Becca said, just as Heyward was saying "Soon."

"You have to wait a year," Annie declared. "It's not fitting, with Rhoda just dead . . ."

"And that's what I want to talk about," Mary said crisply. "Rhoda—and Francine, and the Judge."

"What's the Judge got to do with it?" Annie demanded. "He died a perfectly natural death."

"I don't think so. Sheila didn't think so, and I believe Dolly didn't think so, either. Am I right, Dolly?"

Dolly shook her head. "I wasn't sure, but it was so sudden . . ."

Aunt Mary nodded. "It was puzzling, just like Sheila's disappearance. And I never could stand an unsolved puzzle. It is so unlike her to have left just as she was beginning to get to the bottom of things. I have to wonder if someone has gotten her out of the way."

Becca gasped. "Oh, no!"

Dolly shook her head wordlessly.

"If you think that, we should call the police at once." Marion rose and started across the room.

Mary shook her head. "I've already done that, Marion. They found her car in a vacant lot and are checking it for prints right now. Officer Johnson should have a report by this afternoon."

"I wish I'd known you were worried." Marion resumed her seat and picked up her sherry.

Dolly's face was puckered with worry. "Oh, Mary, this is all my fault. If I hadn't asked her here..."

"Nonsense," Mary said crisply. "She wanted to come." She reached for her little patent leather purse from the floor beside her. "From what she told me about the situation here, I wonder if this means anything to any of you?"

She held up a photograph, yellowing with age, with a smudge of flour in one corner. Dolly recognized it at once. "Of course. It fell out of an old cookbook Francine and Sheila were using to write my little history. But I thought it was in the table beside my bed. How did you get it, Mary?"

"Are you sure it's the same one?" Mary handed it to her.

Dolly gave an exclamation of surprise. "Why, no! Look, Marion, this has you with Mama and Daddy! But I don't understand..."

She passed it to her sister. Marion scarcely gave it a glance. "It must have been taken when I was about three."

"Before Dolly was born," Annie elucidated for anyone who didn't understand. "Does it have a date?" She turned it over to look at the back.

"It says 'Our Wedding Day,'" said a voice at the door.

Nell took a quick step forward. But it was Officer Johnson and his partner who leaped from the hall to hold her as—swearing, screaming, and foaming at the mouth—Marion Wimberly hurled herself at Sheila's throat.

TWENTY-EIGHT

THE END

"I DON'T UNDERSTAND," Becca said, bewildered. "Aunt E[r] killed Rhoda and Francine?"

"And almost Rake. Possibly even Judge Black." Sheil[a] nodded.

"I don't understand, either." Dolly was drowsy with seda[-] tive, but she had insisted that they all come up to her room t[o] talk until she went to sleep. "I can't stand to be alone," she ha[d] said with a whimper.

And so now they sat, leaned, or stood in the large bedroo[m] while she rested against her pillows. "Why?" Dolly pleaded fo[r] the umpteenth time.

"Begin at the beginning," Buddy suggested.

"But first," Dolly said drowsily, "tell me where you wen[t] Sheila, and why."

Sheila and Aunt Mary had already decided on how to an[-] swer that. This family needed no more pain, and Sheila didn[']t want them bearing guilt on her account. "I had to check ou[t] some things, and it was essential for you to think I'd le[ft] Charleston. I was sorry to do it that way" (was she ever!) "b[ut] felt it was really necessary."

"We don't really know the beginning," Aunt Mary began [to] clear things up, "but we think it may have begun when Bel[la] Wimberly died."

"From something Marion said just before they took h[er] away," Jamison contributed, "was there something Bella to[ld] her just before she died?"

Aunt Mary nodded. "I think she must have explained tha[t] she was leaving her shop and money to Marion, but that th[e] house and all the land belonged to Dolly."

"But why?" Becca looked from face to face to see if ever[y] one else understood. Nobody did, not even Dolly.

"Because Marion wasn't your daddy's daughter, Dolly," Aunt Mary told her old friend. "Your mother had been married before. He probably planned to adopt her, but when the war started, he was drafted."

Dolly shook her head restlessly on the pillows. "But why did they keep it a secret?"

"I don't think they did," Sheila said to comfort her. "It was just something everybody knew. It became a secret to the next generation simply because nobody talked about it. If your parents had lived until you were older, they would have told you in time. But they died."

"But Aunt Bella knew?" Dolly struggled against the sedative to understand.

Aunt Mary reached out and held her friend's hand. "Of course she knew. But she also loved Marion very much. As Marion became more and more entrenched as a Wimberly, it became harder to tell her she wasn't."

"Mama Lucille loved her like her own—better, I used to think," Nell contributed from her seat on the cedar chest. Sheila, remembering the old woman's "she became my baby," nodded. Nell was speaking slowly, trying to figure it all out. "So after Mr. Brent died, they must have just put off telling Marion she wasn't born a Wimberly until she was old enough to take it."

Aunt Mary nodded. "I think it was like that exactly, Nell. And since nobody mentioned it, the subject was almost forgotten. Years passed, and they still hadn't told her, until Bella was about to die."

Dolly pulled Mary's hand up to her cheek, where tears were streaming. "I can't bear it, Mary, I can't. Being a Wimberly matters so *much* to Marion. How she must have suffered after she found out!"

"Yes, dear. More than we will ever know." Aunt Mary's husky old voice was almost a whisper.

"When you said to take a sedative before I came downstairs . . ." Dolly tossed her head to and fro on her pillow. "I never imagined it would be like this."

"I'd have spared you if I could," her friend told her, "but you are stronger than you know, Dolly. Cry it out, and rest." She stroked Dolly's hair with her free hand. Dolly wept freely, then gradually her breathing grew calmer, she turned her face to the side, and she slept.

Jamison stepped from the room and returned with a hospital nurse. "Donna will take care of her for now." He led the way as they all tiptoed almost silently down to the living room again.

Annie was the first to speak. "So what you are saying is that Marion was a Yankee! No wonder Uncle Scott was upset."

"A Canadian," Aunt Mary said in a voice like steel. "That's why her name was spelled with an 'o.' But the biggest problem was that Marion's parents were divorced. That's what upset Dolly's granddaddy—his son had married a divorced woman, which his church would not condone. Marion seems to have been about three at the time, but Bella didn't tell her father about the child until a year later, when they were coming home and Dolly was well on the way."

"But what made Miss Marion kill people?" Nell demanded, her voice deep with anger. "She had no cause to kill folks just because she wasn't born a Wimberly."

"She didn't begin by killing," Sheila explained. "She started by covering up. First she put the family Bible in a locked case, because she wasn't in it."

"But I saw her name," Nell objected.

"No, you saw Bella's name and Dolly's name—the two unmarried daughters of the current family. It was Bella's name that Dolly scribbled out." Seeing the puzzled looks on many faces, she stopped to explain. They could all do with a little lightness at this point.

While they were still smiling, she continued. "One thing that puzzled me was how Marion could legally get away with claiming part of the house and the real estate. You put me on the right track, Nell, when you said Judge Black was the family lawyer until he went to the state legislature. Yesterday, through a friend of Aunt Mary's" (dear Charlie, she thought fondly) "we found that he was in Columbia when Bella died. Marion took the will to a lawyer out in the suburbs, someone who didn't know the family at all. She also took Brent Wimberly's will, and discovered—as she had probably suspected—that in the chaos of war and the flu epidemic, it had never been roperly probated. She immediately got herself and Dolly established as joint heirs.''

"So she was dealing with both emotional and financial stress," Jamison mused.

Aunt Mary nodded. ''Marion had learned from Aunt Bella to love Charleston until, for her, it had become an idolatry. To discover in midlife that she had no blood roots in the city must have been devastating.''

"But there was more than that." Sheila picked up the story. "She had grown up expecting to live in this house and inherit her granddaddy Scott's land. Suddenly she discovered that she had no claim to either.''

"Greed," Annie spat out. "Pure greed. Putting on airs about being a Wimberly when she wasn't one of us at all.''

Aunt Mary gave her a look of astonishment. "One of *us*? I thought you were a cousin of Dolly's on her grandmother Dorothea's side, Annie. Didn't your family come from south Georgia?''

Annie subsided against the couch and sulked.

"You still haven't said why Marion thought she had to kill people." Nell rubbed her cheeks with her palms, as if to contain the knowledge she was getting. "The old Judge, now. He wasn't gonna harm anybody.''

"He could have," Aunt Mary pointed out. "He knew who she really was. He must have been nearly fourteen when she arrived, and he'd have heard the story about why Scott had his stroke.''

"You told me he used to tease her about her 'Yankee' name," Sheila added.

"And he was awful the night before he died," Annie remembered. "Going on and on about her mama, and how he knew Wimberly family history she never would. I'd have killed him myself, spiteful old codger. But Marion didn't kill him," she suddenly remembered. "He couldn't reach his medicine.''

"Did she have a key to your front door?" Mary asked.

"Of course. But Marion was at the church with me.''

"Nobody could prove it," Aunt Mary agreed, "but I think she took you to the church and then slipped out—maybe said she was going to help in the kitchen?''

"The library," Annie corrected her. "She said she ha
something she had to look up in the church library. But sh
wasn't gone half an hour! She got back before the vide
started."

"It's a five-minute drive, and takes very little time to wak
up an irascible old man, work him into a frenzy, and withhol
his pills." Aunt Mary ticked the possible series of events off o
her shell-pink nails. "Why don't you explain it from there
Sheila? After all, you've done most of the research."

"I think it actually began the night when Dolly announce
she was asking Francine to write a brief history of the famil
Marion probably protested, but as we all know, when Dolly ge
a bee in her bonnet, she usually gets her way." The others no
ded assent. "Marion brought down some documents for Fra
cine to use, basically harmless documents—old diaries, undate
letters, a cookbook. They were so harmless, in fact, that sh
didn't think them worth removing when Francine was dead.
don't know why she hadn't ever found the pictures in th
cookbook—"

"Because she never learned to cook," Annie said spitefull
"Always let other people do it for her. Was that picture t
treasure Lamar was looking for, then?"

Aunt Mary nodded sadly. "Poor dear, it wasn't such
treasure for Francine after all."

"Where did you find it?" Annie insisted. "We looked
over."

"Marion had put it behind another picture of her parents
her mantelpiece. When Sheila described the contents of Ma
ion's room, I immediately remembered that she used
keep..." She had the grace to pause, give Nell an apologe
look, and stop. "I suspected she might hide something behi
her picture," she concluded.

"Mama Lucille had told me that Marion arrived wearing
'wedding' dress," Sheila came to her rescue, "but I didn't
tally understand what she was saying at the time."

"She comes and goes." Nell sighed heavily. "Lawdy, I wi
my own mind could come and go a bit right now. It's just t
much to take in." She shook her head from side to side, hea
with grief.

"The way Francine's mind worked," Buddy mused, "she probably thought Marion was illegitimate."

"Possibly so." Sheila knew he was trying to distract Nell, and appreciated his effort. "But I think that came later—about the time I arrived, in fact. Before that, hoping to nip the history in the bud, Marion staged a series of harmless accidents to keep Francine busy and distract Dolly."

That was all the distraction Nell needed. "Harmless, huh! I could have been killed by that fan blade!"

"No, because she kept you in the attic all afternoon, and knew Buddy was coming," Sheila pointed out. "She even held you back from going into the kitchen—I saw her do it."

"And she knew as soon as I came in I'd switch it on," Buddy added. "I was the one who put it up in the first place," he explained to the out-of-town guests, "and Nell scarcely ever thinks to use it."

"Nell will never use it again," she informed him. "I'll be hot and never you mind."

"Most of the accidents were carefully calculated," Aunt Mary inserted. "Marion knew that her own tire would go flat somewhere on the sedate drive to church and that the television would catch fire while she was there to make certain it didn't get out of hand."

"What about Dolly's medicine?" Jamison asked. "No matter what else she's done, I don't think Marion would ever hurt Dolly."

"Of course not," Aunt Mary agreed. "But was Dolly ever in any real danger? The bottle capped with a childproof lid was pain medicine, and if her heart had started to bother her, she could have quickly opened her nitroglycerin. I think Marion even expected to hear Dolly call and was horrified that she hadn't."

"She was upset about that," Nell agreed. "Stayed home the next morning from work and fussed around that room like a mother hen."

"Was she really pushed down the stairs?" Becca asked.

"I don't think so," Sheila told her. "A sprain and a faint are fairly easy to fake."

"So is a robbery," Aunt Mary continued. "The object of course, was the Bible, which did not have Marion's name in it.

That's why she had put it in the case in the first place. She'd thrown away the key, and couldn't risk a locksmith opening the case while Francine or even Sheila was standing around. The Bible had to be stolen and 'damaged,' so she could send it out for repair.''

Sheila went into the hall and returned with a parcel. ''We checked several places that do rebinding and found it this morning. Marion has replaced the original page of births and deaths with a new one. It's been cleverly done, but Officer Johnson believes it can be shown that all the names were written by the same hand, using different pens and colors of ink—and written recently.'' She passed it around, so they could all see the page on which Marion's name appeared between those of Bella Wimberly and Dorothea Wimberly.

''Are you *sure* Aunt Em did this?'' Becca asked, bewildered. ''I mean, changing history like that? She—''

Aunt Mary reached over and patted her gently. ''By the end of last week, your Aunt Em was desperate, Rebecca. Not like herself at all.''

''So she decided to frame Francine?'' Buddy shifted on his chair and sat on the front edge, hands clasped tightly between his thighs. ''To kill her and frame her both?''

Sheila nodded. ''It was too good a chance to pass up. Of course, at first I thought it was either you or Heyward.'' Both men gaped at her. ''You both arrived so conveniently,'' she apologized. ''In the chaos after the robbery, anybody could have put sleeping pills in Francine's tea, but I thought it would take a strong person, preferably a man, to slam a woman's head against a table and hold her down while she smothered. Officer Johnson convinced me that Francine was small enough that any of us could have done it, even Becca.''

''Not me!'' the twin squealed.

''You had a couple of good motives,'' Sheila reminded her. ''Francine was either your rival or your potential stepmother.''

''I'd have drowned her,'' Becca said with a grimace. ''Take her out to sea and pushed her off a boat.''

''I see I'll have to watch my step,'' Heyward teased, stroking her cheek with one finger. He looked up at Sheila. ''But why should she kill Mama? She couldn't hope to get rid of everybody connected with historical societies in town." His face was strained and white.

"I think Rhoda was killed because she deduced the same thing I finally did—that Brett Wimberly was not yet married at the time of the Great Hurricane of 1911, when Marion was already born. Marion never expected Rhoda to read those documents, of course, or she wouldn't have left them. The likely person was me—I'd already told her I was interested in history, and as a guest with time on her hands, I was Dolly's likely next choice to write her 'little history.' But when Rhoda showed up at Francine's and offered to help, I asked her to tidy them. She sat down and read them instead. I'm very sorry, Heyward. I feel as if I were to blame..."

He shook his head. "Mama had been wanting to get a look at those papers ever since she learned Francine was working on them. She never could bear to think there was anything about Charleston's history she didn't know personally."

Sheila nodded. "And she would have caught the importance immediately of the letter written after the hurricane. Bella tells how they survived it, then chides Brent for not coming home the summer before. Her father is still well, so he hasn't had his stroke, and she makes no mention at all of Brent's family, which she does in all the other letters. It was obvious that the letter was written before he married. What Rhoda would have known at once, as I did not, was the year in which that letter was written."

"And she'd have known when Marion was born," Heyward said with a sad bitterness. "She had a marvelous memory for anything historical."

Sheila nodded. "I suspect she tried to find her own solution, but when she couldn't, she hurried out to check with Marion. Marion put her off with an appointment for the next morning. Then she arranged for me to be out shopping and Nell to be busy in the third floor, which has no northside windows. She killed Rhoda with one of the bannisters stacked in the back of her shop—I found it the night..." She stopped before she mentioned her abduction in spite of her good intentions.

Luckily, Becca had an objection. "But she couldn't just walk down the sidewalk carrying a bannister without somebody seeing her. There are people all over the place on Saturday mornings.''

"She didn't go through the gate." Annie basked in the stir she created. "I saw her carry a bannister into the little house when I got up to get a drink of water between shows. I thought maybe she was going to fix one, but maybe she went into Rhoda's yard that way!''

Aunt Mary nodded. "If Marion came through the door with a bannister, Rhoda wouldn't have suspected anything other than that Marion was refinishing another piece of wood. It would be easy to hit her from behind.''

"But Marion wasn't left-handed!" Heyward cried.

"Her backhand," Becca said in a strained voice. "It's very strong.''

Buddy stood and paced the room, hands in pockets. "And she poisoned Rake?'' He asked it with his back to all of them.

"I'm afraid so," Aunt Mary replied.

"Rake issued a challenge," Sheila reminded him, "when she said there was someone who would be glad Francine was gone.''

"But that was me!" Becca's voice was choked with tears.

Sheila nodded. "But Marion didn't know that. She thought Rake knew something. So she put a refinishing solvent in her champagne.''

Aunt Mary spoke gently. "Your Aunt Em is a very sick woman, Rebecca, and I hope you will still think of her with love.''

"I think that poisoning Rake nearly killed her, too," Sheila added. "The morning afterward she began to physically fail.''

"Are you sure it was Dolly wanting to write the history that started her off?" Buddy asked. "Could that realtor hounding her about selling land have had something to do with it?''

"Probably so," Sheila told him. "Everything worked together—the realtor and Dolly's idea for a history—even Francine's attempt at blackmail. They were all little pressures building up. Finally she just went over the edge.''

They shifted restlessly in their seats. None of them wanted to remember the raving, screaming woman who had been escorted by Officer Johnson and two paramedics from the room.

"Inexorable grace," Aunt Mary murmured. Seeing their bewilderment, she explained. "It could have all worked for

ood. She was given several chances to admit what she had
one and put things right. Instead, she chose her own way."

Heyward stood and glared around the room. "Well, I've
ever liked history much, but now I can safely detest it the rest
f my days." He started for the door.

"Wait." Aunt Mary put out one hand to stop him. "His-
ory is good in its place, Heyward. Most people in Charleston
reserve a past that we all need to remember. The problem for
our mother and Marion was that they took it out of its place
nd let it consume their present."

"It consumed everything!" His eyes blazed. "Our entire life!
Iama never had time for me because she always had to go to
meeting of the Historic Charleston Foundation, the South
arolina Historical Society, the Colonial Dames—" His voice
roke, and he sobbed rather than said, "And now, now it's
lled her!" He rushed from the room and down the porch.

Becca rose to follow him, but Buddy stopped her with an
nbrace. "Let him go for a while, kitten. He needs to work this
t by himself. And I need you, please?"

She looked from him toward the front door, obviously torn,
en gave a reluctant nod and returned to her seat.

Buddy threw himself into the chair Heyward had left and
ok Becca's hand. As he talked, he gently massaged it. "The
ing I find hardest to forgive is Rake. I mean, her own..." He
opped. "Well, if not her own flesh and blood, certainly her
vn family."

Tears rolled down his cheeks. Becca stroked them away, but
r own eyes were brimming.

"What I still don't understand," Nell said like a dog deter-
ned to worry a bone until all the meat is gone, "is why Mar-
a couldn't take what Miss Bella left her and be happy with it.
e had earned the respect of people in this town all on her
vn—no matter whose daughter she was born."

Buddy shook his head. "Her entire identity was that of
arion *Wimberly*, Nell. You know that. Mama used to tell me
out how cutting Marion could be when outsiders tried to
me into old Charleston society as if they belonged. She could
ver have stood it for people like Mama and Rhoda to find out
e started as an outsider herself."

"Besides," Aunt Mary added with her lips pursed into network of wrinkles, "she'd set her heart on leaving every thing to Charleston—this house, the land outside of tow everything. In her eyes, it was rightfully hers to leave. She an Bella were the only Wimberlys to care about Charleston and th place of their family in it. She was the one who worked to buil Bella's little shop into one of the foremost antique shops in th Southeast. It was she who worked to help build Charleston a ter World War II into the tourist attraction it is today. Do never cared a rap about history, and if you'll pardon me, Do has never done a lick of hard work in her life."

"Unlike others we could name," Sheila murmured under h breath.

Aunt Mary ignored her. "Buddy has the restaurant, and t chances are good that both his girls will marry men who w keep them comfortably all their days. Marion would certain not do anything to harm Dolly, and I think she made certa that each shock was softened as much as possible for her s ter. From what Sheila has told me"—she turned to Jamison "you've been a constant visitor this past week."

He nodded. "I'd begun to think I should move in."

Aunt Mary's mouth twitched, but instead of smiling s turned back to her old friend. "Nell, I think we have to acce that Marion decided long ago that it was her right and pri lege to leave to Charleston the wealth and good name of M ion Wimberly."

"That's not even her name!" Annie rasped like a cro "Who is she, really?"

Nell voiced the sentiments of them all. "She certainly Marion Wimberly, and has been as long as I've known h Anybody says different will have to deal with me. And sh been taken very ill today, as I'll tell everybody who calls ask." She rose and walked heavily to the kitchen.

Becca had been sitting very still, but as Nell began to water in the kitchen she suddenly collapsed into sobs. "I ca stand it! Aunt Em isn't some monster who tried to rob Gr and killed people and tried to kill Rake...I can't stand i can't!" Her voice rose hysterically.

Buddy turned to her, and Jamison had risen, but it Heyward who got there first. He had come back so quietly n of them had heard him, but now he spoke with new purpose in his voice. "Yes, you can, kitten. We both can—if we do it together. I came back because I realized I'd left you, and the only good thing that's come out of this is that I've found you."

"And Marion was many things," Aunt Mary said softly. "She was smart, and refined, and she had exquisite taste. And since she helped raise most of us, whatever she was is a part of us, the good with the bad. She'll need all of you in the days to come."

"What'll happen to her?" Buddy wanted to know.

Jamison shrugged. "She was raving when she left, and I wouldn't expect much change for a long time, if ever. She's put herself under a strain for over forty years, remember, and now she's lost everything in one blow—money, reputation, sanity, family..."

"Not her family," Becca refuted him damply. "If she'll let me, I'll go see her."

"Me, too," Heyward said, keeping her in the circle of his arm. "And before you start work on your medical annex, Jamison, I want to check it out. I might be about to get interested in historical sites."

Jamison looked so chagrined that Sheila nearly laughed. Instead she stood and took his arm. "Speaking of historical sites, I've seen very few of them this past week. What can you show me, Jamison, in the four hours before my plane leaves for Atlanta?"

"Plane?" Aunt Mary raised stenciled brows. "What about your car, dear?"

"Your car," Sheila reminded her. "Your driver will fly in about the time Mildred and I fly out. I arranged that in some of my free time yesterday."

"Where on earth," Aunt Mary demanded, scandalized, "did you get the idea you could run other people's lives like that?"

Sheila smiled. "I've had the world's best teacher," she said fondly. "If you're good, you can use the third ticket and fly, too. But don't make any plans for me tomorrow. I'm on vacation."

EPILOGUE

Dear Sheila,

While Heyward saws limbs and repairs the steps that
Hugo chewed up and spat out, I will thank you for the
lovely silver sailboat. I would have written sooner, but we
had no power until Saturday and I seemed to spend every
waking hour for a week figuring out what we could eat and
how to cook it. It's not every bride who spends the week
after her honeymoon coping with a hurricane! We are glad
Daddy talked us out of getting married the day of the
equinox—even WE don't love the ocean enough to get
married in 130 mph winds!

Of course Daddy didn't anticipate Hugo—he just
wanted us to get married on his anniversary, which we did.
We had a wonderful week at sea and came home three days
before the storm. As you probably already know, Miss
Mary sent Jason with her car to fetch Gram the day before Hugo arrived, and has insisted that Gram stay with
her for a month.

We rode with them to Atlanta, where we learned Miss
Mary had arranged for us to spend the weekend at her
condo in St. Petersburg. It was beautiful, and we hope to
go back some time when we aren't so worried about things
at home—we couldn't get a call through for three days and
I was frantic, since Daddy and Rake had decided to
weather out the storm in the town house.

It was a good thing they did. They spent the whole day
before the storm lugging furniture in three houses to top
floors. Gram's house was built high enough not to take in
any water, but Annie got several inches and in the town
house the water rose three feet downstairs. The carpet is
still covered with mud. They'll just have to take it up and
throw it away. Rake said it was terrifying. Can you imag-

ine Rake frightened of anything?

Daddy's restaurant was terribly damaged—he can't do much until the insurance people are through and won't be open for business for months. Heyward's boats survived better than some, and he hopes to reopen the school by November first.

In Nell's neighborhood trees fell on almost every house. Her own was spared, but a very sad and *strange* thing happened during the storm. For some reason, Mama Lucille suddenly hurried outside. Before Nell got to her, a branch knocked her down, and she never recovered. She died last Friday.

On a happier note, we love your little sailboat, and you were wrong about its having no practical purpose. It sits on our desk to remind us that without you we might never have gotten together. I won't bore you with rhapsodies, but we are *very* happy, even working as hard as we've been working since we got home.

Gram lost part of her roof, which meant the walls are damp and part of the ceiling will fall any minute, but except for the steps, nothing else was damaged in the big house. The little house, being closer to the ground, is full of mud and Heyward is going to have to replace the floor, which buckled. Miramise, however, is still visiting her sister in Augusta, so there's no hurry.

That reminds me, though, that you don't know about all our changes *before* the wedding. Heyward didn't want to live in his mother's house, so he sold it. Miramise moved into the little house as cook and to care for Gram. She's been wonderful—although she talks Gram's ear off, Gram does not seem to mind. Nell and Will still visit often, of course.

The biggest surprise was when Gram told us she was giving us her house for a wedding present! She planned to go to Summerville, where the Presbyterians have a retirement home, but we agreed we'd accept the house only if she'll stay with us as long as she lives. We had fixed up Aunt Em's rooms for ourselves (I say "had" because they got soaked when the roof blew off, and will have to be redone again), and got to enjoy them briefly before the storm. I have realized that this has really been my home since Mama died.

Another surprise was when one of Aunt Em's societies announced they were naming a room for her at their headquarters. They also brought a brass plaque to put on this house indicating that it is now a historical site. We were all so touched that there wasn't a dry eye in the family—not even Daddy's. If she could only know they love her for *herself*!

I visit her weekly, but I don't know how much she understands. Mostly I just sit and hold her hand. Last summer, though, when I said that Rake had gone to work in the shop for summer vacation, she gave a little snort that sounded almost like her old self!

Miss Simmons is managing almost as well as Aunt Em did. She even arranged for a truck to haul everything out of town for the storm. Wasn't that clever? But when Daddy asked her in August if she'd like to buy the shop, she said she doesn't want that much responsibility. Now, this afternoon, as Daddy and Heyward have worked in the yard under my window, they've been talking for the past hour about whether they should diversify and buy Aunt Em out. When Hugo blew out all Daddy's windows, flooded his kitchen, and carried off half his chairs, I guess he began to have second thoughts about owning a second restaurant, especially one out of town.

All I can say is, if they expect *me* to run their shop, they have another think coming. I've taken this term off from school, but will go back after Christmas. I plan to concentrate on marine biology all my life. Wouldn't it be funny if *Rake* wound up with Aunt Em's shop? It would certainly have the most flair of any antique shop in town!

Well, it's time to stop writing and go shovel mud from the little house so Heyward can fix the floor. Sigh. But I don't really mind, for other families have so much more to do. I've learned three things from Hugo—people can be wonderful (people leave their own work to help anyone who's in worse shape), we should count whatever blessings we have, and even *I* can get sick of the smell of salt mud and dead fish!

Thanks again for the silver sailboat. Miss Mary said you have resigned from Markham and are relocating to Atlanta. We look forward to hearing all about your new job, and hope you'll come down next spring and let us take you out on a real boat. Jamison has been looking a little lonely—shall we invite him, too? Only teasing...

Fondly,
Becca Bennett

COFFIN IN THE MUSEUM OF CRIME

A JOHN COFFIN MYSTERY

Gwendoline Butler

MATTERS OF THE HEAD

Life was good for Detective John Coffin—he'd earned a promotion and had just moved into a new home in the tower of a renovated church-turned-theater. True, he now headed his own force and was no longer a street detective, but his business was still crime and there was plenty in the Docklands.

And then a severed human head was found in an urn on the church steps. A hand turned up in a freezer upstairs. It was one of those cases that stretched out long fingers to touch many lives...or, rather, deaths.

"Butler pens a superior procedural." —*Publishers Weekly*

COFFIN

A PORT SILVA MYSTERY

GRANDMOTHER'S HOUSE

JANET LAPIERRE

First Time in Paperback

PORT SILVA—LAND TO KILL FOR?

Situated on California's beautiful northern coast, Port Silva had escaped the rash of land developers eating up the state's prime real estate. But when a posh San Diego firm finally offers small fortunes to persuade the people on historic Finn Lane to sell out, everyone jumps at the chance. Except thirteen-year-old Petey Birdsong. The house belonged to his grandmother. He's not selling. Charlotte, his mother, stands adamantly beside him.

But how far will Petey go to defend his home?

"LaPierre is something else . . . real talent."
—*Mystery Readers of America Journal*

 WORLDWIDE LIBRARY®

Hard Luck

A Cat Marsala Mystery

Barbara D'Amato

First Time in Paperback

HIGH STAKES

Chicago journalist Cat Marsala has just begun her assignment on the state lottery when murder falls into the picture—literally—as a lottery official takes a leap in the middle of the multistate lottery conference.

Suicide...or murder? It's curious to Cat—and to the police—that the guy took his mighty plunge right before his meeting with her. Especially curious since he'd hinted at some great exposé material, like "misappropriation" of lottery funds.

"Cat Marsala is one of the most appealing new sleuths to come along in years."
—*Nancy Pickard*

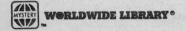

MYSTERY **WORLDWIDE LIBRARY** ®

HARDL